The Church of Arthur Fowler

David Wiley

For Izzy

1

Extract from ArthurFowlerBlog: Entry 21

The first time I met a man from Earth, I slapped him round the face. I have since learnt that this is not the type of behaviour you might expect from the creator of your universe. But then, there are a great many things you seem to expect of your creator, and almost none of them make any sense to me. However, I do appreciate that there exist some people who might object to such a violent act, so I would like to offer something in the way of a defence; there was no malice in it whatsoever. I only hit him because I thought he was having a heart attack.

I have not been here very long, but I have learnt a great deal since those first confusing moments. In fact, I do not think it is an overstatement to say I shall never be the same again. You are a quite fascinating bunch, really, not least because you are so full of contradictions. You are equal parts fascinating and terrifying; inspiring and infuriating; intelligent, yet relentlessly simple. I have enjoyed my time here tremendously, and I am infinitely more proud of my creation to know you are here living and loving and laughing and struggling and suffering within it.

Obviously, I had no idea of any of this when I created it. How could I have? You are, after all, such a terribly small part of it. I was merely happy to have finally created a universe stable enough to not collapse in on itself. For the first time in countless attempts, I had built one that held its shape. All of my previous attempts failed within a few seconds. It was always the same – calibrate the chamber, set the dials, charge the accelerator, flick the switch, and watch in disappointment as a faint flash of light and a barely audible pop and crackle announced that I would have to start the whole process again. But not this time. This time it was magnificent. Well, I say magnificent, but that one may be an overstatement. There are people far more talented than I who have turned universe creation into a fine art. I am a mere amateur – a hobbyist. Very rarely, one of these masters may create something that truly deserves the label 'magnificent'. Perhaps a humble 'very good' would be a more fitting assessment of my own creation. Regardless, as much as I have enjoyed my time here – and I truly have – what I want, more than anything else, is to go home...

2

Genesis

Arthur sat and stared at the sea of lights dancing in front of him, mesmerised by the unfolding shapes. Mere hours after its creation, galaxies churned relentlessly, comets traced arcs across a glimmering backdrop, each dragged into an elliptical struggle by some distant, titanic speck of mass, and tiny flickers of light announced the deaths of stars and the births of richly coloured dust clouds of billowing nebula. Through his magnifying glass, he surveyed the swirling canvas of objects that drew circles around objects that drew circles around objects that drew circles, all the while grinning like a giddy child. It didn't occur to him for a moment that life might be blooming on those tiny lumps of rock. Why would it have? It had never occurred to anyone. His people had always assumed the universes they created were beautiful yet sterile replicas of the real thing. How wrong they were. Sterile or not, Arthur wanted to make sure not to lose the working combination it had taken him so long to discover, so he took up a pencil and, hunched over the row of ten dials that sat between him and his creation, his tongue poking out of the side of his mouth, he carefully marked the setting of each one: gravity, electromagnetism, matter, antimatter and two dials each for the size and frequency of protons, neutrons and electrons. Then Arthur lost himself once more in the glorious and ever changing patterns twirling before him.

He was so entranced he could not say exactly how long he sat there, but eventually the warm glow of the evening crept in through the cobwebs that decorated the single skylight of his dusty attic. Beams of orange light fell on the boxes that lined the shelves all around him, arms and legs and heads poking out of them, hanging limply over the sides and casting long shadows against their bleached cardboard coffins. They were once his pride and joy, but they now served as little more than lifeless monuments to a former life in which he spent what little free time a young teacher could find as a street-performer. It had been many, many years since he had last breathed life into them. Arthur smiled at the memory of crowds watching in wonder as he manipulated the strings and imbued them with animation. It wasn't just children; adults were always amazed by the way he made them jump and dance. So lifelike, they said, and people would gather round in huge numbers, craning their necks and standing on tip-toes trying to see over one another. And, at the end of each day, he would find his case, so easy to carry in the morning, almost impossible to lift due to the weight of the coins that had been thrown in throughout the day. It was a short-lived affair. It was a time of great change, and before long the craft died out. New forms of story-telling replaced the old and fewer people would stop at his little theatre. Those who did stayed for shorter periods, the looks of wonder and amazement fading from their faces. At the end of each day the case would seem lighter and his heart would feel heavier than it had the day before, until eventually people did not stop at all. They walked by without even noticing him and he packed up his case for the last time.

It is, admittedly, a melancholy story, and often the sight of the little wooden figurines, looking like so many little corpses frozen in their attempts to crawl out of their tombs, prompted mournful reflection on the fact some things are simply not meant to last. But not today. Perhaps it was the success in his new hobby that left him thinking

4

more fondly of his old one. Perhaps some things are just too hard to let go completely. Either way, he opened his toolbox, untouched since he last carried it up into the attic, and removed his whittling knife and a character he was halfway through making before he gave up the craft. There never seemed any point in finishing him before, but now, with the taste of success on his tongue, the addiction of completion, he sat back down in his tatty leather armchair and began meticulously shaving the wood. Working by touch, staring at the stars in front of him, occasionally glancing out of the skylight at the stars above, Arthur relaxed, blissfully unaware of the incredible, improbable event that was moments away from unfolding around him.

3

Suffer Little Children

The first time he met God, Victor Dennett punched him in the face. To be fair to Victor, there are two pieces of information that should be taken into consideration before judging him for this. Firstly, he was having a *very* bad day. Secondly, God did hit Victor first.

This type of revelation may provoke all manner of responses. Some may fear for Victor's soul, believing, as so many do, that the consequences of his actions will see him dwelling in a dry land, devoured with the sword, or swallowed by a giant fish, depending on their bible verse of choice. Others may be immediately put off by the phrase 'he met God'. These people Victor could at least sympathise with. He used to be one of them. Belief in God, any leanings in the direction of being in any way 'spiritual', used to turn him right off people. He couldn't understand them, didn't *want* to understand them. They were the antithesis of everything he stood for. But, for all kinds of reasons, things change. The reason for this particular change was simple – Victor had met him. It is very difficult to not believe in someone you have met.

Meeting God was a surprising experience for Victor to say the least. Also surprising was the discovery that he isn't actually called God. His name is Arthur. Arthur Fowler, in fact. It's a simple coincidence, nothing more. It shouldn't render his status as creator of the universe more unlikely. It's strange how some coincidences are treated as indicators of supernatural agency, while others are treated as the exact opposite. Take the relationship between the Earth and the Moon, for example. Many a deist would gleefully point out that, were the moon just a little bit larger, or just a little further away, then life on Earth would be impossible. 'You see?!' they say, 'It's all too perfect to have happened accidentally. Someone *must* have designed it that way.' But tell them God shares a name with a dreary loser from a television programme enjoyed by other dreary losers, or that he happens to speak the same language as them, and suddenly coincidence is proof you are talking absolute bilge.

Victor's bad day began with him giving a tour of his workplace to a group of secondary school children. This was not a task he felt he had evolved to perform. He didn't have the temperament required for dealing with young people. Things may have been different if he had children of his own. But, things being as they were, he was ill equipped to deal with the vacuous herd moping along behind him one morning at the clumsily-named East of England Quantum Laboratory. Victor was sure the name had only been selected because it could be shortened to 'E Equals', which no doubt made some prat in PR feel incredibly clever. He was correct in this assumption. He was clever like that himself. He had to be, given his profession. He was a theoretical physicist involved in a range of research experiments covering things like quantum field theory, string theory, particle physics and a host of others you may have heard of but likely do not understand. There is no need to feel bad about this. Most people, including many of those who study them, don't really understand them either.

Though he did not believe in God at this time, Victor did have an odd habit of allowing him to exist whenever he felt the need to blame something other than his own life choices for whatever miserable situation he found himself in. At such times, Victor allowed a brief, offensive, and one way conversation with God to take place, just so he could tell him what a bastard he thought he was. It didn't make much difference. It didn't even make him feel much better, though he told himself it did. He was still being followed by a group of about twenty pupils from a local secondary school and they still made no effort whatsoever to appear interested in anything he had to say. He couldn't really blame them. Fifteen year olds aren't going to understand what happens at E Equals. You don't inspire the next generation of scientists by dragging them around what amounts to little more than pipes and wires. It wouldn't have made Victor want to study physics. Let them play with Van de Graaff generators and magnets and prisms. Get them to make parachutes and drop them out of the classroom window. Let them drop Mentos into Diet Coke. These were the things that got everyone in this building interested in physics. But apparently that was too simple. Being partly state funded, E Equals was obliged to offer community outreach and educational provision. It didn't matter that the kids didn't want to be there, that the teachers didn't want to bring them, or that Victor certainly didn't want to talk to them. An imbecile in Westminster who had never had a real job thought it would improve GCSE Science results if kids spent a day there and that was that.

And so, Victor drew the short straw and found himself shepherding them along the corridor, wires protruding from their ears, seemingly oblivious to the world that existed outside the ten-centimetre screens they held in their hands and could not divert their attention from without suffering irreparable brain damage. Every now and then their teacher, a tired and defeated looking man in his early fifties, would tell them to pay attention and put their phones away. With expressions designed to suggest they considered this a violation of their basic human rights, those students who did not simply ignore him dropped their phones into their pockets for a few seconds before retrieving them and resuming their feverish screen tapping as soon as their teacher's attention was diverted elsewhere. Occasionally, the teacher threw Victor an apologetic look, which Victor quietly interpreted as confirmation that he was not the only one suppressing an urge to make the relationship between phone and student even more intimate.

They arrived at the main detector, which was essentially a large concrete and steel chamber about the height and width of a train carriage and about half as long, with large pipes connected at either end. In front of the chamber sat a small corrugated iron staircase leading up to an access panel. Two plastic spray bottles full of water sat on the top step, left there by Victor earlier to aid with a demonstration. He climbed the staircase and turned to face his audience.

'Right,' he said, in what he hoped was a confident and authoritative tone. The effect was minimal and he waited with growing irritation for the little shits to acknowledge he was even there at all.

'Can we try and show some semblance of politeness, guys?' asked the teacher, in a slightly too pleading tone. About half of the students fell silent. Victor couldn't tell if the other half hadn't heard him, or thought being polite meant they had to communicate in whispers, sniggers and frantic gestures so they could continue to ignore him without causing too much inconvenience. 'Millie, put the make-up away. Lauren, headphones out please. Curtis, Anthony, can you save the boring conversation for the coach? Thank you. Daniel, phone! How many times? Millie! Put it away!'

'I'm doing it!' snapped an angry looking fifteen year old who, Victor thought upon inspection, had a morning routine that involved covering her hands in makeup and then slapping herself repeatedly in the face. 'My God, there's no need to shout is there? Who's bein' rude now?' she asked, all the while continuing to inspect her face in her mirror.

Victor glared at her with as much contempt as he could gather while she closed her compact and put it into her bag. He hoped that, being an unknown entity to her, she wouldn't be bold enough to be quite so petulant with him. He was wrong.

'Yes?' she barked, through an expression so hateful Victor thought she was trying to set fire to him with the power of her mind. Fortunately, the power of her mind was such that it would have hardly fared any better had it been in possession of a can of petrol and a lighter.

'Nothing', Victor replied. 'I just wanted to make sure you were ready and I could continue.'

'Am I stoppin' you?'

He maintained the glare for a few moments, mainly because he couldn't think of anything to say, and took a deep breath as the teacher dealt with the last of the pupils who weren't paying attention. Within a minute he was looking down at twenty resentful faces sitting atop forty folded arms. He glanced at the teacher, whose brow was beading with sweat, and realised life could be worse.

'This is the most important of our five hermetic detectors,' Victor told them, gesturing to the chamber behind him. 'The accelerator allows us to send billions of protons whizzing through it at close to the speed of light.' The students stared blankly up at him, unmoved by this impressive fact. He reached for the two spray bottles and pointed the nozzles at each other. 'We send them in opposite directions around the collider and sometimes they bump into each other, just as some of the water particles from these bottles bump into each other when they're sprayed.' He squeezed the triggers and a light and unspectacular mist blossomed in front of him and then drifted slowly to the floor. The blank stares remained. One student sighed loudly.

'The problem is,' continued Victor, 'the gaps between the particles are so big that only a few of them collide. So, later today, protons will be redirected through these two tubes, where they will be squeezed into concentrated jets and fired into each other inside this chamber. This should cause far more of them to collide with each other than normal, generating a great deal more energy.' As he spoke, he twisted the nozzles on the bottles and squeezed them again, causing two thin jets of water to shoot out and collide with a splash that ricocheted onto some of the nearest students. They turned to each other and shared sympathetic looks of open-mouthed disgust, before glaring at Victor with such contempt you would think he had just spat at them. He pressed on regardless. 'The sensors in the detector will give us information about the collisions that will help improve our understanding of the origins of our universe.'

The students looked as disinterested and unmoved as they had done all morning, except for Millie and the splash victims, who were all looking at him the way a captive gorilla looks at children who bang on the glass. He stood in awkward silence for a moment, at a loss as to what to do next, until a creature in a navy cardigan and a pair of beige jeans so tight Victor was certain he could see not only the veins in his legs, but a pulse struggling to make its way down them, raised its hand.

'So is it in there you make all the black holes then?'

Before Victor could even attempt to address this asinine misunderstanding, Millie's voice filled the hallway again.

'They make black 'oles in there?!' she asked, aghast.

'Apparently,' confirmed thrombosis trousers boy. 'They're makin' black holes that might destroy the world.'

Millie rounded on Victor angrily. 'What you doin' that for?' she shouted, furious at his stupidity. For a moment he was speechless. Of all the things he had expected today, being treated like an idiot by something further down the food chain than the matter that grows at the bottom of his bin was not one of them. He searched for a response, but his brain simply shrugged its shoulders and sent what he imagined was a rather stupefied grin to set up camp on his face. He looked to the teacher for help, who rolled his eyes and shrugged. Victor silently told God what an utter, utter bastard he was and became suddenly aware of how funny his colleagues would find all this.

The news that he was conducting the day's school trip had caused quite a stir upstairs. He knew there was a great deal of speculation about how he would cope with a group of teenagers. The phrases 'eaten alive' and 'lamb to slaughter' had been thrown about liberally. Sam, a former student and now close colleague, had told him she was running a book on how long it would take him to have a nervous breakdown. At the time, he laughed along with the joke, but he was now starting to feel someone might make a tidy sum on the back of all this.

'They won't destroy the world,' said a timid voice. Every head turned towards a small, blond-haired boy. His face, pasty white until now, glowed red under the attention.

'How d'you know?' growled Millie.

'Because they'd be too small. If a black hole gets made, which it probably won't, it won't have enough mass to hold on to any matter. It'll disappear in a second.'

The boy who rescued Victor stared at the floor as he spoke, his cheeks still glowing wildly. His slight frame made him look younger than the rest of the group and this obvious vulnerability gave Victor some uncomfortable flashbacks of his own school days. He hated being the centre of attention and remembered what it was like to feel embarrassed by his intelligence and passion for science. He didn't like teenagers when he was one, and realised this probably had something to do with how he felt about them now he was in his forties.

'That's right, um...'

'Stanley,' said the boy.

'That's right, Stanley. It looks like we have a future physicist with us here today,' he said, with what he thought was an encouraging smile. There was a moment's silence before Millie let out a snort of derisive laughter. The boy shuffled his feet. Realising he hadn't helped at all, and whatever he said would only make things worse, Victor decided to press on, the only help he could now offer being to take the attention away from him. 'The accelerator really is perfectly safe,' he said. 'All the talk of black holes and the end of the world is another example of how you shouldn't believe everything you read in the newspapers.'

'I don't read newspapers,' said Millie.

'Really?' Victor asked as insincerely as he could, though he feared the tone was lost on her.

'So what if you're wrong then?' she said, after a brief pause.

'I'm sorry?'

'What if it doesn't do all that stuff you just said?'

'Well, then we should still get lots of useful information, because it will mean our current understanding of the big bang is flawed and needs revising.' He felt on safer ground here, like he might be able to explain these ideas so even she could understand them.

'Yeah, but won't you feel stupid? And won't all the other scientists be annoyed if you prove them wrong?'

'We're not really worried about proving each other right or wrong,' he said. 'We want to know how things work. When we're not sure, we come up with ideas and then we test them. If they turn out to be wrong, we come up with different ideas and test those too. And we keep going and we keep finding new things out.'

Millie shrugged, sighed, and started to gaze around the room. Victor took this as a sign the exchange was over and gave the teacher a nod.

'Well, unless there are any more questions for Professor Dennett,' he said. A handful of pupils shrugged. 'Well, then I guess we're done,' he added, somewhat deflated. 'I think we should thank Professor Dennett for his time.'

About six pupils mumbled something Victor supposed could have been a thank you.

'My pleasure,' he lied.

When the ordeal was over, Victor marched upstairs at the increased pace particular to people fuelled by severe grumpiness. He stormed into his office, slammed the door behind him, slumped heavily into his chair, and let out a long, long sigh. Sitting at her own desk a few feet away, Sam's fingers rattled away at her keyboard. She stared at her computer monitor, completely ignoring his dramatic entrance. 'So,' she said, in a mockingly cheerful tone, 'how were they?'

'Inspiring,' he sighed, unbuttoning his collar.

Sam let out a small chuckle. 'No nervous breakdown then?'

'No. I just about survived. So who won?'

'Funnily enough, I was the only one who thought it a likely outcome.'

'Well, I'm glad someone has some faith in me.' He shook the mouse on his desk and watched the monitor spring to life. 'Everything okay for this afternoon?'

'All set and running smoothly,' said Sam.

'We'll see,' he said, unconvinced. There had been so many problems with the accelerator that he didn't trust it when everything appeared to be running as it should. There were several false starts early on. The electromagnets had failed on day one, setting them back months as they ran through an endless list of checks and recalibrations. The press had a field day with that one. They had spent weeks talking about the 'black hole machine', predicting various doomsday scenarios for the day the switch was flicked. Then, after whipping the more gullible members of the public into a frenzy, they reported that the entire project was an abject failure. They lost countless beams to helium leaks and faulty components. And, of course, there was the infamous superluminal neutrino incident, where it looked like they had broken the speed of light because one of the millions of wires in the building had a loose connection. *Running smoothly, my arse*, he thought.

'Still glad you don't have any of your own then?'

'Sorry?' he said, snapping out of his pessimistic daydream.

'Kids,' prompted Sam.

'No,' he laughed. 'Yes, I mean. It baffles me that anyone would want to put themselves through it.'

'You don't know what you're missing,' said Sam.

'If you say so. Are you going to be here for power up?'

She gave him a sideways look. 'Why wouldn't I be?'

He shrugged. 'I don't know. Don't you have to butter up some television producers?'

Sam rolled her eyes. In addition to setting herself apart from every student Victor had ever taught and securing a position on his team that was all but equal to his own, Sam had also carved out a successful second career as a presenter of science-based television programmes. Audiences loved her for her warm, eloquent delivery, and the fact she clearly knew what she was talking about and knew how to explain it so middle England could understand it well enough to feel more intelligent than they actually were. Her warm persona, however, did not always extend to

Victor, especially when he decided to act as though he was bitter about her success.

'Firstly,' she said 'I'm not buttering anyone up. If anything, they want to flatter me into taking on another series. And secondly, you know very well that it isn't until next week.'

'And how long are you going to be away for this time?'

'Only a few weeks. I'm sure you'll be able to cope without me while I'm gone, so you can stop pouting.'

'Never,' he said, allowing a half smile to betray that he was only teasing.

She returned the smile as she stood up and walked towards the door. 'Coffee?'

'Thanks.'

As the door closed behind her, Victor closed his eyes to enjoy the peace and quiet he had been longing for half an hour ago. It was almost immediately interrupted by a commotion spilling in through the open window. Listening carefully, he heard the exasperated voice of the teacher competing with excited chatter, laughter and bickering as he tried to hurry his students on to the waiting coach. As he listened, a voice cut through the crowd as it prattled loudly into a mobile phone.

'Oi, right, I'm at this really borin' place in the middle of nowhere where these people are tryin' to make black holes that are gonna end the world...'

Millie's voice disappeared as she boarded the coach and the door closed behind her. The sound of the engine grew quieter as it pulled away and disappeared down the road. Momentarily, the silence returned and Victor's gaze drifted towards his desk and rested on the photo of his wife. 'I don't know what I'm missing,' he told her.

4

The Work of His Hands

The body of the marionette was all but finished when Arthur first noticed that his universe was not quite as perfect as he first thought. He held the puppet under the lamp, which, but for the soft glow from the centre of the room, provided the only source of light at this late hour. He checked the details of its features, created by the removal of the hundreds of curled wood shavings at his feet until it had taken on the form of a man. He wiggled each leg to ensure the pins in the ankles and knees allowed them to move freely and then did the same with the arms. He turned the head back and forth, nodded it up and down. Everything was working as it should – smooth movements, good balance. *Very good,* he thought. He rested the puppet on his lap and prepared to make the control. His father had taught him to always complete the woodwork before painting and dressing his marionettes. He was an incredible craftsman and his methods were always law when Arthur was learning from him. Arthur had prepared four thin lengths of pine and arranged them side by side on the table next to him. He picked up the two longest pieces and held one across the other to form a cross, marking the area where they met with a pencil. Then, using his whittling knife, he cut a small, square indent into each strip and blew the dust from them before pressing them together. They slotted together perfectly. He ran his finger over the join and was satisfied to find he could barely feel it. Some skills do not leave you. He picked the puppet back up and held the control over it, imagining how the finished marionette would move when he manipulated it.

A flicker in the background caught his attention. He leaned forward and tried to focus on the shifting points of light. The sea of galaxies was still swirling as it had been all evening, but there was something odd about one tiny cluster. Squinting, he was sure he could see a faint pulse, as if the cluster was throbbing. He shifted the chair forward and looked through the magnifying glass. He was right. There was a definite, regular ripple spreading out in a perfect circle. As he watched, he noticed the pulse growing stronger and more frequent and, as it did so, he was able to identify the source of this strange phenomenon as an otherwise unremarkable spiral galaxy. A sense of unease flowed over him as he watched the ripples grow in intensity. He became aware of a humming sound, faint at first, which quickly grew louder and throbbed in time with the ripples. Within a few seconds it was almost deafening. The galaxy shook violently in front of him, blurring his vision.

There was a sound like a million zips being undone all at once.

Arthur was suddenly overwhelmed with nausea. He lost all sense of balance and felt for all the world like he was falling. Onwards and onwards he fell, tumbling ever downward, but he never hit the ground. Then, just as quickly as it started, it stopped. He sank back into his chair, the falling sensation having abated, the puppet and its control clutched tightly to his chest, surrounded by silence and darkness.

5

Numbers

While it is always nice to test a hypothesis and have it proven correct, there are occasions where accurately predicting something turns out to be a real pain in the hole. The frantic noise and activity that greeted Victor as he entered the main control room told him this was definitely one of those occasions. His earlier suspicion that something would go wrong was evidently correct.

'What the bloody hell is going on?!' he yelled at no-one in particular, which was just as well, as no-one in particular seemed to notice. Everyone was too busy answering phones that rang and rang and rang for attention until they were picked up and chattered into and then rang again as soon as the receiver was replaced, or poring over printouts and passing them round so everyone could cast their confused expressions over them. Row upon row of computer monitors displayed graphs and charts and statistics that elicited exasperated exclamations from men and women as they slid from screen to screen on wheeled chairs and tried to make sense of what they were seeing.

Amidst all this chaos, Victor heard his name being called across the lab. He looked towards the source of the call and saw Sam hurrying towards him.

'Have you seen it?' she asked.

'Seen what? What the bloody hell is going on?' he repeated.

'The results are insane,' said Sam. 'We had a massive energy spike the instant we redirected the beams.'

This was confusing. A huge energy spike was precisely what they had expected to see. Indeed, it is precisely what they had *hoped* to see.

'No, a *massive* energy spike,' said Sam. 'Much bigger than we predicted.'

Victor looked around the room again. It may seem like a contradiction, but unexpected data is something those working at the cutting edge of particle physics have come to expect from experiments like this. That alone should have been no cause for this kind of excitement. *There's something else*, thought Victor.

'There's something else,' said Sam.

Another irritatingly accurate prediction. 'Go on,' he said, bracing himself.

'The power is out.'

Victor cast his eyes over the room. The lights were on. The computers were running. The printers were spitting out reams of paper at an alarming rate, and the number of people tapping at their smartphones suggested the wireless network was still live. He looked back at Sam, incomprehension written all over his face. She raised her eyebrows. And then it clicked.

'The power to the *accelerator*?' he asked, his voice barely above a whisper and his heart dangerously close to palpitations.

Sam nodded, her expression sullen.

'What about the generators?'

'They fired up, but the ring isn't using them.'

'Oh God.'

'I don't think he's got much to do with it,' said Sam.

How wrong she was.

Victor had good reason to be concerned about the power outage. While E Equals had been a working research laboratory for almost fifteen years, the main accelerator took so long to complete that it had only been operational for five of them. It had always been part of the original plans for the facility, but the infrastructure necessary to meet the accelerator's power requirements did not feature as part of the initial build, which meant a separate power supply had to be installed later on. This was not an oversight. It was decided a separate, more secure power supply was necessary for both safety and practicality. At peak times, the accelerator's energy consumption rivalled that of a small city. Naturally, conventional supply chains weren't up to this task. It was also essential that it received a constant flow of power while it was running, as a sudden loss of power could have disastrous effects. The beams of protons that travelled around the accelerator rings were steered by superconducting magnets. These magnets had to be cooled to a temperature colder than outer space. A temperature rise of just a few degrees would result in the magnets losing control of the beams and, given that an uncontrolled beam could melt half a ton of copper in the blink of an eye, this could not be allowed to happen. Ever. So the designers of the accelerator devised a method of sourcing power from three different energy suppliers. The aim was to spread their consumption across suppliers and, if one suffered a fault and the supply dropped, they could, temporarily at least, increase consumption from the other providers. In the unlikely event that all three providers suffered an outage simultaneously, a bank of huge emergency diesel generators was installed to provide enough energy to dump the beams safely and power down without a problem, making a sudden total loss of power impossible. Or so they thought.

Victor's first reaction was to get in touch with the engineers for a status report. Had the beams melted the ring? Were they looking at the destruction of billions of pounds worth of particle accelerator? He picked up a ringing phone, put it straight back down, and then lifted the receiver before the caller had time to redial. No sooner had he dialled the extension than Sam put her finger on the switch hook and told him there was no point. They were already doing everything they could and the last thing they needed was another voice asking the same questions they were already asking themselves. Despite his desperate yearning for answers, he had to concede she was correct. He had, however, a little more trouble accepting her next point.

'What *you* need to do is look at the *data*.'

Victor wasn't sure this was what he needed to do. His head was spinning, his ears ringing. He was hardly in the right frame of mind to crunch numbers and study graphs. But Sam, offering him a single sheet of paper, persisted.

'It's the energy report from the last second before we lost power,' she said, staring at him intently.

He scanned the page, working his way down the list of values. Everything appeared normal until he reached the very last figure. His jaw dropped.

'This has to be a mistake,' he said.

'Probably,' agreed Sam. '*Hopefully*', she added. 'But what if it's not?'

'Two times ten to the power of fifty-one joules?'

Sam nodded.

'That's more than the total energy of the *Sun*!'

6

As the Blind Man Gropes in Darkness

Arthur was quite certain he was no longer in his attic, but that was the sum total of his understanding of his situation. He tried fumbling his way around his new environment, feeling the walls for any sign of an exit, but there were too many oddly shaped objects protruding from them and none of them reacted to being pushed or pulled or turned. It quickly proved to be a futile task. He stumbled around with his hands outstretched, searching for his chair, and stepped on the marionette that he must have dropped in his initial confusion. He fumbled around the floor for the control and then sat back down, absent-mindedly running his hands over both items to check for damage as he thought about his situation. There was, admittedly, very little information at hand to consider, but he was acutely aware that thinking was a far more useful activity than groping around in the dark and waiting to stub his toe. It was also his firm belief that if you can't solve a problem by thinking about it, then the next best thing to do is wait, and he was quite content to think while waiting. And so, he thought. Had he jumped the gun in thinking he had finally got all of the measurements correct? When it went wrong, he usually knew about it terribly quickly. There was barely a flash and a pop and a fizzle and then he had to start again. And he had started again so many times. The longest he had ever had a universe survive before was about three seconds. This one had been stable for hours. Once it had been going that long, you would think you were safe. Maybe this was a different problem.

Maybe this one had spilled *outwards* instead of collapsing inwards. This last idea he quickly dismissed on the grounds it was at best ridiculous and at worst terrifying. He returned to thinking, searching for a different, more comforting idea. None came. He waited.

Time passed. He couldn't say how much. And then he heard something – a dull *thud* from somewhere to his right. He had no idea what it was or what it meant, but it was something else to think about at least. He thought about it.

Thud!

There it was again, this time from the left. He thought about this too.

Thud!

This time it came from right in front of him. He barely had any time at all to think about it before it was followed by a much louder noise, more of a *clunk* this time, and then a definite *creak.* And then, moments later, there was light.

7

Deus Ex Machina

'Don't be stupid, Victor,' yelled Sam, hurrying along the corridor behind him. 'We have to wait. Let the engineers deal with it.'

Victor walked at a brisk pace, breaking into a short, nervous jog every few steps. 'I need to know,' he barked over his shoulder. 'So do you.' This wasn't remotely true and Victor knew it. Or, at least, he would have known it had he been acting rationally, which was something he could typically be depended on to do, having such a world-class scientific mind and all. But even the most hardened students of logic and reason have a tipping point. Realising he might have broken the most expensive piece of lab equipment ever built was Victor's. Having reached it, he forgot the thing that had most impressed him about Sam as a student – the thing that ultimately told him he absolutely had to employ her once she completed her doctorate – he could always trust her to challenge him when he needed to be challenged, and he could do so knowing her judgement was often better than his own. Today, however, she couldn't reach him – it suited Victor to believe the lie, so he convinced himself not only that he knew what she was thinking, but also that she was thinking what he wanted her to think. He continued along the corridor, consumed by that peculiar feature of people who pride themselves on being rational – namely that they are never more certain of their rationality than when they have lost all sense of it.

'We don't even know if it's safe,' she pleaded.

'If there's no power, there's no beam,' he said. He wasn't stopping. He had spent half his life on this project. He was not going to wait around for someone else to come and find out if a proton beam had just destroyed billions of pounds worth of equipment, and his career, in a nanosecond.

They reached the detector and surveyed the scene cautiously. Everything seemed fine from the outside. Even the two spray bottles from earlier were still sitting on the steps, apparently undisturbed. They were cool to the touch. So was the wall of the detector – a promising sign.

Victor took a deep breath, walked to the end of the detector and opened the small panel that hid one of the release handles. Gripping it firmly with both hands, he used his body weight to turn it from a horizontal position to a vertical one. There was a dull *thud* from somewhere inside the chamber. He walked to the panel at the opposite end and did the same. As soon as he had turned the handle, the door release panel popped open in the centre of the detector, right at the top of the small staircase. Both their shoulders sagged. A careful listener might have even heard Victor's heart sink. The panel was locked electromagnetically – a security feature designed to prevent the detector from being opened while a beam was active. By opening, it confirmed the power really was out. Ascending the small staircase, Victor approached the door and took hold of the large red lever exposed by the opening of the panel. He pulled on it sharply. There was a final metallic *clunk*. This was it – the moment of truth. He pushed on the door and, as it swung noiselessly into the chamber, peered inside and started to gibber.

It wasn't that the sight before him was confusing. Confusion is the wrong word. Confusion is the sensation that exists between the moment you come to an abrupt halt and the moment you realise you have caught your sleeve on a door handle. This was orders of magnitude further up the scale. There was no word to describe this feeling. Imagine witnessing a rabbit giving birth to a whale. Whatever feeling you would have while watching that is the one Victor had as he peered into the chamber. He stared dumbly, his head throbbing. Behind him, Sam said something but he couldn't make it out. His legs turned to jelly beneath him. He had expected to find glowing bits of melted metal and a sickly burnt electrical smell. While that would have been devastating, at least it would have made sense. What he actually saw made him feel as though his brain had tripped on a raised paving slab. He didn't notice there were no glowing bits of metal. He didn't notice there was no sickly electrical smell. He didn't notice these things because he was too busy noticing the tatty leather armchair in the centre of the detector. It definitely wasn't there when they sealed the chamber several days ago. Neither was the elderly man who was sitting in it and clutching a wooden doll and what looked like a crucifix.

'Hello,' said the elderly man. Victor didn't have time to reply. He was too busy fainting.

8

On the Right Cheek

Arthur struggled to make out the features of the man standing before him. He had been in total darkness for some time and the light the man was silhouetted against was blinding. Someone was talking, but Arthur could tell it was not the person he could see. It was a female voice. 'Victor,' it kept saying, occasionally adding, 'say something,' or, 'talk to me,' with increasing urgency.

'Hello,' Arthur ventured. He regretted it immediately. The shadowy figure pointed into the chamber and made a series of gasping sounds, which was more than a little unsettling. Arthur's eyes, beginning to adjust to the light, could just about make out the man's mouth opening and closing in silent, juddering spasms. His eyes swam in a mixture of bewilderment and terror and he began to rub his chest before his legs buckled beneath him. He clung to a rail with his other hand but could not prevent himself from slumping to the floor. As he fell, his head rocked backwards and made a sickening clang against the metal barrier behind him.

'Oh Christ!' yelled the female voice. She leapt into view and knelt down in front of him, cradling his head. 'Victor? Victor, can you hear me? Victor?'

The man, evidently named Victor, gasped for air as his eyes searched for something to focus on. Feeling useless sitting and watching, Arthur decided he should do something, especially as he appeared to have caused the problem.

'Um, is there anything I can do to help?' he asked. The woman turned, startled, before she too stared dumbly.

'Hello,' he said again, attempting to offer a warm smile that might avoid making her panic in much the same way. She continued staring.

'What... Who... What are you doing in there?' she eventually managed to squeeze out.

'No idea,' he said, far too cheerfully. 'Is there anything I can do to help?'

'What?'

Arthur pointed at Victor. 'Your friend – he looks like he's having a bit of trouble.'

She frowned for a moment before the panic of a few moments ago came back to her in a flash. Her eyes widened and she turned back to Victor.

'Oh, yes. Shit,' she said, and she started to gently pat his cheek. 'Victor? Can you hear me? It's Samantha.'

Quite what she hoped to achieve by this, Arthur had no idea. As fascinating as the spectacle was, he couldn't sit by and watch as she completely failed to tend to a man who, for all they knew, may have been having a heart attack.

'No, no, that's not how it's done at all,' said Arthur, and he stood up from his chair and strode towards the pair of them. He stooped down next to the woman and steered her hand away from Victor's face. 'Allow me,' he said. She yielded, leaning back to give Arthur some room. He studied the man's face for a moment, cradled his head in both hands and turned it left and right, nodded it up and down. He paused for a moment. Then, he slapped Victor smartly across the cheek. This agitated the woman greatly.

'What are you doing?!' she raged. Arthur felt her scolding tone was unnecessary given the ineffective nature of her own intervention.

'Slapping him round the face,' he replied, incredulous. Surely, that much was obvious.

'Why?'

'To see if he's having a heart attack.'

'How does that help you to see if he's having a heart attack?'

'Well, if someone looks like they're having a heart attack, and you slap them round the face, and they actually *are* having a heart attack, then they continue to look like they're having a heart attack.' This explanation appeared to confuse her. Her face turned blank for a moment, as though she was trying to process what Arthur had said. Judging by her response, she failed in the attempt.

'What?!' she spluttered, appearing more irritable than panic-stricken now.

Arthur tried to explain further. 'Well, it doesn't make much of a difference, does it? If someone is having a heart attack, a slap round the face won't change anything, so they'll carry on having a heart attack. But if they're not having a heart attack, a good slap round the face makes them look... well, like him.' Arthur pointed.

She turned her gaze back to her friend. His breathing had slowed down and some colour had returned to his face – on both cheeks, not just the one that was smarting from the strike. His eyes, too, had snapped back into focus and were fixed on Arthur.

'There,' said Arthur with no little satisfaction. 'He doesn't look like he's having a heart attack now, does he? He just looks startled.' He smiled at Victor, ready to accept his thanks.

Victor punched Arthur in the face.

'And maybe a little angry,' Arthur reflected as he sat back up and rubbed his jaw.

9

A Lowly Seat

Understandably, given the circumstances, Victor found his next conversation with Sam rather trying. Receiving a bright and cheerful 'hello' from a man who could not possibly exist does little to foster clear thinking. And he absolutely should not have existed. As far as Victor could tell, he and Sam were the first to open the detector since the proton beams were last active, which meant the man must have been in it during the energy spike. It wasn't simply that he shouldn't have survived it; there should have been no trace of him whatsoever – not even an ashy little mark on the floor. Yet there he was. And now they were faced with the impossible question of what to do next.

It didn't help that Sam kept asking questions about who they should tell, what they should tell them, what the hell had happened, and how Victor was feeling. He said nothing for some time. He was in no state to have a chat about what constituted an appropriate course of action following the impossible discovery of an impossible man in an impossibly expensive piece of machinery that had recently had some impossibly hot photons firing through it impossibly quickly.

Somehow, they arrived at the decision to say nothing until they had at least discussed it further. Inexplicably, they also decided they needed to hide all of the evidence that anything had happened at all. Panic can make otherwise rational people do some very strange things. It made Sam and Victor act like a pair of teenagers who were desperately trying to tidy up after a party while their parents were driving back from the airport, which is why they found themselves smuggling this strange man up to their office to see if they could get some answers from him.

Victor made to head straight off when Sam pointed out they needed to reseal the detector. This led to another problem. What the hell were they going to do with the chair? They couldn't just leave it there. They had to hide it, which was far from an easy task in a tunnel that wasn't designed by someone who had the need to hide armchairs on their mind when they were drawing up the blueprints. They tried behind the pipes on either side of the detector but there wasn't nearly enough room. Victor even wrenched the little iron staircase away and tried to slide it in the space behind it, but it wouldn't fit all the way in and it prevented the steps from lining back up properly. Eventually, they had to settle for stowing it away in a maintenance cupboard down the corridor. If someone found it there, they could at least plead plausible ignorance. Having dealt with the chair as best they could, they led their unwelcome guest off to interrogate him.

10

Hypothesis

Arthur said nothing as he was escorted through the building. Not only did he not know what to say, he was also afraid that if he did speak, he would elicit another violent reaction from Victor, who, based on the small amount of evidence he had gathered so far, might very well have been unstable. Following his presumed panic attack, he was involved in some terribly energetic dialogue with Sam about what they were going to do with Arthur, which was ominously disconcerting until Arthur realised that Victor was merely anxious to keep his arrival a secret from others. This made them seem less threatening, though it didn't make them any less rude. They spoke about him as though he wasn't there, manhandled his armchair into a grubby looking cupboard, and even treated him like he was somehow imposing on them, which he found rather rich. Surely, he had more right to feel inconvenienced – at least they knew where in the world they were, while he had been somehow transported out of his attic and flung into a pitch black chamber who knows where? He refrained, however, from saying anything for the time being because it was as yet unclear whether these two people were responsible for whatever had happened to him or if all three of them had fallen foul of some as yet unidentified agent.

Once they had settled on a plan, they ushered Arthur down the corridor, away from the small dark chamber they had found him in and into an even smaller (though thankfully well lit) one. He noticed it made him feel ever-so-slightly heavier than normal, and surmised that it must be transporting them vertically. Every now and then, one of them turned and frowned at him, as though checking he was still there. He tried smiling, but they snapped their gaze away each time their eyes met his.

When the doors finally opened, Victor issued the bewildering command to look natural. What was it about Arthur's appearance that he considered *un*natural? More confusing still was the way Victor threw furtive glances up and down the corridor. It was as though he thought looking 'natural' involved looking what any person of sound mind would more adequately call 'suspicious'. Whatever he was hoping to avoid, it was obviously making him terribly anxious, and Arthur found himself glancing up and down the corridor as well, uncertain exactly what threats to his safety he was looking for.

Eventually, they steered him through a doorway into a small office and ordered him to sit in a chair that was far less comfortable than his armchair, which was, for reasons he couldn't fathom, currently locked in a cupboard many floors beneath him. Victor sat down opposite, staring at the floor and rubbing his temples.

'So what do we do now?' asked Sam.

Victor offered no answer. Sam didn't press him for one. Arthur continued to say nothing. The question hadn't been directed at him and Victor looked extremely uneasy. He had already punched Arthur once and he did not wish to provoke him further.

He waited and took in his new surroundings, his eyes settling on a strange device on the desk in front of him. It consisted of five small metal spheres suspended from a frame by thin wire threads. He lifted the leftmost sphere and leaned in to take a closer look, running his fingers over the cool, smooth surface for a moment, and then let it drop. As the outer spheres bounced back and forth, he realised it was a device for demonstrating the conservation of momentum and kinetic energy. It had a pleasing beauty and simplicity, and he allowed himself to be almost hypnotised by the toing and froing and clicking and clacking until he noticed the incredulous glares on his hosts' faces. He stopped the device with his hand and the awkward silence crept back into the room.

Victor let out a heavy sigh. When he finally spoke, it was barely more than a whisper, though the seething tone was unmistakable. 'I don't understand,' he said. He turned and looked Arthur in the eye. Something about his expression made Arthur shrink back and grip the arms of the chair. 'Who are you?' he asked.

Arthur, still cautious, spoke slowly and softly. 'My name is Arthur.'

'Arthur,' repeated Victor. 'Is that it? Just... Arthur.'

'Well, my full name is Arthur Fowler.'

Victor looked at Sam and offered a gesture that was equal parts incredulity and irritation. Sam shrugged.

'Fine,' said Victor. 'And where did you come from, Arthur Fowler?' Arthur noticed his surname was dripping with contempt when Victor said it.

'My attic,' he said. This did little to satisfy Victor, whose eyes widened.

'Your *attic?*'

'It's... it's a room at the top of my house.'

Victor pinched the bridge of his nose. 'Yes, I know what an attic *is*,' he said. 'What I mean is what are you doing here? Why were you in the detector?'

Arthur found it odd that someone would ask a question unrelated to the one they meant to ask, but felt it unwise to point this out. 'I'm afraid I have no idea. I was there one moment, and then I was here.'

'What were you doing?' asked Sam. 'In your attic, I mean.'

35

'Not a lot really – I was working on this.' He held up the marionette which he had been clutching since he exited the dark chamber. 'Then I noticed something odd in the universe I'd created and then everything went... swirly.' He uttered this last word quietly, embarrassed that it was the only one his brain could offer.

His hosts exchanged glances. 'Say that again,' said Victor.

'Swirly?' he asked, even more embarrassed.

'No, the other bit.'

'Oh! Well, I've been trying to get it right for years. It's something of a hobby. I build universes. I know many think it a rather wasteful pastime but I do find it rather relaxing. Anyway, it wasn't until a few hours ago that I actually managed to make a stable one. Except it looks like it wasn't quite as stable as I thought. Something went wrong and then... I was here.'

His hosts shared a conspiratorial look. He couldn't tell what they were silently expressing to one another, though the odd question he was asked by Sam suggested a mix of doubt and confusion. 'So... you built the universe?' she said, adding, 'Today?'

'I built *a* universe today,' Arthur corrected her. He was distracted from elaborating by a sudden flicker in the corner of his eye. He had nudged something on the desk as he gestured with his hands, which caused the screen in front of him to spring to life. The image that appeared stopped him in his tracks. It was a perfect universe, awash with galaxies. Believing his new companions must have shared his hobby, he asked, 'Is this yours?'

'Yes,' sighed Victor, 'that's my computer.'

'No. *That*,' he said, pointing at the screen. 'It's remarkable. It looks identical to mine.'

'What?'

'He's talking about the picture,' said Sam.

36

'Yes! Did you build it?'

'That's the Hubble Deep Field,' said Victor, glumly. 'It's just a desktop background.' Neither phrase meant anything to Arthur.

'It's space,' explained Sam. 'A picture of our universe. Well, part of it.'

'So you both built it?'

'Of course we didn't *build* it!' snapped Victor. 'It's *space*. We're *in* it.'

'Oh,' Arthur said. And then he realised. '*Oh*.'

'Oh *what*?'

'This is *my* universe.'

Victor breathed yet another heavy sigh and rested his chin on his hands. 'Of course it is.'

'You think this is the universe you made today?' asked Sam.

'Yes.'

'Well it can't be,' said Victor, who, Arthur felt, had turned unnecessarily morose. 'This one was here yesterday. I remember only too well. It was a much better day than today.'

Arthur got up from his seat and walked over to the window. A nearby star was sinking lazily into the horizon. 'I presume this planet orbits that star,' he said.

Victor rolled his eyes but said nothing. Sam confirmed the fact.

'How quickly?'

'Every three hundred and sixty five days.'

'And how long is a day?'

'Twenty four hours,' she said and, accurately predicting the course of his questioning, added, 'and an hour is sixty minutes and you can see how long a minute is on that clock up there. Every revolution of the red hand is a minute.'

Arthur watched the red hand making its steady sweep of the clock face for a few seconds and recalled the image of his swirling universe. Objects that drew circles around objects that drew circles around objects that drew circles... He had seen galaxies turning at a similar speed. Under the magnifying glass, he had been able to make out individual stars, with tiny little dots of planets looping round them so rapidly they appeared almost as complete circles drawing themselves over and over again. He remembered the throbbing that preceded his sudden arrival in the dark chamber, deep beneath his feet. He considered this all for a moment, turning a possibility over in his head, and then turned to face his hosts. 'I think it is perfectly possible this is my universe,' he said.

'Oh good,' said Victor. 'That clears that up then.'

'Well, I'd hardly go that far. No doubt there are other possibilities we need to discount, but I consider it a reasonable initial hypothesis.'

'You think it's *reasonable?*' Victor yelled, punctuating the final word with a thump of his desk. 'You want to hear my hypothesis? You're a bloody lunatic. How's that for *reasonable?*'

Before Arthur could say he didn't think it at all reasonable, Sam asked Arthur to excuse them for a moment and invited Victor to step outside. Arthur turned back to the window and observed what remained of the star while he waited. It had almost disappeared from view when they returned. It was Sam who spoke.

'Sorry about that, Arthur. My name is Samantha. Most people call me Sam.' She sat in the chair previously occupied by Victor and invited Arthur to sit back down opposite her. Victor took a chair by the door and resumed his troubled staring. 'I have a question about your theory,' Sam said. 'You claim this universe is only a few hours old. How then do you explain the fact that you are talking with people who are clearly more than a few hours old?'

'Well,' he said, 'I believe that as an outside observer I saw time passing very quickly. It's quite possible I saw a great many years ticking by every moment. But now I'm here, I'm experiencing that time very differently. I'm experiencing it the way you experience it.' He smiled at Victor, almost apologetically. 'It's all quite logical really.'

Victor pointed his finger at Arthur and looked as though he was about to say something. Or hit him again. Instead, he smiled, shook his head, and stood up.

'Have I done something wrong?' Arthur asked as the door slammed shut.

11

Evidence

Victor marched out of his office and headed back down to the control room, quietly fuming at what he considered a grotesque misuse of the word 'logical' and feeling somewhat troubled by the rage bubbling within him. Already, he was certain he hated Arthur. He was uncomfortable at the idea of himself as a man who could hate anyone, let alone a man who was, he was also certain, mentally ill. He didn't think it was acceptable to hate someone who was mentally ill, Nonetheless, he was sure he did. In fact, not only did he hate him – he felt like he wanted to harm him. This was the most uncomfortable realisation. In scientific circles, Victor was regarded as the owner of one of the finest minds in the world. It was the sort of mind that could be trusted to remain rational, calm and measured, and definitely not start swimming with violent impulses. But, try as he might, he couldn't stop himself from imagining punching Arthur to the floor. Objectively, he knew this was a bad idea – if today's events didn't end his career, beating up an old man with mental health issues certainly would. He had already taken one swipe at him, but at least he could blame the fact that he was hysterical at the time. Realising this, he acted on the only other thought that made any sense and left the room.

He arrived at the control room to find nothing had changed. The phones were still ringing, the computers were still presenting infuriatingly impossible numbers, the pieces of paper were still being passed around the room and the people reading them were still frowning and scratching their heads. Several of them spoke to Victor, or rather, at him. He couldn't recall afterwards what any of them had said and was dimly aware of answering every question with 'I don't know' and greeting every theory with 'maybe'. They must have been able to sense the breakdown he was close to having because they soon started to put as much distance as possible between themselves and Victor in order to avoid being burdened with the responsibility of helping when it actually occurred.

It was not an environment likely to improve his state of mind, so he trudged off in search of somewhere quiet, eventually finding himself in a quad, thankfully empty now the evening was drifting in. He sat in the fading light for a while and tried to make sense of the mess surrounding him, taking a brief moment, for the second time today, to curse a God he didn't believe existed for placing him in a situation he didn't *want* to believe existed. How could this have happened? How did the mad old git do it? Somehow, Arthur must have entered the facility unnoticed, navigated his way to the depths of the accelerator tunnel, sabotaged the experiment, faked the output data, and locked himself in the chamber. It was simple really, provided he ignored little things like the vast knowledge of particle physics, mechanical engineering and the E Equals computer network he would have needed in order to sabotage the experiment and fake the data, or the fact the detector could only be locked from the outside and the accelerator floor was locked down while the beam was active. It was easy, really, if it wasn't for the fact it was impossible. Unless...

He must have had help.

It was one of those ideas that realises itself and then wonders why it took so long to arrive. It was obvious. There was no way Arthur could have done all this himself. He *must* have had help. Everything became much more possible if there was more than one person involved.

Victor sprang to his feet. If he had help, then he wasn't just some crackpot. Arthur wasn't insane – he was acting a part. This was a set-up! He could hate him as much as he wanted and there was no need to feel guilty about it. The bastard *deserved* it.

He raced out of the quad and back to the stairwell, launching himself up the stairs two at a time. The thought of punching Arthur reappeared in his imagination. He tried to ignore it, but each thud of his feet echoed like a blow to the old man's face. After three flights, the vision had evolved into an image of Arthur admitting through blood and broken teeth that the whole thing was indeed a hoax, before Victor hit him again, just for good measure, just because he could. *That's for making me believe you were crazy*, he said to the sobbing, broken, imaginary Arthur.

After four flights, the energy provided by the fantasy ran out and he had to pause to catch his breath. Leaning on the bannister, panting and sweating, the idea of himself as someone who could beat a man to a pulp finally realised itself to be a hopeless fraud and dissolved almost immediately. It vacated his head without so much as an apology for the inconvenience it had caused and left Victor with nothing but a newfound anxiety about what kind of person he was. He leant against the wall and slid down it until he was sitting on the floor. He rubbed his aching thighs and realised his hands were shaking. Hit with a sudden craving for sugar, he forced himself to stand and made his way back down one flight of stairs to a vending machine he vaguely remembered passing on the way up. He stared at the contents for almost a minute. Then, realising how little he cared which item he ate, he put a coin in the slot and jabbed at the buttons until the machine hummed and a row of chocolate bars slowly drifted forwards. He stared at the one at the front of the line. The chocolate bar seemed to stare back at him. He laughed. An onlooker would have probably described it as a 'maniacal' laugh. He should have expected this. On a day when the impossible had been casually described as logical by no less than God himself, Victor should have known he would be let down by the most dependable of universal forces. For, while gravity has made it its business to wield inexorable power on absolutely everything in the universe, to ensure there is nothing in existence that can escape its relentless influence, it is a well-documented and irrefutable fact that it is yet to permeate the interior of the average vending machine.

It was too much. Victor rested his head against the clear plastic window separating him from the floating chocolate bar and started to sob like a baby. He banged his head against the plastic as tears rolled down his cheeks. Balling his hands into tight fists, his despair gave way to anger once more and he took a step back so he could deliver a vicious kick to the machine. He slapped the sides, the top, the base. He didn't know if he was trying to knock the chocolate bar loose or was simply, madly, trying to hurt an inanimate object as he lashed out again and again and again. But it did no good. Despite the onslaught, the snack wouldn't budge. It hung there stubbornly, impossibly.

He drew his arm back to deliver one final, massive blow, but he couldn't do it. Not because he had finally found some restraint. Rather, he could not physically move his arm. Confused, he turned to see his clenched fist above his shoulder. Casting his eyes a little lower, he noticed another fist clenched tightly around his forearm. This second fist was much bigger than his. It was attached to another arm, also much bigger than his. Turning further, he saw that the arm that was much bigger than his belonged, unsurprisingly, to a man who was much bigger than him. The man who was much bigger than Victor spoke through an expression that was a mixture of concern and confusion, seasoned with a hint of aggressive anger management issues. 'Bad day?' the man rumbled.

Victor nodded. 'It won't fall down,' he squeaked. 'Gravity's supposed to make it fall down but it won't fall down.'

The large man dropped Victor's arm and stepped over to the machine. He struck the top of the plastic window casually with the heel of his palm. There was a dull thud. He reached into the tray and pulled out the chocolate bar. Then, in a display of charity and sympathy that might have brought Victor to tears had he not already been shedding them, he unwrapped it and offered it to him. Victor stared at it for a moment before taking it and biting into it. He offered a meek and muffled, 'Thank you.'

'No problem,' said the man. He was wearing a white shirt with black tabs on the shoulders – the kind designed to look as much like a police uniform as possible without breaking any rules about that sort of thing so the people who saw it would believe the wearer held more authority than they actually did. There was a badge clipped to the shirt pocket with a photo and the name 'Mick Harper' on it. Beneath the name was his job title: 'Security Officer'.

'You alright?' he asked. 'You need me to call someone?' Dealing with emotional people was not part of Mick's job description, Victor could tell.

Victor turned down the offer as calmly as he could. He wanted to beg him not to call anyone but knew, even in his current state, that this would have had the opposite of the desired effect.

'So the vending machine is safe then?'

Victor assured him it was, and realised with embarrassment what a mess he must have looked.

'Is this because of everything kicking off downstairs? You lot are looking a bit stressed out.'

'You've been down there?' Victor asked.

'No, mate. Seen it on the monitors.'

'Monitors?'

'Yeah, the cameras,' said Mick, pointing at the ceiling.

Victor looked up at a small black dome. 'Oh,' he said. A thought occurred. 'Do they record everything?'

'Yep. Why? You worried a video of a bloke losing it with a vending machine is going to end up on YouTube?'

'No. Well, yes, but only now you mention it. No, I was thinking of something else. Do we have many cameras here?'

'Are you joking? A facility like this? They're bloody everywhere. You're lucky you can piss without someone watching you, there's that many of 'em. Pretty much every corner of this place is covered.'

'Interesting,' said Victor.

'Not really,' said Mick.

'I wonder, would you mind doing me another favour?'

The security office was a long, thin room with a bench running along one wall. Spare computer parts and stratified layers of paper littered the shelves and floor, and wires sprawled over the room like weeds growing over that odd collection of cheap furniture and sophisticated equipment that can always be found in such spaces. Several computers sat along the bench and a bank of screens displayed various feeds from cameras all round the site. At the far end, another security officer doubled up as an IT technician as he tinkered with a circuit board. Maybe it was a sign of the way the E Equals budget was stretched to breaking point in every department. Or maybe security just didn't want anyone else touching their stuff.

Mick stood over Victor's shoulder as he sat at one of the computers and stared intently at the monitor while forty-eight hours' worth of video footage played at thirty-two times normal speed. VIctor was not happy at having to scan through it this quickly, but Mick had made it patently clear that he was not happy scanning through it any slower. Victor decided on forty-eight hours because the logs, which Mick could also access, showed the detector had been opened up two days ago for last minute checking and maintenance. They started the video there, and watched at normal speed as an engineering crew closed and sealed the door of the clearly empty detector. From there, Victor wound through the footage, using a control wheel to slow down playback whenever there was so much as a hint of movement on the screen. At no point had the door been reopened.

He re-lived his nightmare with the party of school children, that ugly experience that felt at the time like it would never end racing by in a few seconds, and knew he was reaching the end of the recording. Sure enough, moments later, he saw himself and Sam entering the tunnel and approaching the chamber. He took his hand from the control wheel and it dropped back to normal speed.

'No joy?' asked Mick.

Victor shook his head. 'Could the file have been tampered with? Edited?'

'No point asking me, mate' said Mick. He gestured to his colleague. 'He's the techie one. What do you reckon, Phil?'

The other man spoke without looking up from his circuit board. 'Very unlikely,' he said. 'They'd have to crack the best firewalls money can buy or get into this room, which always has someone in it. Then they'd have to render the video once they'd fiddled with it, which would take hours. And then,' he added, dropping his tools and wheeling his chair over, 'they'd have to replace the original file with the new one. That would leave a trace. The meta-data would be all wrong.'

'There you go,' said Mick, 'What makes you think someone's messed around with it anyway?'

Victor nodded at the screen. Mick and Phil watched as Victor opened the detector, peered inside, and collapsed to the floor. The events unfolded in silence, which was broken only by Mick's 'fuckin' 'ell' as Arthur appeared from the detector and slapped Victor round the face, and then their laughter as Victor's retaliatory punch sent Arthur sprawling onto his back.

Victor took a slow walk back up to the office, his head a mess of cognitive dissonance. He knew Arthur must have opened the door to get into the detector. He also knew the door had not been opened. He also knew both of these things could not be true.

He left Mick and Phil with instructions to check the footage and video file thoroughly, as well as to look out for any evidence someone may have tampered with it, no matter how slight. They had assured him they would, promising extreme vigilance and motivated by the prospect of a serious security breach that could mean both their necks. If there was evidence to find, they said, they would find it. Victor had insisted there was definitely evidence to find.

He considered this as he walked along the quiet, lonely corridor. He had broken one of his own rules. *You can't go looking for specific evidence*, he always told research students. *You simply get what you find. The universe is not interested in proving you right.* He had spent the last two hours ignoring his own advice. He tried to think about the situation objectively, to actually think about this like a scientist for a moment. What conclusions could he draw if he interpreted the evidence in front of him? There

47

was only one – the energy created by the colliding beams must have caused Arthur to appear in the detector. *No,* he thought, *bollocks to the rules.*

As he got closer to the office, the desire to turn and walk in the opposite direction grew. He couldn't stand the thought of facing Arthur again, but he knew he had to. He was starting to feel guilty for leaving Sam alone with Arthur, an unknown and potentially unstable man. Had he been thinking clearly, he never would have done it. He was thinking clearly now, so he had to go back. He wouldn't lose it this time. He would be civil. He would be objective.

He entered the office to find Arthur and Sam deep in conversation. The desk in front of them was littered with pieces of paper covered in scribbled diagrams and equations. There were also two glasses of water and a half-empty packet of Jaffa Cakes. His Jaffa Cakes. They were eating *his* Jaffa Cakes. He took a deep breath and told himself not to let it bother him.

'Hi,' he said.

Sam looked at him with wide eyes. 'Victor, you've got to see this. This man is a *genius!*'

12

The Wisdom of the Wise

'A genius?' Victor said, with not a small amount of mock surprise.

'He knows everything there is to know about particle physics,' Sam explained, making a point of ignoring his facetious tone. 'I started explaining what we've been doing here and he knew it all already. He described our experiment to the tiniest detail.'

This need not have been all that surprising, as Sam should have known. 'Everything we do is in the public domain.'

'Not the results,' said Sam.

'Yes they are. They all get published. They can all be accessed online.'

'Not *today's* results. I told Arthur about our experiment and he predicted the outcome. I gave him the raw input data and he worked out the size of the energy spike with a pen and paper.' As she said this she thrust yet another piece of paper at him. 'Here.' She folded her arms and sat back, a display of confidence all too familiar to Victor. He saw it whenever she was about to prove him wrong. He had first seen it when she was a new student. It had irritated him. She'd seemed over-confident, conceited even. But over time he realised her confidence was justified. Sam knew when she was right, and it didn't matter to her if everyone else thought she was wrong, even Victor. In the end, he couldn't help but be impressed. It was part of the reason she was working with him now.

He read through the numbers. He read them again, and again. She was right. The mad old bastard really had done it. He had predicted exactly what would happen. Arthur had made sense of the input data and arrived at this output data because, as far as he understood, that was what was supposed to happen. That same output data was currently baffling some of the finest minds in the world because, as far as they understood, armed with their collective understanding of every detail of every scientific discovery ever made, it was *not* supposed to happen.

Performing a similar stunt of her own, Sam made sense of the input data provided by Victor's stupefied expression and explained how Arthur did this, which was exactly what he would have asked her to do had he not temporarily forgotten how to speak.

'Apparently this is all rather old hat where Arthur comes from. He says *his* people,' she paused briefly and glared at Victor as she said this; silently acknowledging she was heading into territory several time zones left of left field but warning him not to mention it, 'have already conducted experiments like this and have moved on somewhat.'

'Moved on,' he repeated dumbly.

'Yes. He's been explaining some rather advanced technology,' she tapped one of the diagrams on the desk with her finger, 'that makes it possible to perform such experiments using much smaller equipment.'

'Smaller equipment?'

'Yes. Small enough to fit in an attic, apparently.'

'Right.'

'And,' added Sam, 'he thinks he might know how he got here.'

13

Deduction

'A *wormhole*?' Victor spluttered, failing wholeheartedly to remove the edge of scorn from his voice.

'It seems the most logical scenario, yes,' said Arthur, with infuriating serenity.

There was that word again. In what way could any of this be considered *logical*? Where the tiniest amount of quark-gluon plasma should have appeared for the tiniest amount of time, an entire life-sized pensioner with a superhuman grasp of quantum physics and an absurd claim about having created a fourteen billion year old universe shortly after lunchtime today had turned up instead and wouldn't go away. Not only that, he was now suggesting it was all Victor's fault because his experiment had inadvertently created a wormhole connecting this new universe with what was apparently a much older one at a subatomic level. This wormhole, according to Arthur, was the event that caused everything to go 'swirly', which annoyed Victor for two reasons. First, he felt the whole suggestion carried a rude and unnecessarily accusatory tone. And second, he didn't feel that 'swirly' was the sort of word an extraordinary scientific mind should be using.

'They are perfectly plausible, theoretically speaking,' Sam said tentatively.

'They're perfectly clichéd deus ex machina used by trashy sci-fi writers, realistically speaking,' said Victor. Sam shrank back, obviously hurt. This annoyed Victor further, but only because he knew she didn't deserve to have him take his anger out on her. He turned his attention back to Arthur and forced himself to soften. 'So,' he sighed, 'you think we created negative energy?'

'You created some kind of exotic matter, certainly,' replied Arthur, far too matter-of-factly. 'I'm afraid I can't furnish you with the kind of specific information I sense you are hoping for. Even where I'm from, which strikes me as somewhere far more advanced than here,' he said, in a tone that pushed every one of Victor's buttons, including the big red one that should never be pushed, not even in an emergency, yet for some reason still exists, 'research into exotic matter has yielded only limited results.'

'Yet you know how to create universes?'

'Well, mini-universes, yes. We know how to drive expansion from a singularity of very limited mass,' said Arthur, as though it were the most pedestrian of activities. 'People do it all the time. It's how I created this universe, if it is my universe of course. It never crossed my mind that I might be creating something capable of sustaining life.'

'It never crossed your mind?'

'No-one has ever considered it; the universes are always so small.'

'So why aren't you a giant compared to us?' Victor asked, tacitly aware that he was sounding increasingly like Millie, the student with no idea how stupid she sounded.

'I'm afraid I couldn't possibly say. To my knowledge no-one has published any research into the effects of moving from macro space-time to micro space-time. I can merely deduce that size is dependent on the space-time you inhabit, and the size of a continuum is relative to your position within or without it.'

'You can *merely deduce* that?'

'Well, based on the evidence in front of me, it's... well...'

'Logical,' Victor sighed.

14

Expectations

It was, Arthur noticed, starting to get light by the time Victor switched off his vehicle and announced that they had arrived at his home. By his estimation, the planet must have completed half a rotation since he had watched the star, or Sun, as he had since learnt it to be called, disappear over the horizon.

Victor and Sam had held a lengthy discussion back at the office about what to do with him. The conversation had, on a number of occasions, become quite heated, which undermined their efforts to exclude Arthur from it. It was clear they considered him quite the inconvenience, which was, he felt, unfair, given that he had merely appeared, through no fault of his own, in a room where he was not expected. He was the one who had been dragged through space and time to a completely different universe. Surely this was a much greater inconvenience.

He decided against pointing this out because the discussion appeared to be about providing him with some form of accommodation, which he was most in need of and unlikely to be able to secure for himself in this unknown world.

The disagreement centred on the fact that Sam believed the only place Arthur could realistically stay was with Victor, while Victor believed there simply had to be another solution. Sam told Victor he was being pig-headed and, when Victor said something about a hotel, told him it would be unkind to leave Arthur alone in the circumstances.

Sam couldn't take him – even if she had space for him, her husband and two children would undoubtedly have a few questions when they awoke the next morning. Eventually, Victor relented and accepted that his spare room was the most sensible place to accommodate Arthur without anyone else finding out about him. Even so, Victor's attempts to hide his displeasure failed miserably.

Everything, from the way he had snatched up his keys to the way he forcefully adjusted the odd stick next to his seat, was punctuated with alarming aggression. Even as Victor fumbled in his pockets, Arthur could sense molten rage bubbling away deep beneath the surface.

Victor stabbed the front door with the key, shoved it open and stood inside the hallway, glaring and gesturing into the darkness, which Arthur took as an indication that he should enter. He did so, then started to a halt as the door slammed shut behind him, and then jumped again when Victor brushed past him and through another doorway. There was a faint click and light spilled out of the room Victor had entered. Arthur followed, uncertainly, hesitating and observing from the threshold.

It was a pleasant enough space. He was surprised to find it reminded him of his own home. Two large leather sofas were arranged opposite each other. Between them stood an elegant, low-standing wooden table. The table was perfectly aligned with an opening in the far wall which, he concluded from the blackened interior and flakes of ash on the floor, was a space set aside for lighting a fire. The overall effect was one of pleasing symmetry, which was accentuated by meticulously arranged pictures on the wall above it and large bookshelves on either side.

Victor was standing in front of a small table in the far corner, pouring a golden liquid into a squat glass. He raised the glass and smelled the contents before closing his eyes and drinking from it. He immediately refilled it and placed it on the table between the sofas. He went back for the bottle and another glass and set these down too, the bottle between the glasses, maintaining the pleasing symmetry. He slumped onto one of the sofas and gestured at the one opposite. Arthur interpreted the instruction and sat. He watched in silence as Victor poured a measure of the liquid into the empty glass, pushed it towards Arthur, and then lifted and held his own out in front of him. Uncertain what else to do, Arthur mimicked the gesture, and Victor edged his glass forwards slightly so they clinked together. It was an odd and unnerving ritual, mostly because of the intense eye contact maintained by Victor as he tipped the contents into his mouth. He swallowed and then very deliberately set the glass down.

Arthur sniffed at his glass and was reminded of dry wood and petroleum. His eyes started to water. He was quite sure he did not want to drink it, but the look on Victor's face left him quite sure he was expected to. Despite his uncertainty, he raised the glass slowly to his lips and drank. There was a brief pause as Arthur, desperate not to be rude to his host, tried to maintain control of his body. This was difficult. He looked from the glass to Victor and nodded, forced himself to smile, tried to make a sound to suggest he found it thoroughly agreeable, all the while keeping his mouth closed for fear that his body would reject what he had just poured into it and elect to dispose of it all over Victor's carpet, which, he strongly suspected, it very much wanted to do. Not because of any opposition it had to the carpet – this was soft and deep and perfectly pleasant. Rather, it was due to its objection to being burnt alive from the inside out, which is precisely what Arthur felt was happening. While he did not vomit, his attempt to keep complete control ultimately proved futile. His body erupted in a war between coughs and gasps that it took him almost a minute to recover from. When he finally managed to compose himself again, red-faced, breathing heavily, and beading with sweat, he noticed that Victor had poured another measure into each glass and was completely unperturbed by Arthur's reaction.

'What is it?' Arthur asked, still gasping.

'Whisky,' said Victor. 'Fermented grain. You don't have it where... where you're from?' he asked, clearly uncomfortable talking about Arthur as though he came from a different universe.

'Not as far as I'm aware.'

The second glass went down easier, which allowed Arthur to appreciate the agreeable flavour now that he knew to brace himself for it. They sat in silence for a while and drank another glass each before Victor, his mood apparently slightly softened, let out a burst of laughter.

'This is absurd. You say you're from another universe, *and* you built *this* universe, and here you are drinking with me. I'm drinking with God.' He laughed again.

'With...?'

'God. Creator of the universe. At least, that's what some people believe. A lot of people, actually. In fact, you could give them quite a shock.'

'I could?'

Victor laughed again. 'Oh, they're very sure about their creator. And *you*... well, you'd ruin their day even more than you ruined mine,' he snorted.

He wasn't sure why, but the conversation was making Arthur vaguely uncomfortable. It didn't help that the room had started spinning. 'I'm feeling rather dizzy,' he said, noticing that the words seemed to flop out of his mouth.

'That's just the whisky,' said Victor, pouring himself another. Apparently he was not quite dizzy enough, and kept refilling and draining his glass with remarkable frequency. He offered the bottle to Arthur. He declined. He had no desire to increase the speed of the spin. He was, however, intrigued by Victor's claims.

'You say there are people here who think they know about me?'

'Oh yes,' said Victor, his voice increasing in volume. 'They think they know all about you.' He shouted the word 'all', drew it out and threw his arms wide, as if to encompass everything 'they' thought they knew. 'And if what you have to say for yourself is true, then they are *not* going to be happy.' He laughed again, drank again, poured again.

'May I ask why?'

'Well, for a start, your name's Arthur bloody Fowler.' He was still laughing. Arthur didn't understand why this was so funny, or why it would be a problem, but Victor didn't explain. Instead, he continued, 'And secondly, you're not exactly what people expect you to be. They won't like that at all.'

Arthur nodded. 'Not unlike you.'

'Excuse me?' The laughter evaporated and was immediately replaced with an angry edge.

'Well,' he explained in far too jovial a tone, 'I'm not what you expected from your experiment. And because I'm not what you expected, you are unhappy.'

'No, no, no. It's not like that. They have this image of their god, y'see?' He punched the palm of his left hand with his right to punctuate 'image' and 'god'. As he continued, he elongated an increasing number of words and gestured with more alacrity. 'They think they've got him all figured out. They're so *certain*. It won't matter if you actually are God. They won't accept it. Evidence means nothing to them. If you don't fit in with what they already believe, then they'll just refuse to accept you.'

'Not,' Arthur repeated, 'unlike you.' For a moment he feared he had pushed his luck. He could see the muscles in Victor's jaw clenching. For a moment he wondered if Victor might swing for him again, but instead he sank further into the sofa and swirled the whisky in his glass.

'You don't understand,' he sighed.

'What I understand,' Arthur said, 'is that you have spent every moment since you brought me here trying to prove you did not bring me here. You have an image of this world in which it is not possible to have found me in your machine, and therefore you can't possibly have found me in it. It doesn't matter that you actually *did* find me in it; you will not accept it. The evidence doesn't conform to what you already believe, and so you refuse to accept it. I am not what you expect of this 'God' you speak of. Well, let me assure you that you are not at all what I expect of a scientist. Look at the evidence and *then* come to a conclusion. What is the most logical one you can draw from all of the evidence you have at your disposal?'

Victor, who had been staring into his empty glass throughout this ticking off, finally looked up. His eyes were puffy and red and looked like they had stolen the colour from his cheeks, which were no longer bright with anger but had turned distinctly pale. He wore a far-away stare, apparently considering the evidence at his disposal. Then, he arrived at a conclusion. 'I've had too much whisky,' he slurred, and threw up all over himself.

15

Peal

Whisky, Arthur learnt, did more than make rooms spin. It also impaired the brain's ability to communicate with the body, rendering the afflicted individual with legs that do not always do as they are instructed. He found this out not through his own experience, but as he struggled to guide Victor upstairs without getting himself covered in vomit. It also appeared to curb the ability to make sensible decisions, because Victor ignored Arthur's suggestion that he should try and clean himself up and instead disappeared into his bedroom after pointing vaguely in the direction of the spare room and telling Arthur he could sleep in it. Arthur did so, and woke the next morning to discover that whisky also caused the most awful headaches.

He managed to get up and head downstairs but found no sign of Victor. This was hardly surprising. He could only imagine the horror taking place behind Victor's eyes. If the severity of the headache was proportional to the amount of whisky consumed, then Victor's ought to be very severe indeed. Arthur decided not to wake him and wondered how to pass the time. He was curious to learn more about this world, about Victor, but felt it would be improper to snoop around his home. He settled for simply wandering around and looking at the different rooms. He didn't touch anything, but felt that if Victor had it on display then he must surely be happy for people to see it. Many items were familiar. He recognised books, time-keepers, photographs, decorative objects, and devices for receiving written and audio-visual media – the similarities between this culture and his own really were startling. He was stunned to think he could have accidentally created something that so closely reflected his own world, a species with so many similarities to his own.

He studied the titles of the books on display in the living room and was intrigued by one called *God: The Truth Behind the Lies*. Victor's name was written beneath the title. Remembering the word from his conversation with Victor the previous night, he reached for it, but before he could take it from the shelf a sudden noise from the hallway startled him and he snatched his hand back with a sudden rush of guilt, as if he had been caught prying. Investigating the source of the noise, he discovered it had been caused by something being pushed through a hole in the front door. The item was now lying in a heap on the doormat. He picked it up and studied it. It had *The Times* written across its top, and it featured what he quickly inferred was information about current events likely to be of interest to the recipient. Judging by its size and position on the front, the most important of these events was a violent attack by some people called *extremists*. What it was that made them extreme, other than the seemingly senseless act they had committed, was unclear to Arthur, though he assumed this was due to his lack of familiarity with many of the terms used in the report, rather than any failure on the writer's part. He sat back at the table in the kitchen and laid it out in front of him, glad to have something to occupy the time before Victor woke up. He found the other stories presented similar problems. They all provided parts of various ongoing narratives that he was wholly ignorant of, making it difficult to pinpoint the relevance or ramifications of the information they provided. Many of them hinted at public anger at one thing or another. Much of the time this was directed at figures of authority, whether they be in public office or in charge of large organisations, and it often had something to do with a seemingly arbitrary means of exchange called money that was either not being exchanged for things it should have been or being exchanged for things it should not have been. The solution to this seemed obvious, though this was probably only further evidence of his ignorance. The reports suggested things were far more complicated than he appreciated.

He flicked through a few pages, reading things he understood but could not comprehend, until another odd sound from the hallway interrupted him. He froze when he first heard it, listening until it dissipated into silence, until he was not entirely sure he had actually even heard it at all. He even started to wonder if it was perhaps another side effect of the whisky. But then he heard it again, exactly the same as before – two chimes of different frequencies, one after the other. He stood up from the table and entered the hallway again. The sound disappeared just as it had the last time, making it impossible to establish the source.

He was about to return to the kitchen when yet another noise erupted from the door. This time it was a knocking sound and it was accompanied by the sight of Sam waving at him, her features distorted by the poorly finished glass in the window. He opened the door.

'Hello, Arthur. Sorry, I didn't think you'd heard me.'

He frowned. 'I heard you,' he said. 'That's how I knew you were there.'

She let out a gentle laugh. 'I meant I didn't think you'd heard me ringing.'

'That was *you*?'

'Ringing the doorbell? Yes,' said Sam. She pointed at a small button on the door frame. Arthur reached out and touched it. He learnt that the sound emanated from a small white box next to the door. He pressed it a few more times, looking at the doorbell, then at the box. It was rather fun.

He found it amusing that the first chime came when he pressed the button and could hold the second one at bay by waiting before he released it. He started experimenting, varying the amount of time between pressing and releasing the button. *Ding, dong. Ding...* He let it ring out. *Dong. Dingdong. Dindongdingdong. Ding...* He stopped, the button still depressed, and looked at Sam, smiling quietly as she watched.

'Got the hang of it?' she asked.

Dong.

'Yes,' he said, sheepishly.

'You don't have doorbells?'

'No,' he replied. He pressed it again. He couldn't help it.

16

Something Massively Big

Victor woke up with a ringing in his ears. He had always assumed this was just a figure of speech – another way to describe the dull, high-pitched whine you sometimes get when you feel sick. But this was different. His brain felt like it had been scrubbed with sandpaper, his tongue like it had been replaced with the leathery fold of an iguana's armpit, his teeth like they needed a shave, and his eyes as though someone had been using them as pin-cushions while he slept. Except none of this was true, not literally. No actual sandpaper had been near his brain. His tongue was still his tongue. His teeth weren't actually coated in fur and no actual pins had gone near his eyes. But what he could hear was an *actual* bell. Not the faint, high-pitched hum designed to drive you slowly mad, but a real chiming bell. It took him a few moments in his groggy state to realise that it was the doorbell.

He leapt out of bed in a panic. This caused a sudden rush of dizziness, so he sat back down and cradled his head in his hands. He groaned and wondered why his foot was wet. Inspecting the floor, he discovered he was standing on the shirt he had been wearing when he threw up over himself last night. How typical. Not only did he have a sandblasted brain, a lizard's armpit for a tongue, furry teeth and pierced eyeballs, he also had bits of sick between his toes. Not figurative sick either – actual, tangible lumps of vomit.

As was his custom in situations like this, he cursed God for allowing this to happen. Then he remembered he now not only knew God, but that he had stayed the night having watched Victor drink and then undrink half a bottle of whisky. He tried cursing Arthur for allowing this all to happen. It was no good. It just wasn't the same. He made a mental note to continue to blame Bible God for any and all misery that he caused himself but did not want to take responsibility for, and then started rushing so he could get downstairs before Arthur answered the door.

The shirt was beyond saving so he used one of the cleaner sleeves to mop up the vomit from his foot, an act which nearly induced a fresh deposit all over the floor. Fortunately, his body satisfied itself to simply dry retch as he mopped up the lumps. Standing again, a little more cautiously this time, he took his dressing gown down from the hook on the door and struggled through the wrestling match that ensues whenever someone tries to put on a dressing gown that has one sleeve inside out. Throughout all of this, the doorbell indignantly continued to ring.

Ding.

Victor stormed out of the room to the top of the stairs and then startled to a halt when he saw Arthur and Sam standing in the doorway.

Dong.

'What the bloody hell is going on?' he snapped, dimly aware he had been asking this a lot lately.

They swung their heads up. Arthur smiled and used his free hand to point at his bell-ringing hand. 'It's the doorbell,' he said. He pressed the button. *Ding.*

Victor took a deep breath and rubbed his face and then immediately snatched his hands away again when he remembered what he had just been doing with them. 'I *know* it's the doorbell. It's *my* doorbell. I've heard it before. Why do you keep pressing it?'

Dong. 'Sorry,' said Arthur. 'I thought it was a rather clever little device.' He pressed it again and smiled as it chimed. *Ding.*

'Please,' said Victor, his voice singing with tension, 'don't press it again.'

Arthur pulled his hand away guiltily. *Dong.*

'They don't have doorbells where Arthur comes from,' Sam chipped in with a grin.

'You don't say,' said Victor, edging his way down the stairs. 'I'm starting to wish we didn't have them where I come from.'

Sam started fussing immediately. 'Oh, Victor, look at you,' she said. 'You look awful.'

'I feel awful,' he grumbled, shuffling into the kitchen and filling a glass at the sink. He gulped the water down quickly and refilled it. 'Have you been to the lab?'

'Yes. Nothing has changed. Everyone's confused. Most of them stayed all night, so they're a little fried. I sent an email round telling them to wrap it up and go home. I imagine it's quietened down a bit by now.'

'What are we supposed to do now?

'Well, given that you have two guests, I'd say you're supposed to offer us something to drink. I'll have a coffee. Arthur?'

'Sorry?' said Arthur, who looked like he was struggling to keep up with the conversation.

'Would you like something to drink?'

'Er... I am very thirsty,' he said. 'But I'd rather not have what we had last night.'

'What did you have last night?'

'I believe it was called whisky.'

'Oh, was it?' said Sam, throwing Victor a look that made him shrink back into his chair. She turned back to Arthur. 'Did you have a lot?'

'Not really,' said Arthur. 'It made me feel rather lightheaded.'

'And what about you Victor? Did you have enough to feel rather lightheaded?'

Victor clenched his teeth and glared at Arthur, hoping he would be able to read the complex instructions he was trying to write across his face.

'Don't blame Arthur,' said Sam, demonstrating that uncanny and infuriating ability all self-congratulatory sober people have of saying exactly what a hungover person who is feeling very sorry for themself and knows they doesn't deserve any sympathy but wants it anyway doesn't want to hear.

'I wasn't blaming him for anything,' he said, trying and failing not to sound defensive. 'I didn't even have that much,' he added, defensively.

'It's true,' said Arthur. 'I don't know how quickly it is digested of course, but I would estimate that between fifty and seventy percent of what Victor drank wasn't metabolised. His body rejected it and brought it back up.' Arthur beamed at Victor. The silly old fool actually thought he was being helpful!

'Did it indeed?' said Sam. She clapped her hands, loudly and deliberately, and raised her voice. 'Right, upstairs, now. Go and get cleaned up and be back down here in five minutes.'

'Just let me–'

'Five minutes!' she yelled.

Victor trudged out of the kitchen. He trudged back into the kitchen. He opened a drawer, picked up a roll of bin liners and tore one off. He trudged out of the kitchen.

He returned a little over five minutes later, the bin bag now containing a shirt he never wanted to see again. Sam and Arthur were sitting at the table. They each had a sleek, grey, earthenware mug filled with steaming coffee in front of them. Victor noticed that Arthur also had glasses of water and orange juice in front of him. His incredulity obviously showed on his face.

'Just letting Arthur try a few things out,' Sam explained.

He nodded understanding and dropped the bag in the bin, then poured a coffee for himself and joined them at the table. 'More doorbells?' he asked, gesturing at the drinks in front of Arthur.

'Actually,' said Sam, 'Arthur is familiar with fruit juice, only the fruits are different to ours. At least, different to the ones in your fruit bowl. He is obviously familiar with water.'

'Obviously,' he agreed, with sarcasm even he found unnecessary. The room slumped into silence.

'The juice is lovely,' said Arthur, trying to lighten the heavy atmosphere. As if to prove his sincerity, he took a big mouthful from the glass and offered an expression of overt satisfaction before topping it up with what remained in the carton. 'I'd very much like to try the fruit it comes from,' he persisted, his voice full of saccharine enthusiasm.

'Help yourself,' Victor said, shoving the bowl in the middle of the table towards him. He watched Arthur regard the colourful assortment with uncertainty.

'It comes from these,' said Sam, picking up an orange. 'Though, they are all very nice,' she added, determined to make up for Victor's lack of civility. She turned to Victor. 'How are you feeling?'

He regarded Arthur, who was studiously examining the contents of the fruit bowl, with contempt. How was he supposed to answer that? It is hard to sum up how a deity you do not believe in destroying your career, moving into your house and drinking all of your orange juice makes you feel. 'Bewildered,' was the best he could do, though he couldn't shake the sense that normal words were not up to the task. Perhaps they had some better ones where Arthur came from. He sighed heavily. 'What the hell do we do now?'

'No idea', said Sam. 'But we have to come up with something – Kyle is coming in later.'

'Oh, God,' Victor groaned.

*

Arthur tried to follow the exchange as best he could. As far as he could make out, Richard Kyle, who Sam and Victor both kept referring to as Dick, was an important figure at their place of work. Arthur was quite sure neither of them liked him very much, and his imminent arrival clearly caused them both considerable concern. Victor slumped forward and rested his head on his folded arms as Sam explained that Dick had discovered, in Dick's words, 'something massively big' had happened, and it sounded like the sort of thing that, in Sam's words, 'could only be solved by Dick turning up and asking a load of stupid questions and generally being a total wanker.' Arthur gathered from the tone that the last part of the sentence was an insult.

Before long, they agreed they needed to go back to their office and determined that Arthur should not accompany them. Before they left, Victor told him to treat his house like it was his own. He also gave him some very brief instructions for using his computer. Arthur could, Victor told him, use it to find out anything he wanted about this planet, which he felt should keep him from getting bored. He allowed Victor to explain the process of using search engines to acquire information despite the fact that the concept of a network of linked computers was perfectly familiar to him and that the primitive one this society had created was much like the one he remembered using as a teenager many years ago. Victor apologised for leaving

Arthur by himself, but in truth the prospect of having several hours to explore the knowledge of this civilization was very appealing to him. And my, how much of it there was to explore...

17

An Honest Answer

Victor and Sam watched in silence as little black and white versions of themselves scurried gracelessly across the screen with Arthur's armchair in their arms. They disappeared out of shot, leaving the bewildered Arthur standing in front of the detector, its door gaping behind him. After a moment, they ran back across the screen in the opposite direction, still carrying the chair, Arthur's incredulous gaze still following them as they disappeared on the other side of the shot. They came back empty handed, only to run back after a few seconds of frantic gesturing and head-scratching and return, once again burdened by the chair, to carry it back the way they had done the first time.

As this farcical scene unfolded, Richard Kyle sat in Victor's office chair and gazed from the screen to Victor to Sam and back to the screen at frequent intervals. Occasionally, one of them would try to speak, only to be ushered to silence by Kyle's raised hand – a gesture that inspired silent rage in Victor and made him fidget about in fits and bursts, like a lid starting to rattle on the top of a saucepan as it came up to boil. Next to him, Sam folded her arms and sighed heavily. Together, they stood like two naughty children, summoned to the headmaster's office and forced to listen in silence while the full extent of their ever-so-naughtiness was read out to them in a thoroughly disapproving and disappointed tone. Victor got the distinct impression that Kyle had rehearsed this, and he was not going to let anyone mess with his script before he got to deliver his big line.

On the screen, the little black and white versions of Victor and Sam closed the door to the detector and escorted Arthur out of shot for the last time.

Kyle leant forward and stopped the video. He leant back in the chair and paused for effect. 'Well?' he said. As big lines go, it wasn't as impressive as it could have been.

The pair exchanged a glance. Sam raised her eyebrows. Victor shrugged his shoulders and puffed out his cheeks. They both looked back at Kyle, who was visibly put out by their silence. Presumably, they had failed to say whatever stupid thing they had said in Kyle's head during the rehearsal, meaning Kyle couldn't deliver whatever witless riposte he had lined up.

'Who is he?' Kyle said, in that practised authoritative tone used only by managers who have to go on courses to learn how to speak authoritatively because they cannot manage it naturally.

'We're not *entirely* sure,' Victor said, erring on the side of caution until he could work out how much he was prepared to give away.

'You don't know,' said Kyle, adding to his faux-authority a liberal sprinkling of derision and condescension.

'He's a man who thinks he's God,' said Sam, not only on a different page to Victor, but standing in a different bookshop altogether.

Kyle couldn't have looked more shocked if Sam had walked over and flicked him in the eye. 'Excuse me?' he said.

'God,' repeated Sam. 'That's who he thinks he is.'

'I see,' said Kyle, an automatic response courtesy of the school of Pretending to be in Control of Things. Then he realised he didn't see. 'You mean he's a fucking lunatic? One of those 'I'm the second coming of Christ and the world's going to end when I fart in the key of F' nutters?'

'Actually, no,' said Sam. 'He's never heard of Jesus. He didn't even know he was God. He just made the universe for a bit of a lark and had no idea we were here until the accelerator brought him here.'

Kyle fixed Sam with an icy stare. Unsurprisingly, it hadn't occurred to him that the conversation might branch off in this direction, so none of his prepared lines were of any use to him. Victor felt almost sorry for him, sitting there exposed by the crippling paralysis of a manager without a script. Sam didn't seem to share his sympathy, probably because, as she had often asserted, she believed Kyle to be one of the very worst life forms on the planet – the kind of person who is an argument in favour of terminal illness, she had once said after too much wine.

Somewhere inside Kyle's brain, a reset button was flicked and he turned his attention back to Victor. 'Well?' he said. It somehow seemed a much bigger line this time.

Victor sighed heavily. 'It's true,' he said. 'At least, it's true that that's what he says. It might not be true that what he says is true.'

'It *might* not be?' shouted Kyle after a momentary pause to wade through all the trues. 'You mean you actually think there's a possibility it *is*? You're a bloody scientist, man!'

'Yes,' said Victor, tersely, 'I know.' This was one of the reasons he couldn't stand Kyle. He wasn't a real scientist. He thought science was about maintaining the status quo, about proving what is believed. Discoveries that contradicted the current paradigm were not discoveries – they were failures. He had his own view of the world and he rejected anything that contradicted it. He was a typical ideologue, responding with typical anger. Victor tried to ignore the echo of Arthur's voice saying 'not unlike you' ringing in his ears.

'Then see this for the load of shit it obviously is! He's obviously a bloody lunatic who somehow got into the detector so he could start off his God fantasy with a dramatic entrance.'

'The evidence says otherwise.'

'Evidence?' scoffed Kyle. 'What bloody evidence?'

The lid of the saucepan was really starting to rattle now. 'The evidence you've just shown us for a start,' Victor snapped. 'That video has days of unbroken, unedited footage. Not that we need days – we don't even need an hour. We know the beam was active less than an hour before we opened the detector. We know if he was in there when the beam was active, there would be nothing left of him but a nasty smell and a few stains on the walls. So we know the only opportunity he had to get into the detector was the time between the beam failing and the door being opened.'

'Then that's when he must have done it.'

'So why isn't he on the video?'

'Oh come on, Dennett. The video could easily be tampered with.'

'No it couldn't. It could be tampered with, yes, but not easily. I've already checked. You're welcome to do so yourself. Check every camera in the whole building if you like. If you show me footage of Arthur anywhere in this building before we open the door, then I'm sold. Until then, there's no evidence to support your hypothesis.'

'Arthur? His name's *Arthur*?' raged Kyle.

'Arthur Fowler,' shrugged Sam, knowing how much it would annoy Kyle.

Kyle's eye twitched as he glared at her. Then, he stood up and straightened his jacket before barging between them and muttering something about finding evidence that would show they'd lost their minds. He threw in a few expletives for good measure. He turned as he reached the door. 'Where is this Arthur fellow now?'

'At my house,' Victor said.

'Get him back here,' said Kyle, adopting the Threatening Tone for Dummies. 'I want to have a word with him.'

Sam and Victor nodded in unison.

'And not a word of this to anyone,' he barked, as the door slammed behind him.

'What a prick,' said Sam.

Victor glared at her. 'Why the hell did you tell him?'

'What else were we going to say?' she protested. 'Neither one of us had a convincing lie prepared. I gave him the only explanation we have.'

It did nothing to improve his mood, but he had to concede that she was right. What else were they going to say? If it was possible to invent a reasonable explanation, it would *be* the explanation. Instead, Victor was stuck with one explanation that was impossible, and another that *should* have been impossible, and he was not at all happy about which was which. He sat down heavily in his chair, wondering what to do next.

He was sure they needed to do more to rule out the possibility that Arthur had arrived by more conventional means. But what? Part of him didn't want to – he had a horrible feeling they would find nothing to suggest the detector had been tampered with in any way. He certainly didn't like the idea of being remembered as the man who messed up a physics experiment and brought the creator of the universe to Earth. But, more than this, he hated the fact he had seen so much of his own first reaction to Arthur reflected in Kyle's.

'You sounded like you believed him just then,' said Sam.

'Don't be silly,' said Victor. In truth, he wasn't sure what he believed, though he was certain he didn't believe

Arthur. And he desperately wanted to know what to do about him.

'Maybe,' said Sam, 'you should get to know him a bit better, for the time being at least.'

'Sorry?'

'Well, whoever he is, wherever he came from, I think he deserves to be treated like a person first, rather than a problem. Don't you?'

'Well, yes,' started Victor, 'but–'

'And what other choice do we have? He has nowhere to go. Okay, he might be unwell, but he's not exactly dangerous is he?'

'We don't *know* that.'

'What I'm saying is it's not as though he should be sectioned or anything.'

'I know, I know,' said Victor. 'Fine. Well I suppose I should go home and... get to know God then.'

Sam smiled. 'That's the spirit.'

18

He Prepared a Feast

After several hours sitting in front of Victor's computer and learning about the planet Earth and its inhabitants, human and otherwise, it occurred to Arthur that the internet might be able to help him come up with something he could do to thank Victor for letting him stay. He knew he was causing Victor considerable inconvenience and felt compelled to repay his kindness somehow. The search engine initially provided a huge list of possibilities, most of which required a deep understanding of Victor's culture and a means of obtaining them, neither of which he had. The most popular gift that the search "gifts for host" produced was wine; another intoxicating beverage, in this case made from fermented grapes. Unfortunately, Victor had vowed only this morning that he was never going to drink alcohol again, presumably because of his experience with the whisky last night, so it would have been an inappropriate gift even if he did have the means to acquire it. This also eliminated the plethora of other drinking related gifts he found; oddly shaped wine racks, oddly shaped bottle openers, trays for making oddly shaped blocks of ice to be placed into drinks carried in oddly-shaped glasses, and various prints, novelty artefacts and items of clothing all making some reference or other to the owner's love of things containing alcohol. Alcohol was clearly an important part of giving and receiving gifts in this culture, as was providing the recipient with something oddly-shaped.

He narrowed his search to include only things he could do without a means of exchange and found his options considerably more limited. The only real option available was to make something. Arthur was taken with the idea of finding something Victor already owned and crafting it into an oddly-shaped version of itself, but he had no idea which of Victor's possessions he would be happy for Arthur to modify, nor did he know which odd shapes Victor would find agreeable. Eventually, it became apparent that there was only one thing he could realistically make by the time Victor returned, so he got up from the computer and went to the kitchen to inspect the cupboards.

'And now we get the cream ready,' announced Arthur, doing his best to mimic the inflexion of the host of the instructional video he had found online. He tore the foil lid off a container and threw it aside with a flourish. It cartwheeled through the air and landed with a dull splat on the tiled floor. He turned perpendicular to the hob, held the cream high above the saucepan and poured it in slowly. At precisely the right moment, he punctuated this act by raising his left hand to the air and slowly rotating his hips, exactly as the presenter had done. 'That's the way we do it,' he said, and tossed the empty pot over his shoulder.

Leaving the sauce simmering away, he turned his attention to the foil parcel in the oven, unwrapped it and started carving the roast chicken breast, making sure to chastise it for being a very bad boy at the appropriate moment.

'Having fun?' said a voice that almost made him leap from his skin.

'Victor!' he said, beaming. 'I'm cooking!'

'So I see,' said Victor, a note of scepticism in his voice.

'You're just in time. Take a seat, please. I've made roasted tarragon chicken with potatoes, asparagus and broad beans. Doesn't it sound delicious? It won't be a moment,' he said, as he gestured for Victor to sit at the table.

Arthur noticed that Victor eyed the food rather suspiciously at first, but Arthur was happy it looked as it should. The chicken seemed moist and tender, the sauce silky and creamy, and the vegetables were bright and green and crisp – all was as it had appeared in the video. Arthur placed Victor's plate in front of him and sprinkled a pinch of one last ingredient from a small bowl onto it with a similar flourish to the one he used for the cream.

'A little bit o' lemon zest to finish,' he said. He did the same to his own plate, taking care to utter exactly the same line and perform exactly the same flourish, before whipping the tea-towel from his shoulder and throwing it across the room and, finally, sitting down opposite the gaping Victor.

'Is everything alright?' asked Arthur.

'Sorry? Oh, yes. Everything is fine. I... I just wasn't expecting this, that's all.'

'Why would you have? I wanted to do something to say thank you for letting me stay here.'

'Oh. There was really no need,' said Victor. Noticing that Arthur's shoulders sagged slightly, he added, 'But thank you. It's very thoughtful.'

'You're most welcome,' said Arthur. 'Now, hopefully it tastes as good as it sounds.'

Arthur was nervous as Victor inspected the chicken and took his first tentative bite, but it wasn't long before he began eating eagerly, and by the time he had finished he congratulated Arthur for an amazing meal. His gift had been a success. They sat back, satisfied and full. A few moments later, Victor spoke. Something about his delivery suggested to Arthur that he felt a little uncomfortable.

'What was all that stuff you were doing?' he asked.

'What stuff?'

'All that... moving your hips as you poured the cream, narrating what you were doing, talking to the chicken. That stuff.'

'Oh, it's how the man said it should be done,' said Arthur, as he used the last of his chicken to dab up the remaining sauce.

'What man?'

'The man from the video.'

'What video?'

'On the computer. I've been using it like you showed me. You were right – there's all sorts of information on there. I've been learning all about you.'

'About me?'

'Well, no not *you*,' Arthur laughed. 'Your people. Your world. Your universe, really.'

'You mean *your* universe,' interjected Victor, though with none of the venom from yesterday.

'Quite,' said Arthur. 'Well, I was reading about all sorts of things. Your history, scientific discoveries, geography, all sorts, when it occurred to me I might be able to find out what I could do to say thank you. It suggested cooking a meal, so I started reading about food and I came upon a fantastic... what did you call it?'

'Website?'

'Website, yes, a fantastic website. You tell it what you have available, and it suggests what you can do with it. So I looked through the cupboards, made a list, and told it what I had. That's how I got the recipe for this.' He gestured at the empty plates. 'And there was a video of someone making it. He said all those moves and phrases were important.'

Victor smiled. 'I don't think he meant it literally. That was all part of his act.'

'His act?'

'Yes. You must have watched some TV chef. They all turn cooking into a performance.'

Arthur turned this idea over for a moment. Why would cooking, a strictly functional activity, be a performance?

'People like to be entertained I suppose,' said Victor. 'It's not enough to simply explain what needs to be done. They want a bit of a show.'

'I see,' said Arthur, though he didn't really. He looked around the room at the foil lid, the little pot that had dribbled the last of its contents onto the tiled floor, the tea towel in a heap in the corner, and the various ingredients scattered all over the work surfaces. 'I'm terribly sorry,' he said, feeling more than a little embarrassed. 'I'm afraid I've made a rather unnecessary mess.'

Victor was very gracious about it. 'It's fine,' he said. 'We'll deal with it later. It was worth it,' he added, motioning to the empty plate in front of him. 'So tell me – what else have you been learning about?'

19

Love Thy Neighbour

Victor felt assaulted by the amount of information Arthur relayed. He had gathered a seemingly endless stream of information about the Earth, its size and structure, its distribution of land and water and its biodiversity. The latter, he explained, was a concept he was perfectly familiar with, having come from a planet capable of sustaining life. He was fascinated by the different plants and creatures that had evolved, explaining similarities to creatures from what he called 'back home' and laughing at the absurdity of those that were unlike anything he had ever seen, like the platypus and the narwhal, and a handful Victor had never heard of himself.

He listened as Arthur explained how he had spent hours reading about humans, how their evolution was remarkably similar to what had occurred in his own world, how farming led to civilisation and how this had developed over the centuries. The way he went on, Victor could hardly believe Arthur had spent only one afternoon reading. The depth of knowledge he had already gleaned was remarkable. And, Victor joked, he had learnt to cook a decent meal on top of it all.

'And learn some interesting things about human reproductive habits, too,' said Arthur.

'I'm sorry?' said Victor, his eyes widening.

'Well, they are rather... primitive,' said Arthur, turning, Victor noticed, a little coy.

Victor suspected this was not something Arthur had picked up from Wikipedia. 'I'm not sure the internet is the best place to learn about human reproduction,' he said, making a mental note to delete his browsing history.

'Why's that?' asked Arthur, but Victor was spared the embarrassment of having to explain his species' predilection for pornography by Arthur's new favourite sound. 'The doorbell!' he gasped, and sprang from his seat and rushed out into the hall. As he got up to follow him out, Victor heard the front door open, followed by Arthur's voice, full of the same friendly excitement with which he had been greeted upon his own return from work. 'Wendy! How are you?'

Victor groaned. *Great*, he thought. *Just what we need.* Wendy was Victor's next-door neighbour. He didn't *dislike* her, per se. In fact, in many ways, she was everything anyone could want from a neighbour. She was kind and thoughtful and always said hello. She would check to see if he needed anything from the shops and drop off vegetables from her garden when she had more than she needed. She used to feed Victor's cat when he was staying away from home, back before it made an unfortunate and fatal miscalculation regarding its ability to cross the road without getting hit by a passing Land Rover. They had a key to each other's houses in case either of them ever got locked out. She was that kind of neighbour. But she was also the kind of neighbour that fussed over him a bit too much. She was always so certain he needed looking after and he could never escape the feeling she was mothering him, this woman who was a good ten years younger than him. It was all a bit too suffocating at times, which he could do without right now. She was also a very devout Christian, and, while Victor liked to tell himself this had no bearing on his relationship with her, he couldn't help but feel he was best off avoiding her given his current circumstances.

He took a deep breath and stepped out of the kitchen.

'Hello Wendy,' he said, feigning geniality as best he could. 'How are you?'

Wendy, dressed in smart, light blue jeans and the kind of shirt Victor suspected was what people were talking about when they used the word 'boho', smiled a warm smile. 'I'm well, thank you,' she said. 'I was just popping over to see if Arthur had spoken to you about Sunday.'

'Sunday?' he said, looking at Arthur quizzically.

Arthur beamed. 'Wendy's taking me to church. We wondered if you would like to come too?'

*

'What the hell are you doing?' Victor hissed once the door was firmly closed.

'I told you,' said Arthur. 'I'm going to church with Wendy.'

'Why?'

'She invited me.'

'When?!'

'While you were at work. I was ringing the doorbell and she came out to check that I was alright.'

Time stood still to allow a sense of dread to descend on Victor. 'What did you tell her?'

'I told her I was fine.'

'Not about *that*,' said Victor, the exasperation that was rapidly becoming a hallmark of his discussions with Arthur starting to build. 'Did you tell her anything about where you're *from*?'

'Oh I see,' said Arthur. 'No. You told me it might upset people, so I thought it best not to. I told her we were friends and you were letting me stay here for a while.'

Victor considered this for a moment. It was hard to imagine Wendy, who liked to involve herself in Victor's life as much as possible, allowing that to pass without probing further. 'And she didn't keep asking questions?'

'No,' said Arthur. 'But she put her hand on my arm and told me she understood, although I'm not sure she did. It was quite strange really. She told me not to worry and I would be back on my feet in no time, even though I was on my feet when she said it.'

A suspicion started to grow. 'Was it around this time she mentioned going to church?'

'Yes, it was actually,' said Arthur. 'She said it could help in times of difficulty.'

'Of course she did. Look, Arthur, I'm not sure it's such a good idea.'

Arthur looked crestfallen. 'I was rather looking forward to it,' he said.

'It's... well... you know those people I told you about – the ones who would be upset to find out about you? Well, church is where they go in order to...' he paused. How could he put this in a way that wouldn't invite a torrent of questions? '...talk about you.'

'I know.'

'You do?'

'Yes. Wendy told me all about it. It sounds fascinating.'

'Fascinating?'

'Absolutely. They have something called a faith healer visiting on Sunday. Someone who can heal ailments and illnesses through touch and something called prayer. It sounds remarkable.'

'That's one word for it,' said Victor. Arthur looked at him quizzically. He decided to tread lightly. 'You see, it's not quite as remarkable as it sounds. In fact it's quite frustrating. And sad. Just awful really, and— Why are you looking at me like that?'

'Wendy said you might react this way.'

Victor set his jaw. 'Did she?'

'She did. I have to say I could see where she was coming from. She said you couldn't open your mind to new ideas. It certainly corresponded with my experience of you. I think you should come.'

Victor felt his mouth open and close but found his voice had been paralysed by the deep sense of injustice that occurs when an accusation appears perfectly logical and reasonable to everyone but the accused. He smiled maniacally, wagged his finger and shook his head, but the act failed to jumpstart any actual words. Then he sagged, sighed, and went upstairs to bed.

20

Treasures on Earth

The following day was Saturday – the sixth day of the week, a week being a unit of time consisting arbitrarily and inexplicably of seven days. Victor didn't know why it was seven days – he had made this abundantly clear when Arthur had pressed him for an explanation. Was the number seven important or significant in some way? Why not ten? Or five? At least then it would be a factor of the three hundred and sixty five days that made up an Earth year. Victor wasn't interested, as Arthur learnt when he was told to give it a rest as he mused out loud in the passenger seat.

Saturday, Arthur learnt, was one of only two of those seven days on which the majority of people were not expected to work. The chief pastime of people who did not have to work was shopping. This meant, of course, that those who worked in the shops, who Arthur hoped were compensated with alternative days of rest, were not offered the same reprieve from their employment. Arthur surmised from many of their expressions that they must have one of the more unpleasant jobs on Earth, though it did not take long before he realised the miserable expressions they exhibited were actually shared by many of the shoppers.

They frowned and snarled as they pushed their way through crowds, jostled for position on overcrowded streets, argued with strangers, argued with each other, and argued with the employees of the shops over the price of all of the things they wanted. And goodness, they wanted a lot of things! He looked around incredulously as he and Victor navigated their way through the torrent of sour-faced people struggling along the pavement carrying bags and bags of things and was stunned to discover from Victor that this constituted a normal way for humans to spend the limited amount of leisure time they allowed themselves. What curious creatures they were.

Victor did not share the rest of his species' passion for shopping. He was unenthusiastic about the trip, but had asserted that it was necessary to pick up some provisions for Arthur, who had been wearing the same set of clothes since his arrival. If he must go to church, Victor had told him, he would need something appropriate to wear.

From the moment they had set off, Victor grumbled at other drivers for doing, so far as Arthur could tell, all of the things Victor himself was doing. Perhaps there was some subtle difference in the way Victor manoeuvred his vehicle, indiscernible to his own inexperienced eye, that separated him from all of the 'silly pricks' and 'utter twats' Victor loudly lamented sharing the road with. It was interesting to Arthur that, despite not having encountered such language before, there was something about the tone that left him in no doubt whatsoever about its purpose or intent.

Once Victor was done swearing at other drivers, he swore at the car park, a building which, despite its modern appearance, was barely capable of serving its function given that motorcars must have doubled in size since it was first designed and built. He swore at absent car owners for their inability to park in such a way as to allow Victor to use the adjacent spaces, at a machine that issued little slips of paper permitting the owner to use the facilities for how much it charged, and at his own wallet for not containing the right change, which, Arthur thought, Victor really ought to consider taking at least some responsibility for.

Victor's swearing reduced significantly once they reached the busy streets of the town centre, where it was replaced by tutting and sighing and puffing of cheeks. Arthur could at least empathise with Victor in his frustration at the people surrounding them. The main appeal of shopping appeared to be the trance-like state it induced in human beings. They wandered about with blank expressions, apparently oblivious to everything going on around them. They drifted in a herd-like fashion, following the slow tidal motion of the crowd they had immersed themselves in. They gazed at windows and rows of goods with open mouths, at tiny handheld screens they held a few inches from the tips of their noses, at anything, in fact, except for the direction in which they were walking. It made for an incredibly frustrating experience, yet one over which the pair managed to bond as they pursued a shared goal of getting this necessary evil over and done with as quickly as possible.

Despite his desire to escape the nightmare in which he found himself, Arthur couldn't help but drift into insensible staring of his own as he tried to comprehend what he was seeing. Now and then, he would meander to a halt and watch the crowds, study the shop windows, and take in the vast array of goods in the shops. In response, Victor would stop in his tracks and snap his fingers or call out to him, like a dog owner growing increasingly frustrated with his pet's fascination for sniffing every urine-stained tree trunk it passed, and Arthur would snap out of his reverie and shuffle along to catch up.

Before long, his observations led him to a significant conclusion – humans worship things. He realised the only event that could shake the vacant expressions off their faces was finding a thing they wanted to own and then setting about owning it as quickly as possible. For their part, the shops obviously worshipped money with equal zeal, lending the relationship they had with the shoppers a certain elegant balance. There were still plenty of aspects Arthur didn't understand, such as the number of signs declaring that everything was on sale. Was it really necessary, Arthur wondered, to remind people of this? They seemed to act under a very clear understanding this was how shops worked. He felt it very unlikely they would all forget they could purchase the goods on display if the shop owners took down all of the signs. This too was a subject Victor had no interest in discussing, and he reminded Arthur of their objective to get everything they needed as quickly as possible. Arthur apologised, and they set about purchasing new clothes – a task managed quickly courtesy of the fact that Victor would pay any price and Arthur would wear anything that fit if it meant they could escape the horde of imbeciles bungling their way around the shops with them.

Less than an hour later, Arthur sank back into the passenger seat of Victor's car and let out a heavy sigh. 'Thank goodness that's over,' he said.

'Actually,' sighed Victor, 'it's about to get much, much worse.' He started the engine.

Another thing about human beings, Arthur soon decided, was they had a masochistic attitude to purchasing useful provisions. It was as though they were still clinging to the survival culture they had evolved beyond and had taken steps to ensure a trip to the shops retained a certain degree of threat to their safety. However, in the absence of a physical threat in the clinical and sanitised environment they had built for themselves, they had manufactured a mental one. The supermarket he and Victor had travelled to was a testament to this. From the monolithic lettering that towered menacingly over them as they approached the shop, to the stupefyingly ineffective methods of paying for goods at the end of the ordeal, the entire experience seemed designed with the sole aim of crushing the spirit of all those who entered the building. Almost every feature of it struck

Arthur as instinctively depressing. As they entered, the glass doors hissed open as though the shop was preparing to swallow them whole. Once inside, the combination of synthetic light and brilliantly shining floors conspired to dazzle and confuse shoppers so they were powerless against a layout designed to ensure they all followed the same meandering path through the belly of this beast. The vacant expressions he had seen earlier were nothing compared to the feeble automatons on display here. They drifted through the aisles, blissfully unaware of themselves, let alone those around them. Frequently, as Victor tried to lead Arthur against the current and target only areas of the shop containing the items they required, a wanderer would stray across their path leaving a trolley in their wake. Incapable of shaking them from their reverie, no matter how loudly or rudely he spat 'excuse me' at them, Victor would have to steer his own uncontrollable steel cage around them, a task that should have been relatively straightforward but was rendered nigh on impossible by the fact that the wheels on shopping trolleys had been engineered to always point in four different directions, arguably making the trolleys themselves the most independently minded things in the entire supermarket.

They gathered a few toiletries for Arthur and some food items for the week and then traipsed back towards the entrance looking for a checkout at which they could pay. Arthur's mood sank even lower as he observed with pity the employees who were paid to drag items over a scanner one after another. Could there, wondered Arthur, be a more dispiriting sight than that of a person completing such a mundane and repetitive task – a task that could so obviously be completed every bit as easily by the most primitive of machines? The answer, it turned out, was yes, as Arthur discovered mere moments later in the self-checkout area, where he was greeted by the sight of a person who was paid to tend to all of the machines that failed to do exactly that.

'Please place the item in the bagging area,' said the machine.

'I *did*,' Victor snapped. He picked the bottle of milk up and then slammed it back down forcefully.

'Please remove the last item from the bagging area,' said the machine.

Victor pinched the bridge of his nose 'You just told me to put it there!'

Arthur watched quietly, wondering whether or not to mention his suspicion that the machine understood neither what it was saying, nor what it was told. He decided against it.

Victor looked up and stared at the young man responsible for the malfunctioning machines. The young man stared into space. Victor stared harder. Eventually, the man came back from whatever world he was visiting in his mind and skulked over to them. He swiped a card over the scanner and jabbed at the screen a few times and then skulked back to his post and settled back into his own world. Victor inserted his own card into the machine, jabbed at it himself, and then loaded his bags back into the trolley and headed to the car. Arthur followed in silence, certain he had just witnessed the most bewildering side of human beings. He was wrong.

21

Great and Awesome Wonders

The journey to Wendy's church was a short one, which Victor might have thanked God for, were he as inclined to involve him in the more positive moments of his life as he was those that inspired violent fantasies. He sat in the back, Arthur in the front staring in awe at this new world hurtling past at twenty-six miles per hour – not only did Wendy act like Victor's mother, she drove like her too. For the first time, without even realising he was entertaining the idea that Arthur was not from this world, Victor wondered what it must be like to see all of this through Arthur's eyes. How strange it must all seem. His head was constantly turning, trying to take in every sight, every sound, pausing only when something managed to capture his attention for more than a fleeting moment – a couple walking a dog, workmen repairing the roof of a house, two boys with toy guns arguing over who shot who first.

Victor spent most of the journey on edge, willing Arthur to keep quiet, to not ask any telling questions. There was a brief moment of panic when Wendy had to pull over to let an ambulance pass and Arthur started to speak. He clearly wanted to ask what it was but seemed to remember at the last moment Victor's strict instructions – do not look too fascinated and no questions until they got home. It wasn't so much fear of giving everything away, as it was fear of being unable to explain Arthur's ignorance. How would he explain the fact that a man Arthur's age had never seen an ambulance before?

It was things like this, Victor realised, that gave him no choice but to chaperone Arthur. He needed to keep an eye on him, needed to make sure he didn't make a scene at the church. He could not shake the image of Arthur interrupting and upsetting everyone by saying the kind of things people in churches do not like to hear like, 'are you sure about that?' or, 'logical' or, 'actually I think *I* might be your god'. Victor didn't want to go, but it was for the best. He could make sure Arthur did no more than observe quietly. Preferably from somewhere near the back.

*

Arthur's first impression of the church building was one of distinct disappointment. He had conducted a small amount of research on the internet following Wendy's invitation and had read about St Peter's Basilica, Westminster Abbey, St. Paul's Cathedral, Ulm Minster, Las Lajas Sanctuary, Notre Dame Cathedral, the Cistine Chapel and many others. He was looking forward to seeing what he expected to be a beautiful example of the pinnacle of human architecture. Instead, he entered a modern and rather cheap building that looked more like an unwelcome intruder that had never managed to fully ingratiate itself to the other buildings in its vicinity than the glorious centrepiece each of the churches he researched had been to their own environments. He realised immediately how foolish he was to expect every church to be so grand – it should have been obvious there would be smaller, more functional ones, but the fact is it was not and, for this reason, he entered it in a rather confused and underwhelmed state that would continue for most of the evening.

Attending church, he quickly discovered, was a highly ritualistic affair. From the moment they entered, everything that occurred had the air of a well-rehearsed

93

routine, as though the people were behaving not as a result of conscious thought, but of being programmed to repeatedly perform the same tasks over and over again. The various arrivals asked each other how they were, but few of them answered, electing instead to simply repeat the question back to the person who asked them. They queued at a doorway leading from the entryway to the main church hall and shook hands with a man dressed all in black but for a hint of white at his neck. An elderly woman stood next to him. Wendy introduced Arthur and Victor to the pair of them.

'Victor is a scientist', she said in a tone that Arthur felt was oddly conspiratorial. He noticed it drew one or two suspicious glances from several people immediately surrounding them.

'How interesting,' said the elderly woman. She smiled warmly. 'It's not often one meets a scientist with a mind open to God. We're always being told you can have science or religion. It's lovely to meet someone who bucks the trend and manages to balance the two. Good for you!'

Victor seemed embarrassed. His reply was almost apologetic. 'Well,' he said, 'I'm not so sure I do balance them. I'm here as a sceptic. Wendy invited me.'

'I see,' she replied. Her mouth continued smiling, but her eyes did not. 'Invited you to see the miracles for yourself, did she? Well, we'll see if we can't make a believer out of you yet.'

Victor smiled awkwardly at her and appeared at a loss for a reply. He was rescued when the man, or minister, as Arthur would later learn his title to be, welcomed them to the church and ushered them through to the main hall. Wendy didn't follow immediately, but remained in the entrance hall to talk to the other arrivals. Victor made his way to the back row of seats and gestured for Arthur to enter. He could tell it was something of a security measure on Victor's part – an attempt to control his movement, or rather to restrict it, by acting as a barrier between him and the rest of the church. It felt an unnecessarily parental move, but, knowing it was motivated by nothing more than Victor's anxiety, Arthur paid it no mind and took a seat next to the wall, which he was sure was what Victor was hoping he would do.

Despite his disappointment at its meek construction, Arthur tried to make conversation by feigning interest in the church. It was difficult, given that the main hall was also nothing like the meticulously ornate buildings he had studied, but a plain and apparently hastily thrown together affair. It shared one or two similar touches to those grand buildings, most notably a large stained-glass window high up in the far wall, but against the dull backdrop of the shell of the building it seemed more like a tragic parody of what he had already started to think of as a 'real' church.

'What a fascinating building,' he said. 'What is the picture in the window?'

'Well, according to the people sitting all around us,' said Victor in a muted tone, 'it's your mother being told she is pregnant with you.'

This caught Arthur by surprise. He looked back and forth between Victor and the window. 'My mother?' he blurted.

Victor grimaced and put his finger to his lips as several heads swung round to face them. 'Apparently so,' he whispered. 'An angel is a kind of supernatural being. This one was sent by God to tell Mary she would have a child who would be the son of God.'

This too was puzzling. As Victor had explained it, Arthur *was* this God fellow. Now he was telling him he was his offspring.

'It's a bit strange, I know,' he explained. 'They say he is the son of God, but also *is* God in human form. That's about all the explanation they give.'

'But that makes no sense!'

'Agreed,' nodded Victor. 'But I wouldn't bring it up here.'

'So what is the statue in front of it all about?'

'That one is you, or your son, or both, being executed to atone for the sins of all mankind.'

'Executed? Why was he executed?'

'For claiming to be the son of God.'

Arthur's mouth opened to speak, but his brain couldn't find any words to send out of it before it closed again.

'There's more to it than that. I suppose this lot,' Victor gestured vaguely around the room, 'would accuse me of simplifying it.' He leaned forward and picked up a book from the back of the pew in front of them. 'It's all in there, if you want to try and make a bit more sense of it,' he said, handing it to Arthur.

Arthur flicked briefly through the pages, but was too distracted by the activity in the hall to pay the vast amount of text any meaningful attention for the time being, so he continued observing as the seats filled up. As the last few people trickled in through the doorway, the door was closed by the woman who had spoken to them as they entered. She looked around the hall with purpose until her eyes met Arthur's. He acknowledged her with a smile, which she returned, but without the warmth she showed on the way in. She ambled to the front of the hall and spoke into the ear of a slightly overweight, scruffily dressed man. As they were talking, the man gazed searchingly around the room until his eyes also rested on Victor and Arthur. He looked away abruptly as they exchanged words Arthur was too far away to hear. Then the service began.

The minister introduced himself to the congregation and welcomed the large number of new faces, the appearance of which he attributed to the growing need for God's help and the news it could be found in this very church today. Several voices near the front called out 'amen', which seemed to serve as an indication of their agreement. He then conducted something called an 'opening prayer' another obvious ritual that caused everyone to bow their heads in unison and clasp their hands together. Not wanting to embarrass Victor, Arthur felt it would be pertinent to try to act appropriately and adopted this position himself. However, unsure as he was of the etiquette, he couldn't help but look up every now and then to check everyone else was still doing it. In doing so, he noticed Victor sat quietly and respectfully, but remained upright, apparently making something of a show of not participating despite the fact everyone in the room was oblivious to him. Another man, sitting to Victor's left, did the same, though the next woman along screwed her eyes tightly shut and clasped her hands so firmly that they shook. At the end of the prayer, the minister uttered the same word – 'amen', which everyone else then repeated. This signalled the end of the prayer and the people ceased bowing their heads. The minister then introduced the next activity, something called a 'hymn', called "Be Thou My Vision". Seeing others do the same, Arthur reached for another book tucked into the back of the pew in front of him and stood up – another ritual which was performed uniformly and without instruction by everyone but Victor and the man next to him. Arthur had a moment's hesitation as he realised this and worried he had made a mistake, but felt that to sit straight back down would be the most conspicuous thing he could do, and he was keen not to embarrass Victor by drawing unnecessary attention, so he remained standing. As they stood, a group of people towards the front of the hall began playing some of the most extraordinarily beautiful music Arthur had ever heard. He decided there and then that there could not possibly be anything more perfect anywhere in this or any other universe. And then, somehow, there was. The people started singing. Words poured out of them in perfect time, perfect unison, perfect harmony. They combined with the music so delicately that each individual instrument and voice became more than just a part of something and became the thing itself, until it was no longer possible to tell where the voices ended and the music started. He filled with a feeling so complex and contradictory that it was like humility and importance in equal measure. Their voices stirred something in him he did not know existed. It was as though a part of him, the most important part, had awoken for the first time, and he was suddenly changed, had become more than he had ever been before. This was the real beauty of his creation. The swirling universe he had thought so perfect when he had viewed it from his attic paled into insignificance when compared to this tiny moment in this tiny corner of this tiny speck of it. What other wonders it might contain, in other corners, on other specks, he could not begin to imagine. But he knew they must exist, and they existed because of him. The thought moved him to tears.

As the music finished and he sat back down, Victor looked at him with concern. 'Are you okay?' he asked.

Arthur nodded and wiped his eyes, feeling foolish now the silence had returned, a silence that would forever feel larger and emptier for the absence of what he had just heard.

'Why didn't you stand?' Arthur asked once he had composed himself.

Victor struggled to explain. 'I'm not... this,' was all he managed, encompassing the church and everyone in it with a wave of his hand.

Before Arthur could ask anything else, the minister started speaking again, introducing a very special guest for a second week running. A man, he claimed, who regularly performed miracles for those in need. The man in question was, in fact, the overweight and underdressed man standing at the front of the church before the service began – the one the woman from the entrance had spoken to. He walked onto the stage and accepted a microphone from the minister. He introduced himself as Billy Leigh in an accent that was rougher and less refined than those Arthur had so far encountered. He was, he said, a travelling preacher and healer. He told stories of his younger life as a heavy drinker, drug user, gambler and violent thug, before explaining that, during a time of difficulty, Jesus entered his life and gave him renewed purpose. It was a tragic story, full of confession and humility. He was warm in his delivery and punctuated every other sentence with 'amen', or another word – 'hallelujah', which was repeated by members of the congregation each time. He said he liked to dress casually when preaching but decided to make an effort for this evening, drawing laughter from the crowd. At this point in the proceedings, his tone shifted. The warm, good-natured delivery disappeared almost immediately and was replaced by an authoritative, almost threatening tone. He announced he would now invite people to accept Jesus into their own lives. Up until now, he claimed, they could be forgiven for not knowing any better, but from this point on they could never claim they did not know something called Hell awaited them if they did not submit entirely to Jesus. 'It's now or never,' he asserted with his eyes fixed on Arthur and Victor, before he bowed his head to lead another prayer.

Arthur didn't bow his head this time. Unlike Victor, he didn't refuse as an act of open rebellion, but because he had no idea why he was expected to. Despite the claim he now knew better, he felt none the wiser about this Hell that awaited him. Without a more detailed explanation, Arthur was reluctant to commit to what sounded increasingly like complete subservience to the unknown entity called Jesus. It was all well and good hearing a third party's testimonial, but how could he be sure Jesus would have a similarly positive effect on his own life? Given his unavoidable ignorance, he would just have to hope this Jesus fellow would understand his initial misgivings and let him submit later, provided he gave a satisfactory explanation as to why Arthur should acquiesce to him, of course.

With the prayer completed, Billy Leigh then embarked on the most confusing section of the service. He announced he had a gift. A gift so remarkable it proved the power of God and Jesus beyond all doubt. He could, he said, heal people through prayer. He said he had cured all number of ailments – from minor injuries to terminal illnesses. He stated that he had not only cured a person's deafness by touching their ears and praying, but also to have restored the vision of someone who was not only blind, but who had no eyes. He claimed to have placed his hand over the empty sockets and prayed and, upon removing his hand, revealed a pair of startling blue eyes that could see perfectly. Arthur found the story ludicrous and might even have laughed out loud were it not for the startling reaction of everyone else in the hall – a selection of celebratory amens and hallelujahs that indicated their unquestioning acceptance of his outlandish claims. Gobsmacked, Arthur watched as people accepted an invitation to join him at the front of the church if they were in need of a similar miracle. They lined up behind him, a selection of men and women, a mix of young and old, each presumably suffering with one ailment or another. Arthur noticed one of them was the woman from their row, whose husband did not join in with the prayers.

Billy spoke to a woman at the end of the line. She looked sad and tired, and it was difficult to estimate her age, though she appeared comparatively young.

'What's your name?' He asked.

'Jessica,' she replied, timidly.

'And what can I help you with Jessica?'

Her response was imperceptible from the back of the hall, and Billy repeated it as a question.

'You have tumours all over your liver?'

She nodded and wiped tears from her eyes.

'Now don't you cry, Jessica,' he told her. 'You're in the Lord's hands now. There's nothing to fear.' With that, he placed the palm of his hand flat against her body and began praying. It was not like the other prayers, muted and with head bowed. This time he raised his head, as though calling out to the ceiling. 'Lord,' he said, 'we ask you to reach out your hand and deliver Jessica from her pain and suffering. We pray you remove these tumors from her body and restore her to full health so she may live a long and happy life and stand as a testament to your power and glory. We pray this in Jesus' name. Amen.'

Once more, the church was filled with the collected voices repeating the final word in unison.

'Now Jessica,' he said. 'I want you to stop worrying. I want you to leave here tonight free of fear. Because I promise you, Jessica, next time you go to the hospital, next time they scan you, they will find the tumors are gone. The Lord works through me. I've seen it thousands of times. He has worked through me tonight and you are going to be cured. Do you trust me Jessica? Do you have faith in the Lord and all He can do?'

She nodded again and then broke down sobbing and was escorted away. Arthur turned to Victor. 'Is that all he does?'

Victor nodded and flicked his finger to his lips. He looked exceedingly angry. Arthur had so many questions he desperately wanted to ask, but they would have to wait until later. In the meantime, he could only watch as the bizarre scene continued to unfold. More people stepped forward, stated their illnesses and complaints, and received short, intense prayers and promises. Most members of the congregation continued to cry 'amen' at the appropriate times, but some seemed to get lost in their own prayers, whispering to themselves with their eyes clamped shut and hands pressed together, or with arms outstretched and heads tilted back. One man left his seat and knelt on the floor with his arms held wide, while another woman began to shake and shudder and stood up in a manner that suggested her movements were not her own, as though someone else was controlling her. She lurched into the aisle between the rows of seats and raised her arms too, shaking ever more violently, before stopping suddenly and falling backwards. Fortunately, a man several rows ahead of Arthur's had positioned himself behind her with a blanket in his arms. She fell into the open blanket and he lowered her slowly to the floor, wrapping her up in it as he laid her gently down. How odd, Arthur thought, that he could have predicted he would need to do this and so brought the blanket with him and positioned himself so perfectly. Stranger still was the way he left her on the floor, seemingly unconscious, and returned to his seat without any apparent fears for her wellbeing.

Arthur spent the remainder of the service feeling somewhat detached from what was happening around him. He was shocked and confused and weighed down by a sense of great discomfort he could not quite understand. The prayers ended and another hymn was performed, this one called 'Just As I Am'. Lyrically, it seemed an odd choice given the events that preceded it. This time, Arthur didn't feel moved in the way he had been earlier in the evening. He remained seated, his head full of questions, waiting patiently as the hymn was finished, as the minister spoke to the congregation and thanked Billy Leigh for bringing his gift to the church, as people dropped things into a number of fabric pouches being passed around the rows of seats, and as a final prayer was conducted. Eventually, Victor turned to him and asked, 'Ready to leave?'.

He was.

22

The Conviction of Things Not Seen

The journey home was painful. Wendy, who was more than aware of Victor's views on religion, courtesy of several previous conversations which had all resulted in the same impasse, was eager to hear their thoughts on the service. Victor found this was often the case with religious people – no matter how many times you tell them you don't believe, no matter how many times you explain your reasons, they possess a relentless belief that it's only a matter of time before you realise your mistake and come round to their way of thinking.

She overflowed with enthusiasm about the privilege of bearing witness to 'true miracles'. Victor tried to keep his responses evasive, telling her he found the stories tragic and moving, while avoiding direct comment on the 'miracles' she believed they had seen.

'And what about you, Arthur?' she asked, when she eventually accepted today was not the day Victor would succumb to The Truth.

Arthur shifted uneasily in the front seat and turned to look at Victor in the back, presumably seeking some indication it was okay to share his views.

'I'm just as interested to know what you made of it all,' Victor told him.

He sat quietly for a moment and then said, 'I liked the hymns.'

Victor smiled to himself, quietly pleased Arthur had chosen to be evasive too. Clearly, he didn't want to offend

Wendy, which suggested he saw everything that had happened at the church for what it was.

'Beautiful, aren't they?' she replied. 'And what about Billy Leigh? Wasn't it moving to see the power of the Lord working through him?'

'It was... interesting,' said Arthur. 'Though I am not entirely sure what I just saw. I can't see how what he did could possibly make a difference to the ailments described.'

'That's what makes it a miracle,' said Wendy. 'The power of the Lord works through him.'

'I see. And has this power been shown to work in the past?'

Arthur was treading on dangerous ground now. Victor was tempted to suggest he read about it online when they got back, if only to try and put the brakes on a conversation that could quickly turn quite uncomfortable, but a rebellious part of him thought it would be interesting to see how Arthur would respond to what he knew was coming. Besides, they were less than five minutes from home, so they wouldn't have to sit in stony silence for too long if he did say something to offend. Plus, if he did, Victor would have the added bonus of being given the cold shoulder by Wendy for a few weeks.

'You heard his stories, didn't you? He has helped the deaf to hear and the blind to see!'

'Yes, I heard him make those claims. But have you ever seen anything like it yourself? Or have you only witnessed him healing things you cannot immediately measure the effects of?'

'Well,' Wendy began, with a notable change in her tone, 'what about the woman tonight? Why would she and so many others break down in tears if not because they were overwhelmed by the knowledge God will heal them?'

Victor had to bite his tongue. Because they were terrified, he wanted to say. Because they knew it represented a last, desperate hope in a likely futile struggle. Because they were bloody *dying*. Years ago, he wouldn't have been able to, but he kept quiet. He had had this conversation with Wendy enough times to know there was no point pursuing it. Instead, he waited to see how Arthur would play it.

'I think people can be quite emotional,' said Arthur, throwing a telling look back at Victor. 'They can break down for any number of reasons, surely?'

'And,' said Wendy, tactically ignoring this, 'there are countless testimonials from others who have had their illnesses miraculously disappear after praying with Billy Leigh. It happened in our church last year. A woman who was diagnosed with cancer prayed with him and it had disappeared the next time she went in for tests. How else can you explain that?'

'I think there could be a number of explanations,' he said, thoughtfully. 'But I would suggest the most likely one is that a mistake was made in the original diagnosis.'

There was a brief lull as Wendy considered this. 'I don't think so,' she said, though Victor thought he noticed a slight crack in her conviction.

'Really? Surely there is plenty of evidence that individuals are capable of making mistakes, while there is presumably very little to suggest medical conditions can be cured by prayer?'

'When the Lord fills you with faith, you don't need hard evidence,' said Wendy.

'I see,' said Arthur, and then a pause, before, 'doesn't it make more sense the other way around?'

'What do you mean?'

'Well, it would make much more sense if you said 'when you have hard evidence, you don't need faith', don't you think?'

'I don't think you quite understand the nature of faith,' sighed Wendy.

'Oh,' said Arthur.

They were about three minutes away from home. They were filled with stony silence.

23

We Are Powerless Against This Great Horde

'But it makes no *sense*,' said Arthur.

Victor rubbed his temples. There were only so many ways he could try to explain what they had witnessed, and he had tried almost all of them in the half hour since they arrived back at his house and closed the door safely behind them. The irony of an atheist defending religion to a god who was made angry by it started off as amusing but was now wearing thin. 'I agree,' he protested. 'Completely. But that's the way it is. They believe it. All of it.'

'Even though they can prove none of it?'

'Yes,' said Victor, for what felt like the hundredth time.

'Even though much of what they claim can be *dis*proved?'

'Yes.' One hundred and one.

'Why?'

Victor sighed. 'I don't know. All sorts of reasons I suppose. Because they've been taught to since they were too young to know better. Because they're scared of death. Because they want it to be true so they have convinced themselves it is.'

Arthur stared at him, dumbfounded.

'Look,' said Victor. 'I know it seems mad. I know it seems almost as mad that I'm so blasé about it. Don't mistake that for me disagreeing with you. I've just had more time to get used to it than you.' He suppressed the voice in his head telling him he was talking to Arthur as though he really was from another world and pressed on. 'The fact of reality is there are a lot of people who believe something that makes no sense to us and there is nothing we can do about it. Believe me, I've tried. I've written entire books about it. And I'll keep doing so. But I don't really hold out much hope of success. Some people can't be reasoned with.'

Arthur deflated, the energy of his frustrated confusion seeping out of him in a hefty sigh as he contemplated a world full of people who believe things that make no sense. He imagined it was probably not a very happy one. How reality must trouble humans, that they are so eager to reject it for fantasy. With the benefit of hindsight, he understood Victor a little better now. His reluctance to visit the church was based on sound judgement, not on the narrow-mindedness Wendy had accused him of. It even explained why he found it so difficult to accept the fact of Arthur's origins. Unexpected truths must be difficult to accept in this world, where they probably resemble, at first glance at least, the impossible lies the people all around you are happy to accept. Victor's scepticism was simply the result of his failure to reconcile what he observed with what he expected. It was not obstinate or ignorant of him to require further evidence – it was simply a requirement for any rational being in this irrational world. He turned to Victor. 'Humans are an odd bunch, aren't they?'

Victor smiled wryly and nodded his head. 'Yes.' One hundred and two.

24

Incredibly Shiny

Of all the people Arthur met during his time on Earth, Richard Kyle proved to be the single most obnoxious one. 'He's a complete arsehole,' Victor warned him before their meeting. By now, Arthur understood that this kind of hyperbolic metaphor was meant to convey a sense of character, and so he concluded that Kyle would prove to be unpleasant, though he was still surprised by just how rude the man he found himself standing in front of early the next morning turned out to be.

'So,' said Kyle, jabbing a finger towards Arthur and pacing back and forth in irritable fits and starts, 'you're the fruitcake who thinks he's God are you?'

Arthur looked him up and down. He was dressed in a dark suit with thin white stripes stitched into it. His skin was dark, though it looked to Arthur as though this was the result of overexposure to ultraviolet light, rather than genetics, and his hair was meticulously crafted. He also wore the shiniest shoes Arthur had ever seen. He found himself staring at them, his gaze drifting down frequently throughout their meeting as he marvelled at the fact he could see his own distorted reflection in them.

'I'm up here, idiot,' barked Kyle. Arthur snapped his head up to meet his gaze but said nothing. Kyle continued. 'Do you have any idea how much trouble you've caused? Or how much trouble you're in?'

Arthur looked at Victor and Sam, who stood beside him in their office. They had assured him he could say anything he wanted – Kyle already knew how they had discovered him and what Arthur had concluded about this being his universe. 'Be honest,' Victor had said. 'There's not much else you can do. And it'll probably irritate the shit out of Kyle,' he added. It seemed Victor deemed this a desirable outcome. Arthur considered this a little juvenile at the time, though he was beginning to understand and share Victor's desire to cause the man some frustration.

'Don't look at them. I'm the one talking to you,' said Kyle, making the mistake of thinking rudeness was synonymous with assertiveness.

'I'm afraid I don't quite follow,' said Arthur. 'You say I've caused trouble, but I rather feel I am the one who has been inconvenienced.'

'Oh you do, do you? How'd you work that out?'

'I didn't choose to come here,' said Arthur. 'I was merely sitting in my attic admiring my universe. It was your actions that brought me here. Any trouble you feel has been caused is your own doing.'

Kyle stared at him dumbly, his face glowing red and his forehead already beading with perspiration. 'Now you listen here,' he said, wagging his finger at Arthur. 'This heap of shit story you're spinning isn't fooling anyone. We all know we didn't "bring you here",' he stopped wagging to make speech marks with his fingers. 'We both know you got yourself into that machine, and you're going to tell me how you did it.'

Arthur frowned. How could this man know he did something if he had no idea how he did it? He put the question to Kyle.

'Don't you try and get clever with me,' said Kyle, wagging his finger again. Tiny droplets of saliva had started to erupt from his mouth as he spoke. 'I could have you arrested at the drop of a hat.'

'I'm sorry,' said Arthur, maintaining a calm, soothing tone. 'I don't know what that means.'

'Not so clever now, eh? It means I could have you locked up,' barked Kyle. 'Or chucked in some loony bin.'

Victor felt it necessary to intervene. 'Calm down, Richard. You're not having him arrested.'

Kyle rounded on Victor. 'Don't you bloody start. He's obviously mental. Needs help, this one.' He eyed Arthur with loathing. 'Locking up is the best thing for him,' he said, allowing, as the ignorant and self-righteous so often do, his malice to masquerade as empathy. Victor could have punched him. 'Look at him,' Kyle continued, 'what's so fascinating about my fucking shoes?' he snapped his fingers in Arthur's face.

Arthur snapped his head back up again. 'Sorry?' he said.

'Last chance,' warned Kyle. 'Tell me how you got into the detector.'

Arthur told him. He explained that by compressing the beams of neutrinos as much as they had, E Equals had caused a subatomic collision that created so much energy it tore a temporary hole in spacetime. This caused the universe he had created to open up and, essentially, swallow him, dragging him all the way through to the source of the tear. He explained that he had no idea this had happened, nor that it was even possible, until he had studied the data Sam had provided him with and realised this was the most logical conclusion.

Arthur realised from Kyle's dumbstruck expression that he had completely failed to understand this explanation. And it wasn't just a failure to understand how the events Arthur had described could have happened – he genuinely had no idea what much of what Arthur had said actually meant. It was a revelatory moment for Arthur, because, in that moment, he realised it was possible, in human society, for a person to secure a position of responsibility for which they were completely unqualified. What kind of lunatic, he wondered, would think it was a good idea to employ someone who lacked even a rudimentary grasp of physics in the most senior position of responsibility of an organisation such as this? He hoped it was not a common problem and that elsewhere, people with important responsibilities, such as designing policies for healthcare, education, and economics, for example, knew what they were doing. He was shaken out of this musing by Kyle once more addressing him unnecessarily abruptly.

'Is that it?'

Answer everything honestly, Victor had told him. 'Your shoes are incredibly shiny,' he said.

Mere moments after they had stormed out of the office, Kyle and his shiny shoes stormed back in, flanked by two security guards. 'That's the one,' he said, pointing at Arthur.

One of the guards approached Arthur. 'Excuse me sir, but we need you to come with us.' The other guard, Victor noticed, was Mick. He threw Victor a shrug and an apologetic look, which he interpreted as saying *'sorry mate, he might be a twat, but he's the twat who pays me'*. Surprisingly, this was precisely what Mick was trying to convey. They escorted Arthur out of the office and down to the building's reception area where, after a short while, two more men in similar yet subtly different uniforms to the guards told him he was under arrest.

25

There is Liberty

Sam glanced at her watch for the fourth time in ten minutes and wondered what secrets the builders of police stations knew that prevented the normal laws of time from passing within their walls. She considered approaching the desk sergeant again to ask how much longer she could expect to wait, but decided against it on the grounds that asking for an eighth time was probably pushing it a bit. She was wrong, at least as far as the desk sergeant was concerned. The desk sergeant felt that asking for a second time was pushing it a bit. Asking for an eighth time would have been pushing it over a cliff, having already pushed it one step too far, pushed it to the very end of its patience, and then promptly pushed it down the stairs. What part of 'he'll be out when he's out' didn't she understand? In Sam's defence, she had been sitting in the waiting area of the station for a little over two hours, and hadn't arrived until four hours after Arthur's initial arrest. She looked at her watch yet again. Ten past five. *I'll give it another ten minutes*, she told herself, *and then ask for an update.*

What felt like a good fifteen minutes passed. She checked her watch. Thirteen minutes past five. *Sod it*, thought Sam, and she stood up.

The desk sergeant, whose peripheral vision was finely tuned for spotting angry members of the public, took a deep breath and prepared to explain that no, there hadn't been any update, no, he didn't know what was taking so long, and no, he couldn't just run along and check, and, as ever, Arthur would be there when he'd be there. He decided he would say it all before she had even asked. In fact, he would say it all in one breath. However, just as he had primed himself to deliver all of this in the most delicately poised tone, right on the cusp of being tolerant but clearly expressing an enormous weight of exasperation, a doorway flew open and Arthur was steered into the waiting area. The sergeant deflated and went back to his paperwork.

'Arthur!' exclaimed Sam. 'How are you?'

'Er,' said Arthur. 'I feel fine... but apparently I have delusions of grandeur.'

'Excuse me?'

'But on a positive note, they are quite certain I'm not schizophrenic, paranoid, or a danger to myself or others.'

'The police told you all that?' asked Sam.

They had not. What had actually happened, Arthur relayed, was he had spent some considerable time trying to explain he was God, but not the version of God they knew about, because that version of God wasn't real, and trying to explain how he had come to be on Earth with the aid of diagrams and mathematical explanations. The diagrams and maths were tricky at first, because the police officers interviewing him weren't keen on the idea of giving him a pencil. Arthur found it an odd decision to struggle over but let them take their time until eventually they relented. In the end, the police decided what they really needed, more than an explanation of how Arthur was God and how he had got here, was a psychiatrist, so they sent for one. It was the psychiatrist who had given the diagnosis of delusions of grandeur but not schizophrenic, paranoid or dangerous after a short interview with Arthur and an even shorter chat with the police officers who had performed the clever police trick of making 'please tell us we can get shot of him' sound like 'is this man dangerous and does he need help?' They added a silent yet perfectly clear, 'Bear in mind that saying 'yes' to either of those questions means more time spent in his company and a lot of irritating paperwork for all of us.'

And with that, Arthur was free to go.

'What about the trespassing charge?' asked Sam.

'Oh, that was dropped hours ago,' said the very tired, very fed up officer who had been listening to Arthur all afternoon.

'Really? Why?'

'No idea. We'd have given him the boot as soon as they were dropped if we weren't so worried about his... y'know.' He tapped his head to avoid saying anything Arthur could hear. It would have been a far more considerate gesture had he been out of Arthur's field of vision at the time.

26

Comfort

Arthur was left to his own devices again the next morning. Victor was in a tense and uneasy mood as he left because he had another meeting with Kyle to look forward to. He was full of concern for Arthur before he left, frequently asking whether he would be okay on his own despite Arthur's repeated assertions he would be fine. Arthur found it an odd peculiarity of humans that they tended to repeatedly ask the same question, as though they never quite trusted an answer to be honest. He was actually more eager to be left alone than he was last time – he had much to research following his visit to the church. He wanted to find out more about faith healing: the processes, the basis for people's belief in it, the *evidence* for it. As soon as Victor was out of the door, Arthur sat down at the computer and started searching. After nearly four hours ploughing through a wealth of material, he reached a number of conclusions:

1. Faith healing is a method of curing an individual's ailments via an appeal by or on behalf of the afflicted person to the supernatural entity called God.
2. God's response had to be magical. It seemed the prayer was only believed to have worked when the person was cured in a seemingly miraculous way. The application of modern medicine rendered the prayer void.
3. Given that he was the likely creator of this universe and had no powers, divine or otherwise, that he

could use to cure afflicted individuals, his very existence was proof that belief in faith healing was erroneous.

4. Even if Arthur's hypothesis turned out to be wrong and he was not the creator of this universe, there was still no meaningful evidence to support faith healing, spiritual healing, or any other religion-based alternative to scientifically-proven medicine. All evidence suggested that prayer was a pointless and impotent response to illness.

It was baffling. How could any intelligent being believe in something so contradictory to the evidence their species had collected? The only explanation he could come up with was that this important evidence had not been dispersed widely or effectively enough, which was disgracefully careless on the part of those who had gathered it or whose responsibility it was to distribute it, given their failures had certainly led to the countless deaths of people who would have no doubt used an alternative method of tackling their illnesses had they been better informed. This explanation was, obviously, wrong in pretty much every respect, and eventually dawned on Arthur that there was a far more straightforward explanation – the differences between himself and the human beings of planet earth were much greater than he had first realised. Unfortunately, this realisation didn't occur to him before he made the decision to take his findings next door and share them with Wendy in the firm belief he was about to change her life forever.

No less than five minutes later, Arthur found himself sitting on Victor's doorstep like a child enduring a popular form of discipline among human parents. As it turned out, everything he had discovered had indeed been shared with Wendy before, and she did not appreciate being reminded of it. The visit had started off promisingly. Wendy invited Arthur in. Arthur thanked her. Wendy told him how nice it was to see him. Arthur thanked her. Wendy asked what she could do for Arthur. Arthur then told her everything they had witnessed on Sunday was a complete farce, that there was no evidence prayer could heal any illness, and Billy Leigh was almost certainly a charlatan. This was where, Arthur reflected, things had taken a downward turn. He endeavoured to explain that he was only trying to help – he didn't want Wendy to waste her time with prayer should she ever fall ill, and he had her best interests at heart. Wendy didn't see things this way.

'You're no different to Victor,' she said. 'You agreed with me the other day that he should be more open-minded, and yet here you are now trying to undermine my faith. And for what? What difference does it make to you what I believe?' Arthur tried to protest, to point out it wasn't about the difference it made to him, but to her, but she wasn't finished. 'Did he put you up to this?' she asked. 'Is this your idea of a joke?'

He told her it was not his idea of a joke, that he couldn't see how it could conform to anyone's idea of a joke. She kept asking why he had come, even though his explanation only increased her anger each time he repeated it.

'I think you should leave,' Wendy said. Again, he tried to explain. Again, she interrupted. 'Please, Arthur, I don't want to talk to you,' she said, holding the front door open. Arthur exited sheepishly and offered a final apology as the door closed behind him. He walked the short distance back to Victor's front door and realised he had left the key Victor had given him inside the house. He stared at the door foolishly for a moment, indulging in a similar kind of denial that drivers experience shortly after they hear the sound of metal scraping along concrete in multi-story car parks, and assured himself this did not mean he would have to sit on Victor's doorstep and wait for several hours for him to come home. His shoulders sagged. He sat down.

As was his custom, he spent the time thinking. He started by trying to imagine how a person could contend that a hypothesis was true in the face of overwhelming evidence it was not. He wracked his brain for a logical explanation but could come up with none. If he had to point to a single moment when he began to understand that there existed vast differences between his own people and human beings, he would have to conclude it was during that brief spell on Victor's doorstep. Back home, ideas were rejected as soon as they were disproven. The possibility that someone would continue to subscribe to them would be considered absurd. Indeed, it would be seen as a sign of mental illness or a worrying neurological problem. He briefly entertained the idea that this may have been the case with Wendy, but then thought about how many humans shared her views. He thought it unlikely such a large proportion of a species capable of reaching the level of technological advancement required to bring him to their universe would be mentally defective. There must have been something he was missing – some piece of information that would surely help to make all of this clear. For the time being, however, it eluded him. His inability to work this out was, in itself, worth thinking about. How stupid he had been to presume he knew enough about this world to share knowledge and wisdom with its inhabitants. This planet, indeed this universe, was unknown to him. Should he not be gathering information, rather than sharing it? If only he could have spoken to Wendy, he was sure she would have been able to help. But he couldn't call on her again. She had made it clear she didn't want to see him and he could imagine no circumstances under which this would change for the foreseeable future. As if making a point of proving him wrong and underlining just how little he understood this world, Wendy chose this moment to exit her front door. She looked at Arthur and frowned.

'What *are* you doing, Arthur?' she asked.

Arthur made sure to take a moment to think about this. Not because it was a difficult question to answer – far from it. But the answer was so obvious, he thought it an incredibly stupid question to ask. Surely, Wendy was capable of deducing that he was sitting on a doorstep through simple observation. In fact, a recently twitched curtain suggested she had already done exactly this and was merely feigning surprise when she exited the house and looked over. However, he was at this moment acutely aware of something that had been slowly dawning on him for some time, which was that his initial interpretation of anything anyone on this planet said could not be trusted and required more consideration than he had been giving it. After some thought, he realised this was another situation where the question being asked was not, in fact, the one the asker sought an answer to. Furthermore, he surmised, it made more sense that Wendy wanted to know *why* he was doing what she could clearly see he was doing. He fought the urge to ask if this was the case, which protected him from having to fight the further urge to point out she should really just ask the question she sought an answer to, and answered the question he assumed she wanted answered. 'I seem to have locked myself out of the house,' he said.

'And you are just going to sit there on the doorstep until Victor gets home?'

'I couldn't see an alternative course of action.'

She shook her head and smiled. 'Come on,' she said. 'You can't sit there all day. I'll put the kettle on.'

'Are you sure?'

'I don't like to leave things on an argument,' she said, ushering Arthur back inside. 'Make yourself at home.' She directed Arthur towards the living room and then disappeared into the kitchen. 'Do you take sugar?' she called.

It seemed a bizarre enquiry, bordering on invasively rude, but this too had the potential to be something he had misinterpreted and, keen not to say anything to offend Wendy again, he thought it best to answer honestly. 'Er, no,' he said. Gazing around the room, he noticed a number of motifs he recognised from the church. There were two crosses on the wall, one bearing a likeness of Jesus being executed, which he was finding an increasingly uncomfortable image. It seemed odd that his death would be the event his followers would choose to repeatedly depict. Were there no other events and acts worthy of commemoration? Arthur made a mental note to check when he finally got back into Victor's house. Odder still was the knowledge that the man on the cross was, to all intents and purposes, him. Or his own son. Or both. Granted, it bore no resemblance to the *reality* of Arthur, but he still found it unnerving to think this, in the absence of any knowledge of who he was, was the image that seemed most obvious to those who speculated about what he might be like. He tried to ignore it, which was difficult while its harrowing, pleading eyes followed him around the room. He scanned the bookshelves. They contained three Bibles and a number of books which, based on their titles, appeared to be about the Bible or God or Jesus in some way. To the right stood a wooden cabinet, on top of which was arranged a collection of photographs of a young boy, ranging from a few weeks old, up until the age of about nine or ten. In most of them, he was alone, but in two of them he was sitting with Wendy. She looked a few years younger – in her late twenties or early thirties, and infinitely happier. In one, she was sitting with him on a beach, both of them holding orange cones with a white substance on top.

'My son, Luke,' announced Wendy, reentering the room and offering Arthur a cup. He took it from her, quickly transferring it to his left hand so he could hold it by the handle. It contained a brown liquid that was so hot the skin on his right hand felt like it had started to melt.

'He seems a happy chap,' said Arthur, trying not to whimper.

'He was,' said Wendy. He noted both the past tense and the enormous sense of sadness that emanated from her.

'Oh,' he said, and added, 'I'm sorry.'

'It's okay,' she sighed. 'I like to think he's always like that now. Smiling down from Heaven, waiting for mummy to come and join him.' She smiled as she spoke, but it contrasted jarringly with the emotion hiding behind it, pressing against it like water behind a cracking dam. 'God is looking after him until I get there,' she added. Arthur obviously had good reason to suspect this was not the case, but even in his ignorance of human beings he was aware this was not an appropriate time to share his thoughts. A moment of silence passed as they gazed at the picture of the smiling child. 'That was almost four years ago,' Wendy continued. 'He was diagnosed a few days later – a rare cancer. He was so brave. He never stopped smiling. We prayed and prayed, but God clearly felt he needed him more than I did. He took him a few months later.'

Two things dawned on Arthur. First, he realised how insensitive he must have seemed earlier. To lose a child was devastating enough. For humans, who, based on his interactions with them so far, experienced much stronger emotional responses than his own people, it must have been utterly overwhelming. If Wendy's beliefs were part of her method of dealing with the loss of her child, then to attack them was to attack her grief. The second was the missing part of the puzzle he had been trying to work out while he was sitting on Victor's doorstep. This was why a seemingly well informed person could continue to believe in something that was contradicted by all of the information at their disposal – their emotions overwhelmed everything, including their ability to think logically. It essentially resulted in a form of denial, not only in terms of her loss, but also regarding the evidence disproving what must have been a very comforting fantasy about her child's continued existence. Humans were not stupid creatures, he realised – but they were burdened with such strong emotional responses that they had to resort to illogical thinking as a coping mechanism. A wave of guilt washed over Arthur and he apologised profusely for both her loss and how inconsiderate he had been.

'Thank you,' she said. She placed her hand on Arthur's arm and invited him to sit.

He did so, taking a surreptitious sniff of the drink as Wendy took a seat on the sofa opposite him. It had a vaguely earthy smell. Seeing Wendy do the same, he placed the cup on a small table in the middle of the room.

'I'm sorry I lost my temper,' said Wendy.

'There's really no need,' Arthur replied. 'I understand completely. I feel quite foolish.'

'Well, don't we make a right pair?' she said. Arthur wasn't sure what she meant by this, but agreed anyway, which seemed the desired response. Unsure what to say next, Arthur picked up the cup of tea and took a sip, realising as he did so why Wendy had asked about the sugar. It was not, as he had foolishly assumed at the time, a random and rather forthright enquiry into his consumption of an addictive and harmful substance. She was asking if he wanted any added to the drink. It had a terribly bitter taste, as though it had been made by straining hot water through dry leaves. In light of this, he couldn't help but feel he had answered incorrectly, though when asked how it was, he assured Wendy it was lovely.

'So,' said Wendy, 'I assume you've been reading up on faith healing.'

'I have,' Arthur said. 'But we don't have to talk about that.'

'It's fine, really,' she replied. 'I'd be happy to discuss it.'

Despite her assurances, Arthur was reluctant to bring it up again having so recently managed to make peace. Not only did he not want to cause Wendy further upset, he certainly didn't want to be asked to leave again. He would rather finish the cup of bitter leaf-water than go back to sitting on Victor's doorstep for the rest of the afternoon. Erring on the side of caution, he decided to run with his recent resolution to focus more on learning from the people of Earth, rather than trying to educate them, at least until he had a firmer grasp of what he was dealing with. Recalling the last thing Wendy had said to him, Arthur said, 'Last night you said I didn't understand the nature of faith. I was wondering if perhaps you could explain it to me?'

'You want me to explain faith to you?' Wendy asked, demonstrating another peculiar feature of humans Arthur was picking up on – the tendency to seek clarification of a request that is already perfectly clear. Nevertheless, he told her yes, he did want her to explain faith to him.

'I'm not sure I would know where to start,' she said. 'What do you think it means?' This struck Arthur as an absurd thing to ask. Why would his ignorant ideas about faith affect what faith was? The concepts of time and gravity and magnetism and friction do not change depending on the preconceptions of the person to whom you are explaining them. They simply are what they are. How could this be any different?

'I have no idea what it means,' he said.

'Really?' She asked, clearly surprised. 'No idea at all?' Arthur sensed this was one of those situations Victor was keen for him to avoid – one in which he demonstrated a suspicious ignorance of something he should have at least some knowledge of. He was going to have to tread carefully now.

'Well, it's obviously an important part of your relationship with God,' he said, trying to keep things as vague as possible.

'Of course.'

'Perhaps you should start there. What makes it so important?'

She sat back and contemplated the question for a moment. 'I suppose it's why I believe that, no matter what happens, God has a plan for me, will protect me, and wants what's best for me,' she said.

'So it's about trust?'

'Precisely,' she said. 'I trust God to keep watch over me and to guide me and that His plan is for the best.'

Arthur struggled his way through the conversation; through Wendy's assertion she did not know what the plan was but knew there was one, and through her explanation that she felt God guiding her actions, yet could not explain the nature of that guidance beyond something she 'just knew' she was receiving. The key to understanding all of this was the Bible, which she kept referring to as the source of her faith. His sole experience of it so far was Victor's flippant remark in the church implying he should not consider it a reliable source of information. Wendy, on the other hand, clearly felt it qualified as empirical evidence to support her beliefs. Arthur had just resolved to conduct extensive research into it when Wendy stood up and took a volume down from her bookshelf.

'Here,' she said, handing it to Arthur. 'Why not have a look for yourself?'

'Thank you,' said Arthur.

'You're welcome. Hopefully it will help you understand. It was a source of strength and comfort for me after I lost Luke. I only wish it could have done the same for Victor.'

Arthur frowned. 'What do you mean?'

'Well, I thought it might help him after Martha.'

'Martha?'

'Oh, sorry. I assumed you must have known, what with you being friends. Victor was married. Martha was his wife. She was killed in a car accident. Terribly sad. Almost a year ago now.'

27

Leak

Sam sat opposite Victor in their office with her mouth forming an astonished O. They had achieved next to nothing all morning. Although the initial shock from the accelerator data had largely dissipated, the confusion it left in its wake was proving a far tougher stain to shift. Nevertheless, the building was much quieter. The phones had calmed down and the frenzy of the control room was over now the staff had all retired to their respective offices to continue scratching their heads and struggling to make sense of the results in private. Of course, Sam and Victor had additional information at their disposal crucial to achieving this, but they couldn't, or wouldn't, share it with anyone, so it was a thoroughly fruitless affair for all involved.

For the first time in days, they saw an opportunity to sit down and take a breath. They took it gratefully, catching each other up about recent events. Sam filled Victor in about her trip to the police station and the puzzling fact of the dropped charges against Arthur. They were sure Kyle must have decided against pressing charges, though they quickly gave up trying to work out his reasons, despite their shared suspicion they were less than benevolent.

Victor gave Sam a blow-by-blow account of the church service he and Arthur had attended. Sam's stunned expression was the result of Victor reaching the point where William Leigh had promised to make a glut of tumors disappear.

'I know,' said Victor. 'And instead of shouting "rubbish", like any sane person would, they all shouted "hallelujah" and "amen".'

'Like one of those American evangelist churches.'

'Exactly.'

'I didn't know that even happened over here.'

'Apparently it does.'

'Wow. What did Arthur make of it all?'

Victor did a sort of half-smile, half-frown and bobbed his head from left to right. 'He was,' he began, 'odd. He cried during one of the hymns.'

'Really? Why?'

'I'm not sure,' said Victor. 'It was like he'd never heard music before. Not like that, at least.'

They fell into a moment's contemplative silence, both of them trying to imagine what it would be like to live in a world without music. In doing so, they both realised at precisely the same time that they had subconsciously accepted, for the moment at least, that Arthur could potentially come from such a world. Fortunately, they were spared the embarrassment of acknowledging this to each other by the phone on Victor's desk, which started to ring.

'Victor Dennett.... Sorry? Er, no, I haven't... No, sorry... No... No... No, look, who is this? And where are you calling from?' He slammed the phone down.

'Everything okay?' asked Sam. He frowned at her but said nothing. 'Victor, what's going on?'

'We might have a problem,' he said.

'What sort of problem?'

'A Daily Star sort of problem.'

'What?'

'Someone has leaked it.'

'Leaked what?'

'Arthur,' explained Victor. 'It was a journalist. Wanted to know if it was true I'd found God.'

Sam's eyes widened. The phone rang again. They looked at it. They looked at each other. They looked at the phone. Victor picked it up.

'Hello?' said Victor. 'No. Listen, I–... Look, I don't know who you've been talking to but– No, I–... No... argh!' He slammed the phone down again.

'You know they won't take no for an answer,' said Sam. 'They'll keep ringing and ringing. It's what they do.'

'That wasn't the same one. That was the Mirror,' said Victor, rubbing his temples. What was he going to do now? How the hell had they got wind of this? His brain leapt into action and tried to find a way of rationalising that it wasn't as bad as it seemed, of reassuring itself everything would be okay. It failed. This, it told him, was sure to spiral into an absolute disaster. And not just a run-of-the-mill, everyday disaster. This was thermonuclear. This was his personal Chernobyl. He would be a laughing stock. Kyle would see him out for sure. It wouldn't matter that none of it was his fault. He would always be the scientist who 'found God'. Who would want to touch him? He would never work in another lab. No university worth a damn would take him. Dear God, he might even end up having to teach. He shuddered as the ghost of an obnoxious teenage voice echoed through his head. *'Won't you feel really stupid?'*

The phone rang again. Victor picked up the receiver and put it down without speaking. It rang again. He picked it up, put it down, picked it up, and flung it across the table, leaving it bungeeing up and down against the side of the desk. He relaxed for a moment, and then immediately tensed back up as his mobile started vibrating in his pocket. He pulled it out and saw 'unknown caller' written across the screen. He swiped to answer, shouted 'No!', hung up and switched it off. He took a deep breath and made another attempt to relax his shoulders, but the world was having none of it. His computer chimed to inform him that an email had arrived. It did it again. And again. It continued to do so with increasing frequency until it sounded like the machine was trying to communicate with him in Morse code. Sam's started to do the same. While Victor was leaning across his desk to switch it off at the plug socket, Sam was glancing down the list of subject headings.

'Victor,' she said.

'What?' snapped Victor, ripping the plug out of the socket for good measure.

'I'm getting an awful lot of messages telling me to turn on the news.' She started streaming and turned the monitor so Victor could see it. Video footage appeared on the screen, the building they were currently sitting in visible in the background. They could even see their office window in the corner, just over the shoulder of a young reporter talking into the camera.

'...live at the East of England Quantum Laboratory, or E Equals...'

Though he had no reason to doubt this, Victor raised his hand and waved. A second later, he saw his hand appear in the window over the reporter's shoulder. He lowered his hand and rubbed his temples again.

'...no official comment as yet, but we have received unconfirmed reports that an unknown man has been found inside the particle accelerator. Our sources tell us the man claims to be God...'

Victor stood up and looked out of the window to see several vans, some making their way up the driveway towards the building, others already having camera equipment unloaded from them.

'...but Professor Victor Dennett, the lead scientist on this experiment, has so far been unavailable for comment.'

'Did she just say my name?' hissed Victor.

'She did,' replied Sam.

'Oh Christ.'

Sam straightened suddenly. 'You need to get home,' she said with alarm.

'Are you mad? I'm not going out there with that lot waiting for me.'

'You need to get home *now*,' she said.

Victor stared at her for a moment. Then, barely perceptibly, the tiniest of changes crossed his face to indicate that he suddenly understood why Sam was so insistent. 'Oh, *shit!*' he said, and ran for the door.

28

Bible Study

Arthur found the bible a difficult and confusing read. On the face of it, he thought, it should be perfectly clear to anyone that the contents, or at least those he had made his way through thus far, were rather fanciful, and perhaps not meant to be taken literally. As he read it, it occurred to him that this book, which was supposed to make things clearer, was actually filling his head with an ever increasing list of questions. The story of the creation itself was not entirely inaccurate. There really was nothing but a formless void in the tank before he had created it, and it was indeed dark. However, the description of how he had gone about creating it was rather contrived. If it was as easy as issuing simple commands like "let there be light", it would have been a damn sight easier than it actually was, and he would not have suffered so many infuriating failed attempts. Yet, for a species that had no concept of Arthur's existence less than a week ago, let alone several thousand Earth years ago, it was an interesting allegorical representation of the processes he had been through to get the universe up and running. It even captured the sense of pride he had felt on its completion, and his decision to relax for a while afterwards.

Things got a bit much for him with the introduction of Adam and Eve and the talking snake. He started spotting contradictions, absurdities even. How did the snake learn to speak? What was so special about the tree in the middle of the garden? How did God not know they would end up eating from it? Wasn't he omniscient? Arthur was certain

Wendy had told him he was. Didn't everything happen according to God's plan? How could it, if he did not know they would eat? How could he justify punishing them if it *was* part of his plan? Or was punishing them part of the plan in the first place? Wouldn't that be rather sadistic? Why did God need to ask Cain where his brother was when God knew everything? Why did Cain need an identifying mark when there were so few people in the world, and where did his wife come from? And so on. Then, of course, God grew so angry with it all that he decided to wipe everyone out with a flood. Everyone, that is, except Noah and his family, who were given one week to build an enormous ark and gather two (or, if their hygiene allowed, fourteen) specimens of every animal and cram them all aboard for forty days – a feat that, if Arthur was to believe what he read, Noah actually managed. Not only did it seem highly unlikely given the logistical challenges, it was also a much more difficult task than the actual creation of the universe.

Nevertheless, Arthur attempted to plough on, reading about people who purportedly lived for hundreds of years, agreed to kill their offspring without so much as a token protest, and seemingly went out of their way to provoke God, who struck Arthur as an incredibly unhinged and vengeful character utterly undeserving of the worship he demanded.

Eventually, Arthur turned to the internet in the hope it could help him make sense of it all. His early searches did not help. He found that, broadly speaking, there were two camps. The first was made up of people indignantly stating every word Arthur had just read was true. The second was populated by people who didn't believe it was true and who, rather than explaining why in clear, logical terms, called the people in the first camp rude names. There were, he found, a small number of people who fell between the two groups, often arguing it is possible to treat these early books of the bible as figurative, rather than literal. These people were generally attacked by both of the more extreme camps for not being devout enough or for being apologists for those who were too devout, depending on who was doing the attacking. The way to make the most people angry, Arthur learnt, was to try to be as reasonable as possible.

In due course, however, Arthur did manage to find more moderate, intelligent commentary from both sides of the divide. He found a number of people who claimed the laws and teachings of the Old Testament were fulfilled with the arrival of the Messiah, Jesus Christ. His story began in the New Testament, and it is here that modern Christians should turn to for guidance. This sounded fair enough to Arthur. Perhaps Wendy, as a modern Christian, did this. It would have been nice if she had told him and saved him from wasting all this time, but never mind. He sat back down on the sofa to read the New Testament. Then, the doorbell rang.

29

Go in Haste

'Oh shit shit shit shit shit,' hissed Victor as he navigated the fine line between a little bit too fast and really very fast indeed. Yet another set of traffic lights conspired to render yet another quarter of a mile of driving like a maniac redundant, forcing him to slam on the brakes so hard he was practically standing. The traffic light glowed red. Victor seethed. It continued to glow red. It did so obstinately. It did so, Victor felt, with an air of smug satisfaction he had hitherto never encountered in a traffic light. He continued to seethe. It continued to glow red, like it enjoyed being red, like it would, if given the chance, never change from red ever again, such was the pleasure it took from being red. The car he had roared past about a minute ago rolled up behind him. In his rear view mirror, he saw the driver indicating with a wide and varied range of obscene gestures that he felt Victor was a man of limited intelligence and that the manoeuvre by which he had overtaken him had been dangerous and perhaps a little unnecessary. Ordinarily, Victor would have gestured back, for he was no more immune to the idea it was okay to drive like a dangerous lunatic when *he* needed to and that the rules of the road only applied to other people than anyone else who has ever sat behind the wheel of a car. The traffic light however, chose this moment to decide that glowing red could get boring much quicker than it first imagined and decided to give amber a go. It would probably try green next, but Victor wasn't hanging around to find out. He roared off, only to slam the brakes back on to avoid ploughing into the side of someone who had gambled at the adjoining lights. He blared his horn and shrieked something unprintable at the driver who, unlike Victor, did feel he had time to offer his thoughts via juvenile sign language. Once he had completed his offensive semaphore, the man crawled forwards deliberately and painfully slowly. In his blind rage, Victor lifted the clutch too quickly and stalled in the middle of the junction. Horns blared out from all directions, with the notable exception of immediately behind him, where the previously irate driver was now applauding and laughing hysterically. Victor turned the key, revved the engine, and sped off down the road.

He had travelled less than five hundred metres when he spotted a woman approaching a pelican crossing. *I can make it,* thought Victor, as she reached to press the button. He buried the accelerator. *I can make it.* He was wrong. He realised this with slightly less than the required stopping distance for his current speed remaining. He stood on the brake pedal again and skidded to a halt with the front of his car hanging over the stop line. He yelled a further obscenity. The woman glared at Victor and he remembered with embarrassment that his window was open. He raised a hand apologetically. Then he shrugged and ran the light, treating the speed limit like a high score he intended to double.

In this fashion he somehow managed to make it back to the road on which he lived without maiming or killing anyone. He screeched round the final turning to find two white news vans and a small group of journalists gathered outside his house. Arthur was standing on the doorstep, apparently locked in cheerful conversation with the assembled journalists. Victor planted his hand onto the middle of his steering wheel and let the horn blare out, hoping to either silence Arthur or render him inaudible to the journalists and their means of recording him, and to inform everyone that yes, he did intend to park on his drive and no, he did not intend to wait for anyone to get out of his way first so they had better get a bloody move on if they wanted to avoid being run over.

30

The Judges at the Door

If the expression that befell Arthur's face when he answered the door had to be described in one word, it would be this: befuddled. Or bamboozled. Or flummoxed. Whichever word you prefer from those offered, the point is this – his expression could only be described by the type of word no-one really uses but that exists quite happily in thesauruses for those instances when mundanities like 'confused' or 'taken aback' simply won't do.

The reason for his confusion was a crowd, three people deep, on Victor's doorstep. It was armed with strange devices that flashed and beeped and pointed at Arthur, and it was shouting a lot of questions. The questions were difficult to discern, because they were being shouted several at a time, one after another, with no opportunity for Arthur to answer any of them. For a short while, Arthur maintained his dumbfounded expression. This was not a conscious decision or deliberate strategy to deal with what was before him – it was simply the inevitable result of being utterly dumbfounded. Or thunderstruck. Or flabbergasted. When he had recovered sufficiently to realise he should perhaps try to respond to the crowd of people shouting at him, he pondered the best way to go about doing so. It was pointless trying to engage with any of them at this time, so he elected to wait patiently for a more suitable opportunity. With any luck, they would all eventually calm down and he would be able to try and make sense of the situation. So he waited. And, as was his habit, he thought. What he thought was,

Well, this is interesting. I wonder what it's all about. The immediate result of this was that Arthur's expression changed from stupefied to patiently curious. And the result of *this*, was the eventual abatement of the questions as the crowd of people mistook it for an indication he was ready to answer.

'Hello,' said Arthur. 'I'm Arthur. What can I do for you?'

With this, the gathering once again erupted into a chorus of questions, all of them rendered inaudible by each other. Arthur sighed.

'Wouldn't it be easier,' he offered in a loud tone that fell just short of shouting, 'if you asked your questions one at a time so I might actually answer them?'

The crowd fell silent. It was their turn to look confused. And a little embarrassed. It was as though this was the first time they had encountered this idea and they were not sure what to do with it. They glanced around at each other searchingly, as though they were all waiting for someone to be the first to take a bold step into this uncharted territory. Arthur pointed at a man in the front row.

'You, sir. What was your question?'

The man rocked back slightly and bumped into the people behind him. A faint look of terror descended on his face as everyone's eyes fixed on him and he felt the weight of pressure to make this opening question count. 'Er,' he said. 'Um,' he continued. 'Who are you?'

'I am, as I have already told you, Arthur. Arthur Fowler.'

'Like the bloke from Eastenders?'

'I'm afraid I don't know what that means,' said Arthur. He pointed at a woman standing next in line. 'Madam?'

'Where are you from?'

Arthur took a moment to consider his response, acutely aware of the consternation he could cause Victor by answering truthfully. 'I'm afraid I cannot answer that at this moment.'

'But is it true,' shouted the next person in line, you were found in the detector at E Equals a few days ago?'

Arthur was about to say he couldn't answer that either, but then it struck him that there were only three people, as far as he knew, in possession of this information. If the people in front of him were now also aware of it, then they must have obtained it from one of those three. In light of this, was there any reason not to answer? Before Arthur reached a firm conclusion to this question however, the next person in line yelled out one of their own.

'And is it true you claim to be God?'

'Well,' said Arthur, deciding that if they also knew this, then they really must have spoken to Victor, Sam or the rude little man with the shiny shoes, 'that is a difficult one to answer. I think there is a great deal of difference between what you think that word means and what it actually means.'

'So is that a yes or a no?' yelled yet another person.

'For now,' said Arthur, 'it is a possibility. A working hypothesis, if you will.' A few members of the assembled crowd started sniggering, though the reason for this escaped Arthur. To coincide with this, the flow of questions grew into a torrent again.

'Where do you stand on gay marriage?'

'Is this the second coming? Have you come to pass judgement on humanity?'

'Should we be expecting the rapture anytime soon?'

'Are the four horsemen saddling up as we speak?'

Arthur apologised and told them he had no idea what they were talking about.

'You might want to brush up then mate,' said someone at the back of the crowd. 'You're not doing a great

141

job of being omniscient are you?' Another round of sniggering rippled through the crowd.

'Oh, I see,' said Arthur. 'I think this might be an example of that difference between what you think 'god' means and what it actually means.'

'What does it mean then? You saying you're not here for the Christians?'

'I'm not here for anyone.'

'So what then? Are you starting a new religion?'

'I am not starting anything,' replied Arthur, growing increasingly frustrated by a method of questioning that appeared to involve nothing more than ruling out a potentially infinite list of assumptions by throwing them out in no particular order and then either ignoring the answer or not even bothering to wait for one. 'Allow me to explain,' he said.

And Arthur explained. He told them about his attic, about his constant struggle to create a stable universe and his eventual success. He told them about how everything went swirly, how he found himself inexplicably occupying a dark and stuffy chamber, how he and Victor had exchanged blows, all the way to the moment when he arrived at the conclusion that the universe he was now in was very possibly the one he had created in his attic, including a brief overview of the data analysis that was carried out in order to reach it. There were about three seconds of stunned silence when he finished. Then, as one, the entire crowd started firing off a new round of questions. Arthur couldn't distinguish a single one, but was quite certain they were all entirely unrelated to what he had just told them.

'Listen!' he yelled. The crowd shrank immediately back into silence. The respite was short-lived, however, as a blaring monotone prevented Arthur from explaining, once again, the virtues of asking questions one at a time.

All but one member of the crowd looked down the street to the source of the noise and saw Victor's car racing towards them. The one who did not look down the street was instead looking to the sky. He had grown up with a particularly strict Catholic grandmother and, while he would eventually go to his grave having never confessed this to anyone, for a fleeting moment, the nature of the questions and answers got the better of him and he was filled with guilt-ridden terror by the thought he was hearing a trumpet from heaven signalling the start of the rapture. He realised his mistake just in time to leap out of the way of Victor's car as it screeched onto the driveway. Arthur looked on in confusion as Victor barrelled out of it and pushed through the crowd.

'Get out of my way, please,' he snapped. 'In fact, better still, why don't you all piss off completely?'

The journalists dodged Victor's question and volleyed with an assault of their own.

'Professor Dennett, what are your thoughts on Arthur's claims?'

'Do you think he's telling the truth?'

'Are you off to repent for your sins?'

'Has your stance on religion changed?'

As Victor reached the doorstep, he placed his hand squarely on Arthur's chest and pushed. Arthur staggered backwards and then watched as Victor turned around to face the people outside. He held up his palms and waited for them to fall silent. 'I have,' he said, 'just one statement to make at this time.' He paused as microphones and cameras and digital recorders were positioned and adjusted. 'Get off my fucking property!' he yelled, and slammed the door.

31

False Witness

Victor rounded on Arthur. 'What the hell was that all about?' he barked.

'I'm not entirely sure,' said Arthur. 'I was rather hoping you would be able to explain it to me.'

Victor rubbed his temples and took several deep breaths, steeling himself for a conversation that would, he anticipated, fall somewhere between quite frustrating and incredibly distressing.

'How much did you tell them?' Arthur didn't reply, but Victor noticed the way he shifted and fidgeted. 'You told them everything didn't you?'

'Not,' said Arthur, '*everything*, no. But I fear I may have told them rather more than you would have liked me to.'

Victor sagged and sighed and made his way into the living room and virtually threw himself onto the sofa. Arthur followed and sat down opposite, just as he had done on his first night on Earth. It was he who broke the silence. 'I'm sorry, Victor. They knew things only you and your colleagues could have told them. I thought they must have spoken to one of you.'

Victor looked long and hard at Arthur and then buried his face in his hands. He didn't have the energy to stay angry with him. And why should he? Could he really blame him? Wherever he came from, and regardless of whether or not he was telling the truth, he was obviously very confused by all that was happening. It would be inappropriate, cruel even, to direct his anger at him. He took one more heavy breath and said, 'Sod it. I don't even care any more. Let's get something to eat.'

Arthur had once again been exercising his culinary skills and had prepared what he apologetically called 'a rather simple affair' consisting of roasted salmon fillet with red onion and new potatoes. It was, Victor declared, even better than the chicken dish Arthur had made. They ate in relative silence, or at least they did so once Victor disconnected his home phone and delivered a very clear message from an upstairs window to the now smaller but still substantial collection of journalists outside that the next one of them to ring his doorbell would have their own bell rung for them.

After they had eaten, they returned to the living room to discuss their unwelcome visitors, Arthur filling Victor in as best he could on the information he had provided them, and Victor trying to explain who they were and what they did. Victor found this a difficult task. There was something inherently frustrating about the way Arthur found everything he had to say about the press so positive, when he was sure he was painting them in the negative light that they, to his mind, absolutely deserved.

'But how could it be anything but a good thing that information about the world be shared with the entire population?' he asked.

It was not so much the sharing of information that was the problem, Victor explained, but the way in which it was shared – the way only certain facts were selected for sharing while others were ignored so as to elicit the desired response from those who received them.

'So,' said Arthur, 'they don't really present data at all. They present the conclusions they want others to draw from it?'

'Pretty much.'

'But that's ridiculous,' said Arthur.

Victor couldn't argue. It was clear Arthur found it difficult to reconcile that people could be aware this was happening, yet still treat these providers as valuable sources of information. Why, he wanted to know, did people simply not source their information from more objective, honest sources?

'Ignorance? Stupidity? Confirmation bias? Take your pick,' said Victor.

This too threw Arthur. 'I thought you said most people know what they read in newspapers can't be trusted?'

'Not ignorant in that sense,' explained Victor. 'Ignorant in the sense that they just don't care. Working things out for themselves is simply too much effort for most people. They would rather be given a conclusion than take the time to arrive at their own. Does that make sense?'

'I think so. What you're saying is human beings are more interested in feeling like they know what is going on than they are in actually knowing what is going on.'

'Precisely,' said Victor.

'What a horrible state of affairs,' said Arthur.

'Agreed.'

It was with a degree of morbid curiosity seasoned with a hint of trepidation that Victor turned on the evening news a short while later, though he was relieved when there was nothing in the opening headlines and he grew more and more relaxed as the programme wore on with no more than the usual serving of political scandal, death and destruction in some far away corner of the planet, gloomy news about the dwindling economy, and a human interest tragedy. It wouldn't be long before they were onto the sport and weather.

'Well, we won't know for sure until we've seen tomorrow's papers, but maybe there is nothing to worry about after all,' he said, turning with a smile to Arthur.

'Nothing to worry about?' exclaimed Arthur through a horrified expression. 'Forgive me Victor, but it seems to me your entire civilization is on the verge of collapse! How can you watch that and not be filled with consternation about the state of this planet?'

'Oh, it's always like that.' Victor waved a dismissive hand at the television. 'That was a fairly typical day's news.'

Arthur's jaw dropped. 'You think that makes it *better*? You mean similar information is shared with everyone on a daily basis and the standard response of even intelligent people such as yourself is to shrug their shoulders and do nothing?'

Victor reeled at the outburst. He struggled to say anything for a few moments. Then he came a hair's breadth away from an overly defensive response full of 'but what can I do?' and 'I'm just one person' sentiments. Ultimately, however, and with a sense he was finally getting the hang of how best to talk to Arthur, he decided on cold, hard facts.

'I'm doing my bit,' he said. 'I'm pushing the limits of human knowledge and understanding of the universe. That's my role in all this – to try and improve our lives through science. The problem is there are so many people who aren't doing anything. Trying to make a difference is like trying to make the wind blow in the opposite direction by flapping at it with your hands. I know it's frustrating, I really do. But I've been frustrated by it all for decades and there is only so long you can stay angry before you resign yourself to the way things are.'

'It's been like this for *decades*?' asked Arthur, even more incredulous.

'Longer. That was pretty much a microcosm of human history.'

'And nobody has thought of a way to improve things?'

Victor bobbed his head left and right. 'They have improved by degrees,' he said. 'But that's not to say things are actually good,' he added, embarrassed. He could tell Arthur was struggling with this. Or, at least, gave the appearance of struggling with it. Why, he wanted to know, were things not actually good? Victor shrugged. 'A range of reasons I suppose. Stupidity. Self-interest. People don't think it's their problem. They have their own little problems to deal with and don't have time to think about the bigger ones.'

Arthur fell into a thoughtful silence. Victor decided to let him mull things over, mainly because it would protect him from having to answer any more difficult questions. He sank back into his chair and closed his eyes, allowing his thoughts to drift and trying to unwind after yet another stressful day. He managed one deep breath before every fibre of his body once again turned rigid when he heard Arthur's voice coming not from the seat opposite him, but from the television. He sat bolt upright and stared wide eyed at the screen.

How could he have been so stupid as to think he was home and dry? No news broadcast was complete without the silly, light-hearted non-story designed to make the viewers feel better after all the terrible things they had been told. Today, *he* was that story. He gaped at the image of Arthur chatting away on the doorstep.

'*Well, I fell through a sort of swirly hole,*' said Arthur, '*and landed in a small, dark room.*'

They cut to a wide shot of the exterior of E Equals as the reporter fleshed out the story. '*It was supposed to be a big day at E Equals for very different reasons...*' Cut to stock footage of the control room. '*The scientists here were hoping to discover...*' Cut to stock footage of the detector.

'The last thing they expected to find was...' Cut to black and white CCTV footage of Victor opening the door to the detector.

Victor cradled his head in his hands. The interviewer intersected with a question. *'And how did Professor Dennett react when he saw you?'*

'He punched me in the mouth,' said Arthur, as it cut back to the shot of him.

Arthur frowned and filled with indignation. 'That wasn't how the conversation took place!' he exclaimed. 'They left out –'

'Shhh!' hissed Victor, waving at Arthur to be quiet without taking his eyes off the screen. The reporter returned and delivered a piece to camera.

'Unfortunately, Professor Dennett, a leading physicist at E Equals and the man in charge of the experiment, was in no mood to comment.'

Victor groaned as they cut to shaky footage of him arriving home and addressing the journalists on his doorstep. Two bleeps were inserted over his profanities. His humiliation complete, the reporter wrapped up their segment and threw it back to the main presenter in the studio, who smiled into the camera.

'Fortunately there is one person from E Equals who is prepared to give a statement,' she said. *'We are joined in the studio by Richard Kyle, Chair of the E Equals finance committee. Good evening Mr Kyle...'.*

Victor laughed a twisted, seething laugh, as a suspicion he had barely even registered was confirmed. 'Yes,' he said, nodding his head. 'Yes, of course you did, you *wanker.*'

32

Bringing Good News

The following day, Arthur finally settled down to make a start on the New Testament. On the whole, he found it a more palatable read than the confusing and contradictory Old Testament. He liked the sound of this Jesus fellow, particularly his advocacy of such virtues as forgiveness, mercy, compassion and humility – there was nothing to argue with there. Despite this, it failed to hold his attention for very long. The continued presence of far-fetched ideas frustrated him. The virgin birth stuff, for example, seemed rather dubious, as did the stories about healing, especially in the light of his recent research in this area, and other fantastical elements like the bits about wine, walking on water, cursing the fig tree and rising from the dead. He could see it was a more measured collection of tales designed to inspire readers towards a healthy moral compass, but these supernatural elements did little to assuage the sense it should not be taken at face value. He was also distracted by his desire to learn more about the reporting of news, and so he eventually put the book down and spent the rest of the day glued once again to Victor's computer.

When last night's news programme had finished and Victor had finally calmed down, Arthur asked him to explain why the producers had altered his conversation with the journalists. Did they not want people to know the truth? Did they think their viewers would fail to understand the full exchange? Or was there some other reason that hadn't occurred to him? Victor did his best to explain. He said the people whose job it was to report the news also thought it was their job to decide how it should be interpreted, so they often presented it in such a way as to ensure it would elicit a specific reaction. They could usually rely on this to work because most of the people who watched it were, also according to Victor, idiots with shit for brains. He was further surprised to learn that news reports were affected by time constraints. There was only a certain amount of time in which to divulge important information, and therefore some of it had to be left out to prevent the programme from overrunning. Arthur wondered what happened on days when there were more newsworthy events than usual to report. Some of them simply would not be reported, Victor told him. This confused and troubled Arthur and so, once Victor had gone to bed, he stayed up to see what could possibly be so important that it was necessary to limit the sharing of vital information in this way and was stunned to discover the subsequent programming amounted to little more than people answering questions about past sporting events, discussing cars, and following people through the process of buying houses and working to make them habitable, only to sell them to someone else the moment they had done so. Unable to make sense of any of this, he turned to the web in search of answers. Interested as he was in finding more detailed discussion and analysis of world events, it should come as no surprise that he eventually stumbled upon the phenomenon of blogging.

A blog, he learnt, was a kind of online notebook or journal the owner could use to share their knowledge, wisdom, experience or, more often than not, ill-informed opinions regarding any subject of their choosing. It was obviously a popular activity – there were literally millions of them, covering almost every sphere of human activity: how to be happy, how to be healthy, how to exercise, how to be a parent, how to be a child, how to cook, how to eat, how to build and fix things, how to grow things, how to clean things, how to spend your money, how to save your money... there were even blogs about how to blog. Whatever a person's interests, no matter how niche or strange, there would be a blog, usually a large number of blogs, all about them somewhere out there on the internet. Whatever their beliefs, a person could be sure to find an abundance of content reassuring them they were correct and just as many explaining why they were not. The full range of human experience was represented in this medium in the most exceptional detail. And it was here, Arthur discovered, that human beings attempted to enter into a reflective and nuanced discussion of important current events and that they, for a range of reasons, almost always failed in this endeavour. It was not that they were badly written per se. Far from it. Many of the ones Arthur glanced at were perfectly eloquent and articulate. But they almost always gave Arthur the sense he was reading the public prevarication of a person who did not really understand the topic they were writing about. Very simple ideas were presented in the most convoluted ways in an apparent attempt to make the author seem like they were saying something profound. Often, this was used to try and persuade the reader to exchange money for a book or product or access to additional content.

When it came to blogs about news and politics, he felt like he was learning more about the author than he was the subject of their writing. Everything was so subjective, rendering it as far from objective news as possible – it was merely the thoughts of a layperson on the objective news. Those thoughts prompted comments from readers. Most of the time, they expressed hearty agreement and incredulity that the people who disagreed with the subjective thoughts could not see why they were the *correct* subjective thoughts. Nobody was really learning anything. They were simply expressing their opinions to like-minded individuals, who then rewarded the writer with affirmation, which the readers themselves had already received by reading something they knew would tell them their own subjective thoughts were correct. On the rare occasion when a person who disagreed made a comment, they invariably did so merely as a provocation. They made insulting, belittling, and snide remarks designed to inspire outrage and offense. This was called 'trolling', and it achieved little beyond turning the entire discussion into an exchange of juvenile insults and attempts to score points by highlighting the shortcomings in each other's arguments – a simple task courtesy of the fact that, as Arthur had already noted, nobody really understood the topic of conversation as well as they would have their readers believe.

Not every blog was like this. There were many well-informed writers out there. But it was difficult for Arthur to discern the good from the bad, especially with his limited knowledge of human culture and the sheer mountain of them to search through. It was a wonder, given the amount of time and effort that must have gone into writing them, that anyone had any time left to read them. Perhaps, thought Arthur, this imbalance was part of the problem – if all anyone wants to do is teach, they leave themselves no time to actually learn anything.

Despite all of these problems, and all of his misgivings, Arthur saw some real potential in the format for himself. For all of its faults, blogging appealed to Arthur on the grounds it provided an opportunity to express himself in his own words. There would be no need to worry about being censored or manipulated or taken out of context. There would be no need to talk to the reporters again. Instead, he could communicate directly with anyone who wanted to know about him. He typed "starting a blog" into the search engine.

33

In the Lap of Fools

Richard Kyle held up a hand to indicate that he would be just a few moments, thank you very much. It was a simple gesture, but it rather knocked the wind out of Victor's sails. For the last ten minutes, he had been deliberately working himself up into a rage. The anger he had felt on seeing Kyle interviewed on the news last night was so teeth-grindingly, fist-clenchingly, blood-boilingly vengeful that he spent a good hour failing to fall asleep because he couldn't stop thinking about increasingly creative ways of telling Kyle what an odious little cretin he was. It wasn't until he finally settled on the phrase 'odious little cretin', which he even wrote down so he wouldn't forget it, that he was finally able to switch off and succumb to sleep.

When he woke up, Victor discovered his fury had all but abandoned him during the night, and he started to contemplate going to Kyle and talking to him calmly and rationally. There was, however, the tiniest sliver of anger tucked away in the corner of his mind. Sensing this was its moment, it crawled out of those dark recesses and back to the very forefront of his consciousness. It smothered his prefrontal cortex and told him in soothing tones that he wanted to feel angry, that Kyle deserved his anger, and that, despite years of experience informing him that it always leads to regret, this time was different, and he was *right* to act on his anger. It took hold of his decision making abilities and set about sustaining itself, encouraging Victor to revisit memories of every annoying thing Kyle had ever said or done, refine every seething outburst Victor had rehearsed but choked back at the last moment, and recall every decision Kyle had ever made that was detrimental to Victor's work and E Equals as a whole. Before long, it had such a perfect hold over Victor's thought processes that it had him reading through old emails to remind him of how livid he had felt when he first read them. It made him pace up and down the office. It made him practise the delivery of every ranting, finger-wagging sentence in front of a mirror. It made him imagine throttling the life out of Kyle until his eternally asinine smile finally disappeared from his lips. Finally, when it was certain it was in complete control and was ready to deliver the most perfectly scathing yet utterly justifiable tirade ever conceived, it made him storm into Kyle's office, where it was greeted by fleeting eye contact and the palm of Kyle's hand, who either ignored or, more likely, completely failed to register Victor's thunderous expression or the finger he had raised, armed and ready to start wagging. Ill-prepared for this scenario, Victor's anger went scurrying back to its hiding place, leaving him standing in the doorway looking like a lost child. Kyle wrapped up his call and put down the receiver.

'Victor. What can I do you for?'

'Er,' said Victor. And then, 'Um.' His anger crept forward and gave him a push before running back into the shadows. 'What the hell was all that about you odious little cretin?' When he rehearsed it, he imagined this question landing like a punch to the face, but in reality it landed more like a graceless splat on Kyle's desk, leaving Victor devoid of all the righteous indignation he had felt moments ago and instead feeling somewhat guilty for making such a mess. It didn't help that he had forgotten everything he was going to follow it up with, such as the accusation Kyle leaked the story himself, or the assertion that he was a disgrace to the entire organisation.

'I presume,' said Kyle, with the air of someone who had also rehearsed his own version of this conversation with arrogance, rather than anger, directing the action, 'you are referring to my appearance on the news last night.'

Grateful for the reminder of why he was actually standing there, Victor gathered himself slightly. 'Of course I bloody am! What were you thinking? You leaked it yourself, didn't you? Didn't you?!'

'Whoever is responsible for the leak,' smarmed Kyle, ' I thought it best someone take control of the situation–'

'That you created.'

'Someone take control of the situation,' Kyle continued, not missing a beat, 'before it got out of hand.'

'Out of hand for who? I've got journalists camped outside my house! I had to fight my way through another load of them to get here this morning. What do you think is going to happen next? You know what sort of rubbish they're going to start writing. You're turning us into a laughing stock.'

'Oh, come now, Victor,' said Kyle, as though he were trying to calm a stroppy child. 'Look at the positives here. A little bit of publicity will do us some good. The economy is in the toilet. The public aren't happy about having their taxes spent on research they don't care about or understand.'

'You know how important this work is!' snapped Victor.

'Of course I do, of course I do,' replied Kyle, soothing Victor slowly out of his tantrum. 'But the people out there don't. This could be good for us. A bit of lively debate, a bit of exposure, a bit of lighthearted news. It will all help to improve the public's view of us. We'll let the cameras in, give a few interviews – it could be a good way of generating a bit of extra cash for research with the budget cuts that are inevitably coming.'

'This is why you dropped the charges against Arthur, isn't it? You realised you could make some money out of him – money that'll be useless to us when no-one wants to work with us because they don't take us seriously.'

'Don't be so melodramatic, Victor. It's just one of those silly stories they report to distract people from all the important and depressing stuff that goes on. It'll be over before you know it. The important thing is to make the most of it while it lasts.'

Victor clenched his jaw. That was the important thing? What about the fact that his house was under siege from a group of journalists hoping to talk to God? Or that, for the rest of his career, Victor would always be associated with this story? *Important thing, my arse,* Victor wanted to say, but he couldn't, because Kyle's phone started to ring again.

'Sorry Victor, I have to take this. I'll speak to you later. Expect an email about an interview. I've told a few outlets you'll be happy to speak to them. Oh, and no more swearing at the press – play nice when you get home. We need to keep them on side.' He picked up the phone. 'Richard Kyle.' And with that, he disappeared into another conversation and, to all intents and purposes, Victor ceased to exist. He turned on his heel and skulked back out of the office. His anger crept forward again and told him he'd feel better if he slammed the door. He slammed the door. He didn't feel better.

34

ArthurFowlerBlog: Entry 1

I suppose I should start by saying hello. My name is Arthur Fowler. You may have recently heard or read about me through what passes for your world's news outlets. I am the man who was found in the detector at the East of England Quantum Laboratory following a high energy proton collision experiment. It is quite likely that I am the creator of your universe. I understand this may cause some of you a great deal of concern. For this, I can only apologise. I have no desire to upset or offend anyone. Of course, I had no desire to end up in the detector at all, but some things cannot be avoided. My limited experience of life on your planet suggests this is especially true with regard to upsetting and offending those who seem to aspire to being upset and offended as often as possible.

I will keep this opening post quite brief. My main objectives here are only to introduce myself and to get to grips with the process of writing and publishing a blog entry. I think this may be a good way to communicate information about myself to anyone who is interested in me, and the presence of your news media outside the house in which I currently reside would imply that there are at least some people who are. Unfortunately, I do not think it is wise for me to engage them in conversation following what I have learnt about them since my arrival here. Reading the websites of your major news outlets, I am inclined to agree with those who have advised me they cannot be trusted to provide a full, detailed and honest account of the facts. They strike me as unnecessarily negative and disingenuous, presenting stories, rather than reports, intended to manipulate readers for ideological purposes. Judging by the comments submitted by readers, these stories do little to aid their understanding of whatever they happen to be about, though they do an awfully good job of making people very angry. Little appears to be done by the news outlets to reduce the anger felt by their readers. If anything, they appear to me to have been written with this outcome in mind. For reasons that so far elude me, the readers themselves appear reluctant to turn to outlets that make them less angry. It's almost as if they enjoy it.

Reluctant as I am to allow any information regarding myself to be manipulated by these duplicitous organisations, I have taken the decision to communicate directly with any interested parties via the medium of blogging. So, here I am. I look forward to sharing more about my experiences with you and reading any responses you may have. Thank you for your time.

35

What Shall I Do?

Victor sat with his head in his hands and let out a long sigh. It was an inauspicious sign, so Arthur was tentative as he asked, 'What do you think?' There was a pause as Victor let out another sigh. Arthur pressed on. 'I thought it would be a good way to set the record straight. I can talk to people without anyone changing what I have to say.'

Victor drew a deep breath, as though about to speak, and then sighed yet again. He rubbed his face and then placed both palms on the desk in front of him and said, very slowly and deliberately, 'What the hell were you thinking?'

Arthur said nothing, mainly because he felt he had answered precisely this question a moment before Victor had asked it.

'Please!' snapped Victor, slapping the desk suddenly. 'Explain. What exactly did you think this would achieve?'

Again, Arthur said nothing. This, he was sure, had also been answered.

'Are you doing this on purpose? Do you not think you've done enough damage already? This,' he said, gesturing to the screen, 'isn't helpful. You talking to the press isn't helpful. In fact, everything you have done since the moment you arrived, *including* your arrival, has been the perfect example of something that is utterly *un*helpful. I don't know who you are, Arthur. I don't know where you're from. I don't know if you're nuts or if you have some sinister motive or if you are actually God. I don't even care anymore. I care about my career, which is in the toilet because of you.

And I am desperately trying to figure out how to save it and I can do without this,' he gestured contemptuously at the screen again, 'blindsiding me and making things infinitely more difficult.'

Arthur shifted uneasily where he stood. 'I'm sorry,' he said.

Victor took a long breath and shook his head slowly. He made as if to speak but instead let out a short humourless laugh.

'I'm not sure what else I can say, Victor,' said Arthur, quietly. 'I've been nothing but honest with you since I arrived. I really was trying to help.'

Victor threw his face into his hands again. This was too much. His conversation with Kyle, the email he had subsequently received detailing the interviews he was expected to give, and the fight he had to put up just to get to his own front door without swearing at anyone had worked every single nerve he had, including a few he didn't even know about. He felt as though he were teetering on the edge of an abyss and had forgotten how to step backwards. His breathing was growing heavy, his throat closing up, his eyes filling with tears. Before he knew it, he was sobbing uncontrollably into his hands with such intensity he didn't even register the sound of the front door being opened or the chorus of voices that followed it.

Some time later – he had no idea how long – Victor was sitting on his sofa with a blanket over his shoulders and a cup of tea cradled in his hands. Next to him, Wendy gently rubbed his back and made generic soothing 'there there' statements. He sipped at the sickeningly sweet tea.

'That's it, get it down you. You'll be right as rain after a good cuppa.'

While he was far from feeling 'right as rain', he couldn't deny the calming effect it was already having. He took another mouthful and sank back into the chair as Wendy explained that Arthur, realising he could, as the cause of Victor's anguish, do nothing to help, had turned to the only other person he knew how to contact. He had fought his way through the mob outside and asked Wendy to come and check in on him. Wendy, ever the model Christian, had come to her neighbour's aid. Victor noted the irony with a sardonic chuckle.

'Well, it's funny, isn't it,' he said as his laughter drew an inquisitive look from Wendy. 'All these years you've believed you were doing God's work. And now here you are, doing exactly what Arthur asked of you.' He laughed again. Wendy looked at him pityingly and he felt a pang of guilt. 'Sorry,' he said.

'It's okay. We'll put it down to you feeling under the weather.'

They sat in silence for a minute or so, as Victor sipped his tea and contemplated Wendy's gift for understatement. Then he frowned and looked about him. 'Where's Arthur now?'

'At mine. He thought it best to give you some space for the time being. I know you don't want to hear it, Victor, but this really isn't his fault. You do see that don't you?'

Victor balked. 'You *believe* him?'

'I'm not saying that. He may just be very confused and more in need of help than the scorn and derision he's probably in for now.'

He knew she was right. And, if he was honest, he knew Arthur hadn't done much wrong. The blog wasn't actually a bad idea, and it didn't do any more harm than Kyle and the press were doing. It was simply one unexpected thing too many. Arthur didn't deserve to be the sole target of his frustration. 'Maybe I should go and apologise,' he said.

'You might not need to,' said Wendy, turning her head to listen. Sure enough, the voices outside rose and they heard the front door open and close. A moment later, Arthur appeared in the doorway to the living room.

'Hello,' he said, sheepishly.

'Hi,' replied Victor, avoiding eye-contact.

'I'm sorry. I won't stay long. I wanted to check if you were okay.'

Victor made a wry smile. 'I will be,' he said.

'I'm glad. Look, Wendy has been kind enough to let me stay with her for now. It's unfair of me to keep imposing on you, and I think it's fair to say you could do with a break.'

Victor turned to Wendy. 'You really don't have to.'

'Nonsense,' said Wendy, smiling warmly. 'It's no trouble at all.'

Victor acknowledged her smile with a brief one of his own and a single nod of his head. He turned to Arthur and offered him the same gesture.

'I really am sorry, Victor,' said Arthur. 'I didn't mean to make your life difficult.'

'I know.' Victor believed him. Not about everything, but about this. Arthur might have been dragged kicking and screaming out of another universe. Or he might be incredibly delusional. Either way, Victor was in no doubt about Arthur's sincerity. His concern was written all over him and, while Victor couldn't say how, he knew it was genuine. 'I'm sorry too. You didn't deserve all that.'

'Thank you. I doubt it's any consolation,' said Arthur, 'but I understand how you are feeling.'

Victor bridled slightly. It was one thing to accept an honest apology, but this, he felt, was pushing it. 'I'm not sure you do,' he said, struggling to hide his irritation.

'Of course I do. You feel as though your whole world has been turned upside down and torn apart. I have been torn out of mine completely. I have a wife, Victor. She had called up to say goodnight shortly before you brought me here. I wanted to finish one more part of my marionette, so

I told her I would be a few more minutes. And then I was here. And, given your limited understanding of what you did to cause that, I have no idea if I will ever see her again. I don't know if you have the technology to get me back. I'm not even sure how we would go about trying to achieve it, and I think we have safely established that my knowledge in these matters is superior to yours. So yes, Victor, I do understand.'

With that, Arthur left the room and made his way back to Wendy's house. Victor leaned forward in his seat, his elbows resting on his knees, his head cradled in his hands.

'He certainly is convincing, isn't he?' said Wendy.

'I thought you didn't believe him,' said Victor.

'Well,' she said, 'the way I see it, we have two possibilities. Either he is very unwell and in need of help. Or,' she added with a pause, 'he's telling the truth and in need of help. You've always lectured me about the importance of evidence, Victor. Which way is it pointing today?'

Victor looked at her with raised eyebrows. It shouldn't have surprised him. Why wouldn't Wendy be open to the idea that Arthur was telling the truth? If you can believe a faith healer can use magic to cure cancer, you can believe anything. Still, he was taken aback by her implication.

'I'm just saying there is much about life we don't understand. And I have always believed you scientists are a bit too confident you have it all worked out. You've thrown the same accusation at me. Who knows? Maybe he'll prove us both right by proving us both wrong.'

36

A Time to Throw Stones

Arthur woke late the following day. He wasn't typically a late riser but he had struggled to sleep worrying about the previous day's events and the toll his presence was taking on Victor. He dragged himself up with the headache and sluggishness that a poor night's sleep leaves in its wake, yawning and stumbling for balance as he dressed himself and shuffled downstairs. Despite the late hour, the curtains were still drawn and Wendy was sitting on the sofa looking pensive.

'Is everything okay?' he asked.

Wendy spoke as if coming back from some distant dream. 'Have you looked outside?'

Arthur parted the curtains slightly and peered out of the window. The press throng lining the road looked as though it had at least tripled overnight. 'Oh dear.'

'We should probably check on Victor.'

'How are we going to get through that lot?'

Wendy thought for a moment. 'We might not have to.'

Fortunately, the press were yet to discover that the row of houses was accessible from the rear, which meant Wendy and Arthur were spared the indignity of having their attempts to get Victor's attention caught on film. The gardens backed onto an alleyway which all the houses could access via a rear gate. Unsurprisingly, Victor's was locked. Wendy had attempted to reach him by phone to inform him of their intentions but it was permanently engaged, most likely because Victor had disconnected it to stop it from permanently ringing. All of this meant Wendy and Arthur had to resort to jumping up and down and waving furiously from behind Victor's gate to try and get his attention.

'He's definitely in,' said Wendy, looking through a hole in the fence. 'I can see him in the kitchen. Hold on. He looks like he's turning this way. Not yet... Not yet... Now!'

Arthur jumped into the air and waved his arms but, his knees not being what they once were, the effect of the leap was negligible.

Through the hole in the fence, Wendy saw Victor glance out of the window as if he had seen something in his peripheral vision. He frowned for a moment and then returned to whatever he was doing. She sighed. 'It didn't work. I wonder,' she said, looking around and picking up a pebble. She hurled it over the fence and heard it ping off the window pane. She looked back through the hole and saw Victor staring out of the window with an unmistakably furious expression.

'Yes, that worked. He's looking. Now! Now!'

Arthur leapt into the air again and waved his arms maniacally. He crashed back down with a yelp and clutched at his poor knees.

Victor's furious expression was replaced by one of open-mouthed incredulity. Wendy watched him unlock and open the back door. He walked across the garden and opened the back gate to find her looking sheepish and Arthur bent double, rubbing his legs and panting for breath. 'What on earth are you doing?' he said.

Victor barely had time to put the kettle on and sit down with Arthur and Wendy before the noise outside picked up. Wendy crept into the living room and peered through the curtains to investigate the cause of the excitement. Seeing

Sam fighting her way through the sea of cameras and microphones while a torrent of questions was thrown at her, she dashed to the front door to open it as Sam arrived on the doorstep. Sam rushed in and Wendy closed the door quickly behind her.

'Hello, Samantha. Lovely to see you. How are you?'

'Surviving,' said Sam. She gestured to the door. 'Although I could do without all that.'

'Couldn't we all? I'm sure it'll blow over soon,' said Wendy, though her tone was hopeful rather than confident. 'Can I look forward to seeing you on the television again soon? I really enjoyed your last programme.'

'Thank you. It's funny you should ask,' said Sam as she followed Wendy to the kitchen. 'I had a meeting a couple of days ago. I'm presenting a four-part documentary about the different moons in our solar system. We'll be filming in a couple of months and you'll be able to watch it early next year.'

'Oh, wonderful,' said Wendy. She led Sam into the kitchen where they found Victor preparing a pot of tea. Arthur was sitting at the table and grimacing as he rubbed his shattered knees. Victor put the teapot and four mugs on the table and then they all sat down to discuss the latest developments.

'But I feel absolutely *fine*,' said Arthur.

'Not like that,' said Victor. 'Your *blog* has gone viral. It spread, like a virus, across the internet as more and more people discussed it and shared it online.'

'Oh, I see,' said Arthur.

Arthur's blog, Victor explained, had so far been read by nearly three million people across the globe, making it slightly less popular than a two-minute video of a man being chased by a pigeon. The result of this was a dramatically increased interest in the story, hence the growth of, in

Victor's words, 'that crowd of vultures out there'. It also had an effect Victor had not foreseen, namely a positive reaction from the scientific community.

'I've had emails from all over,' said Victor. 'Beckett's been in touch. So have Belicec and Levinsson. I even had an email from Brundle to tell me he thought it was as hilarious as it was interesting. Then he tweeted to confess his jealousy that he wasn't in on the action.'

Arthur had no idea who any of these people were, or what 'tweeting' was, but that was neither here nor there. Everything sounded very positive and Victor seemed to be feeling much better than he had been yesterday. Sam saw it, too, and found herself smiling at Victor's relief.

'Rumours of your career's death were greatly exaggerated, then?' she said.

'It would seem so. In fact,' he said, 'I've had a job offer.'

'What?'

'Just Rush sniffing around again. I suppose if all else fails, I can sell my soul.'

'After all the crap you've given me about not joining him?'

'If all else fails,' he repeated, with a smile of his own.

Elijah "Eli" Rush was an American technology entrepreneur with a maverick reputation. With the billions of dollars at his disposal, he had pretty much single-handedly funded the construction of a particle accelerator even more powerful than the one at E Equals. His reasons were the source of much speculation. Some suggested it was a philanthropic gesture – a donation to the scientific community to be made available to teams from all over the world, particularly those that had interesting hypotheses but no funding. More cynical commentators felt it was nothing more than a big vanity project tied to his rather extravagant space exploration ambitions. Whatever the reason, he had contacted Victor and Sam on a number of occasions to try and poach them from E Equals. Sam had been his main target because, Victor suspected, of the reputation she had built as a television presenter in the UK, but he had made his interest in Victor clear before today.

'So,' said Wendy, 'what do we do now?'

'Well,' said Victor, 'I don't know about you, but I don't fancy dealing with that lot out there, so I think I should put the kettle on again. And,' he added with a glance at Arthur, 'how would you feel about writing another blog post?'

37

The Blazing Furnace

Arthur was beginning to feel like he would never get the hang of dealing with humans. Yesterday, Victor acted as if his world was falling apart because Arthur had written a short blog entry and he didn't want anyone to read it. Now, having discovered that an enormous number of people *had* read it, he was as happy as Arthur had seen him since his arrival and even wanted him to write another one – all because a few people had said nice things about it. How could one person's attitude to an outcome swing so dramatically based on such limited feedback?

Arthur scrolled through the comments left by readers. They made for fascinating reading. Victor was right – they were largely positive, though Arthur was mildly concerned about the tone of the more negative ones. He had already read several that wished horrible illnesses on him, or wished him dead, preferably by slow and painful means. Others had taken time out of their day to express their satisfaction that he would burn and suffer in Hell for all eternity whenever this did eventually occur. He would, they said, be judged by God. The irony tickled him, but the venom troubled him. Victor assured him it was nothing to worry about – the internet, he said, was full of crackpots Arthur should pay no attention to. Still, Arthur couldn't discount the possibility that Victor's indifferent attitude was just as foolhardy as the rest of humanity's dismissive approach to horrifying news about itself and its bleak future, and so he took this advice with some caution.

The concern generated by the negative comments was largely moderated by the fact they were so heavily outnumbered by the sheer weight of the positive ones, even if there did appear to be a very limited amount of interesting and intelligent discourse – most of it was puerile and banal. But they all had one thing in common; they all expressed admiration for Arthur.

finally a religion i can get behind!
Luv it! This is gona b intrestin.
this bloke is my god! even if hes not lol
Great stuff. Wouldn't it be funny if the atheist scientist proved the existence of God?!
What a LEGEND!!!!1

And so on.

Plenty of comments fell between the two extremes. Some thought it was mildly amusing. Others thought it was just silly. An alarming number appeared to have nothing to do with the content of the blog at all, and there were many exchanges between users that, while beginning on topic and respectful, quickly descended into name-calling and desperate attempts to discredit each other with ad hominem arguments. There was, Arthur noticed as he was scrolling through them, an inverse relationship between the extremity of the views expressed, and the quality of the spelling, punctuation and grammar.

The conflicting views expressed in the comments section reflected Arthur's own internal struggle. On the one hand, he was encouraged by many of his readers' contributions, as well as by Victor's own desire for him to write more. On the other, he felt worse about the idea now than he had when writing the first one. He reflected on the possible reasons for this. Perhaps it was nothing more than his inability to shake his sense of regret following Victor's initial reaction. Was he unnecessarily concerned about further unintended consequences? Maybe. Or maybe it was the sudden weight of expectation. While he knew he was using a platform which allowed him to communicate with huge numbers of people, he had not expected to reach quite so many, and the sheer scale of the response had caught him by surprise. Now that so many eyes were on him, and so many of them were either violently opposed to his communication, or had such high expectations for what would come next, he felt a huge pressure to get it right that hadn't been there before. Or perhaps he was allowing the more aggressive responses to put him off. Even though the positive comments outweighed the negative ones by a significant margin, the tone of those opposing voices made him distinctly uncomfortable. Why were they so convinced he would, and should, burn? Why was it so important to them that he should suffer? And what was this 'Hell' place they all thought he should be taken to? He recalled first hearing it at Wendy's church. Billy Leigh had said he was destined to end up there, but he hadn't thought to look it up. He decided it was time to find out. He typed 'Hell' into the search bar and spent the next few hours growing increasingly horrified at what he discovered.

38

ArthurFowlerBlog: Entry 2

Hello again. It appears my recent activity has caused quite a stir. I think I should start by apologising to those for whom this is a terrible inconvenience. I have met some very kind people recently and I am all too aware that their association with me has made their lives difficult. For this, I am truly sorry. The discomfort I have caused them left me unsure about writing any further entries, but those same people have been extremely supportive and have encouraged me to do so knowing it will almost certainly bring more disruption to their lives.

I was, at first, uncertain what I might discuss. I did not start this blog to make regular contributions. Rather, I thought it might be a useful platform to communicate about an issue as and when I felt it necessary to do so. Yet here I am ostensibly writing for the sake of it. My new friends have suggested something about my background may be of interest. While this feels terribly self-indulgent, I may touch upon it at a later date. Today, I would like to take the opportunity to address some of the responses my first post provoked.

I am delighted so many of the comments are positive. Your kind responses have helped to alleviate much of the stress that my sharing it with you has caused. I am unfamiliar with many of the subtleties of your culture's written communication. Much of the humour and irony was lost on me when I first read your comments. However, following a lengthy discussion with my host, I now understand many of you were amused, interested, or feel I have somehow helped to affirm your personal beliefs. I hope my future contributions will prove to be as satisfying for you.

Although the majority of the comments were positive, I have spent most of today reflecting on the negative responses I received. The vitriol directed at me has been extreme, to say the least, and I am unsure what I have done to deserve it. My host has found it difficult to explain this particular phenomenon to me and believes I should dismiss it. However, I have already seen how eager your species is to dismiss things that are incredibly important and deserving of your immediate attention and action, such as your attitude to the devastating impact your behaviour has on your environment, so I am worried he may have been a little too quick to suggest this.

I have been called a liar, offensive and evil. People have openly wished illness on me. Others have gone as far as wishing death. And, far from being shocked, my host has told me this is quite typical, normal even. For someone who is not used to it, this seems rather alarming. You may share his view that such comments do not merit a response because they are so commonplace. But, my status as an outsider notwithstanding, I would still encourage you to consider what it says about your culture that such behaviour can be taken so lightly.

The most alarming comments of all were the ones related to Hell. I must confess, I had no idea what this was when I read them, but the comments carried an unsettling tone. They were vengeful, angry and satisfied all at the same time. They caught my attention not solely through the repeated use of this unfamiliar word, but because they were so often paired with the assertion I would burn and suffer because of it. For eternity, no less! My concern was such that I have spent a considerable amount of today reading about Hell, which I now understand has no actual physical location to speak of, and have found myself horrified and reassured in equal measure. Horrified, because the very idea is appalling. Reassured, because it is also absurd.

As I understand it, Hell is a place for sinners. Sinners are people who do not behave according to God's expectations. As a punishment for this, they are cast into Hell and tortured until the end of time. This concept took me a while to grasp, because it is so disconnected from my own experience of people who claim to be followers of God (who seem perfectly pleasant, if a little misguided). My reading and interactions so far suggest people of faith subscribe to the idea of a benevolent deity who has the interests of his followers at heart. How, if they believe such a thing, could the idea of forcing me to suffer for eternity because I wrote a short blog entry in which I explained how I created their universe provide them with such satisfaction? Why would a benevolent being inflict this on an individual? The answer is, of course, it wouldn't. I expect this is why my friend finds it so easy to dismiss it. In the absence of any evidence of its existence, and the absence of any logical reason to believe it might exist despite the lack of evidence, dismissal is the sensible choice. That is the choice I too have taken, which is why I feel reassured. Yet the question remains, why do some people believe in it despite the lack of evidence or logic? The *only conclusion I have so far managed to reach is fear. And that fear is, sadly, rooted in a deep lack of intelligence. They have been told Hell is real. They have not questioned it. Perhaps they lack the critical autonomy to ask themselves why the God they believe in would need such a place to exist. But it doesn't matter – to believe in Hell is to show a complete lack of understanding of the thing they claim to believe in, because it is completely incongruous with those beliefs, as is the satisfaction they take from believing I may be destined to end up there. To enjoy the thought of anyone, absolutely anyone, suffering for eternity, is the antithesis of what faith stands for, is it not? And yet, self-professed believers in a benevolent higher power are cheered by precisely that.*

Fortunately, I have knowledge protecting me from Hell – I know I did not make it. And I did make everything else in your universe. That, of course, is the real bone of contention for all these happy condemners. It is rather telling, and rather ironic, that the people most eager to reject me are the very people who most fervently claim to believe in me, or their own vision of me, at least. Perhaps they hold the fact that I do not conform to their expectations against me. After all, if you have devoted your life to a creator who is all-knowing, all-powerful, and offering you an eternal paradise after you die, then the arrival of a creator who didn't even know you existed, is powerless to do so much as get himself back home, and can offer you nothing more than one life and one measly universe to spend it in, is likely to irritate. Yet that is the way of it. This was the best I could do. I am sorry if it is not enough.

39

Free Will

'No!' snapped Victor. It wasn't the first time he had said it this morning. Nor was it the second, or the third.

Kyle placed a hand on Victor's shoulder. 'Listen,' he said, in that tone of voice unique to people who are blissfully unaware of just how stupid they are relative to the person they are talking down to. 'You know we're strapped for cash. And you know those tossers in Westminster are going to cut our funding even more as they drag the country further back into the dark ages. This could be a massive win for us. People *like* Arthur. If we play this right, who knows how we might capitalise on all this new public interest?'

Victor shrugged Kyle's hand off and stepped away. Wasn't Kyle, just days ago, convinced Arthur should be committed? And, now he had pound signs in his eyes, he wanted to put him in a television studio and point cameras at him. Was that an acceptable way to treat the mentally ill?

'Perhaps I was a little hasty in my judgement,' said Kyle.

'Or perhaps that assessment is less convenient now you've found a way to exploit him.'

'Exploit him?' said Kyle, aghast. 'I'm making sure he gets the opportunity to tell his story, in *his* words.'

'Bullshit. You couldn't care less about Arthur. You want to throw him into a full-scale media circus so you can benefit from it personally.' Victor sat down at his desk and shook his head. 'You're not putting him on television, Dick. I won't allow it.'

There was a flicker of annoyance from Kyle at the abbreviated form of his name – something that, until now, Victor had only ever used when Kyle was well out of earshot – but he composed himself quickly. 'We don't actually *need* your permission, Victor. And it's not like he'll be there by himself – he's going to be accompanied by a representative from E Equals.'

Victor goggled. 'Me?'

'You?!' laughed Kyle, even more incredulous than Victor. 'God no. The last time your name was in a national newspaper it was printed right after the phrase "The loudest and angriest atheist in Britain". A review of your last book, I believe. It wasn't particularly positive if I remember correctly.'

'It was the Mail,' Victor growled through gritted teeth.

'Be that as it may, you can't sit next to Arthur on a faith-based ethics programme and expect him to be treated fairly. It'd be a total hatchet job.'

'So who's going with him?'

'I am,' said Sam, who had been sitting quietly at her desk and despairing as she watched them squabble.

Victor's disbelieving gaze bounced between Sam and Kyle as he tried to organise his thoughts. It took a few seconds, but he finally managed to form a response. 'No,' he said.

Kyle smiled an infuriatingly silky smile and spoke in an infuriatingly silky tone. 'You seem to think you have considerably more control over this situation than you actually do, Victor.'

'You're not sending Sam,' he said with finality.

'I'll send whoever I like,' said Kyle. 'And I think it makes much more sense for Arthur to be accompanied by everyone's favourite TV scientist than by the man who said "the only thing more pointless than God is the life of anyone who believes in him".'

This was unfair. Victor had never actually said or written those words, though it was possibly the quote most frequently attributed to him. It originally appeared in a tabloid headline that deliberately misparaphrased a paragraph from one of his books. What he had actually claimed was an omniscient deity, should it exist, would render life less meaningful because that deity, being omniscient, would know all human actions and decisions in advance, meaning they must have been preordained. Unfortunately, Victor didn't get the opportunity to explain this to Kyle because Sam chose this moment to take control of what was becoming a very tiresome exchange.

'Firstly,' she said, 'I'm not being *sent*. I'm choosing to go.'

Victor moved to respond but Sam held up her hand to demand silence.

'And secondly,' she said, 'it's not up to you, is it? It's my choice, and I'm happy to do it.'

'Well said,' said Kyle. 'That, Victor, is what a team player sounds like,' he added, as he breezed out of the office.

Sam managed to put up with Victor's surly silence and furious typing for about three minutes before she couldn't stand it any longer. 'Why are you so upset about this?' she said. 'Arthur actually wants to do it.'

Victor didn't take his eyes from his screen to deliver his curt reply. 'Really?'

'Yes, really. As you'd know perfectly well if it occurred to you to ask him about it, rather than trying to decide on his behalf.'

'And what about you? Do you *want* to? Or are you doing it because you feel like you should?'

'They're not mutually exclusive reasons.'

'Fine,' he said, and went back to his emails. He typed for about five seconds before trying another angle. 'But what about the impact on your career? You're the face of serious scientific broadcasting in the UK. Do you really think producers are going to be as keen to have you presenting for them once you're associated with all this? Any negativity is bound to rub off on you.'

'Don't be silly. It's one hour on daytime television. And,' she added, 'so what if it does? This is the right thing to do. If doing it upsets people, to hell with them.'

It was clear he wasn't going to win her over. He switched off his computer and picked up his keys. He had one last angle – he would have to try and talk Arthur out of it.

'And no trying to talk Arthur out of it,' said Sam.

He stopped at the door and clenched his jaw. When he first offered Sam a job, he had been warned by a senior colleague that he was making a mistake. 'She's too clever,' they had said. 'You don't want a research assistant who is smarter than you. Take on a harmless plodder from the middle of your class – someone who will do as they're told and has no chance of usurping you.' It was a joke, of course, but he was starting to see some merit in the idea. She hadn't remained his assistant for long. She soon graduated to research associate and then associate professor. Her intellect was formidable. There was no fooling her. But that didn't stop him from trying. He turned around, poised to protest he was planning to do no such thing.

'Yes you were,' said Sam, before Victor had so much as opened his mouth.

40

A Just Balance

Sam's claim that Arthur wanted to do it may not have qualified as full-blown dishonesty, but there were certainly enough lies of omission to call it misleading. While it was true Arthur was interested in appearing on television, Sam neglected to mention that he took some convincing it was a good idea. She also left out that she was the one who had done the convincing. She knew she would never get Victor on board, so she had to try and make it happen without his involvement. His intentions were noble enough – he did genuinely want to protect Arthur. But his judgement was clouded by the stress he had been under lately. And, though he would never admit it – perhaps wasn't even consciously aware of it, he also wanted to protect his own reputation. She knew Victor would have seen a television appearance from Arthur as a threat. Sam disagreed. She knew television. She knew her audience. And she knew they would love Arthur. If she could just get him on screen for an extended period, she was sure a significant portion of the viewing public would warm to him, which would make it much harder for the news media to continue treating him like a figure of fun without upsetting their readers and viewers.

Arthur's initial attitude to it was characterised by relentless indecision. At first he was resolutely against the idea. He'd started the blog so he wouldn't have to risk being misrepresented by the press. Wasn't he opening himself up to that very same problem if he agreed to do it?

Having resolved to be completely honest with him, Sam told him yes, this was a distinct possibility. 'However,' she added. 'This isn't the same sort of thing as the news you've seen. It's an open debate. I do think you're much safer here. But you don't have to do it if you don't want to.'

'But you think it's a good idea?'

'I do.'

This left him more open to it. He was, he acknowledged, intrigued by what he felt could be an interesting experience. Then he realised Victor would think it was a terrible idea and decided he didn't want to do anything to upset him. Then he found out Kyle had already made the arrangements and felt it would be rude to let him down.

'Stop worrying about those two for a moment. What do *you* want to do?'

Ultimately, Arthur wanted intelligent and nuanced discussion. The fact that the news was so lacking in this was the main reason he held it in such low regard. If this programme had the potential to facilitate debate, he was interested. 'You'll definitely be coming with me?' he asked.

'I will.'

'Then I think we should go.'

*

AUDIENCE MEMBER: *I think it's appalling you're giving this man a platform in the first place. The things he has to say for himself amount to the ugliest of blasphemies.*

PRESENTER: *Would you care to respond, Mr Fowler?*

ARTHUR: *I'm afraid I'm unfamiliar with the term.*

PRESENTER: Blasphemy? It's the act of insulting or wilfully showing disrespect to something people consider sacred.

ARTHUR: I see. So it's a means of trying to prevent people from criticising religion?

PRESENTER: Well, some people find attacks against their religion or against God terribly offensive.

ARTHUR: That should hardly be grounds for protecting it from criticism. Maybe their religion needs attacking. As for offending God, I don't see a problem myself. As the creator of this universe, I think myself best placed to know what will and will not cause me offense. I certainly don't think I'm guilty of saying anything I find offensive. In fact, if blasphemy means saying things that would offend the creator of the universe, then one would be hard pressed to find a more abundant source of it than the pages of the Bible or the mouth of a church minister.

VARIOUS: [indecipherable shouting]

*

AUDIENCE MEMBER 2: But how are we supposed to take you seriously when you look and sound just like us? You claim you come from another universe, yet you appear no different from humans and you share our language.

ARTHUR: That is an interesting point. It caused me some concern at first. As you might imagine, I too was rather surprised to find myself not only on another planet, but *also surrounded by such similar creatures to myself. However, it is not such a strange state of affairs as it may seem. We know intelligent life can only exist in an environment capable of sustaining it. We can therefore hypothesise that it takes intelligent life to create the conditions that allow a universe to exist and to create the conditions that allow wormholes to exist. Therefore, any life form that creates a wormhole joining its universe to the one containing its creator is likely to encounter another intelligent lifeform. It appears that, in the only two cases any of us are aware of, evolution favours this basic appearance for intelligent life.*

AUDIENCE MEMBER 3: Nonsense! If life on another planet, or in another universe even, shared the same basic form as human beings, then it would be further evidence it was deliberately and painstakingly designed by a higher intelligence.

ARTHUR: Not necessarily. It may simply mean, just as life can only exist under specific conditions, so too can high levels of intelligence. There could be any number of different life forms in this universe. But if this humanoid form is the only one that allows sufficient intelligence to build universes and create wormholes to develop, then it makes sense that they would be more likely to be brought together than two vastly different species.

PRESENTER: But that doesn't explain the fact we speak the same language.

ARTHUR: True. But language evolves with form. Perhaps it is only this particular language, or collection of languages, that facilitate the path towards the kinds of scientific discoveries our respective species have made. Maybe there are planets and universes out there full of creatures that are, to all intents and purposes, identical to us. But, due to differences in the way they communicate, they are not nearly as technologically advanced. Or maybe it's all a remarkable coincidence. Who knows?

*

PRESENTER: Let's say, for the moment, for argument's sake, you are responsible for creating this universe. What do you make of religion?

ARTHUR: Well, I think it's safe to say it's all about death. Much of the bible seems to be about death. Many of the hopes religious people have hinge on what will happen after death. The most iconic moment in the life of the Bible's most important figure is his death. Death is an idea humans seem to find it difficult to come to terms with.

PRESENTER: Which in itself could be the result of a steady decline in religious faith.

ARTHUR: I don't think so. Those with religious faith seem to be the worst affected. No matter how many times they tell themselves they are immortal, they cannot look upon death with anything but unending terror. Instead, I would argue it is the result of a lack of application of the scientific method. Death is a mystery. Mysteries are solved through investigation. You never know – an objective view of death, considered and explored from a scientific approach, could reveal enormous potential for something akin to the afterlife so many of you desire. At the very least, I believe it would be more reassuring than your religious fantasies. These I know for a fact are not real – I cannot offer the life

I have created another life when it ends any more than you can offer one to a flower you have planted once it dies.

PRESENTER: Just to be clear, you're telling us there is no Heaven, is that correct?

ARTHUR: Indeed. And no Hell. This, I feel, is a point worth stressing. Hell is, after all, the most absurd of concepts.

PRESENTER: How so?

ARTHUR: Well, it's such an illogical idea. If you look at the universe, really look at it, all you see is balance. Everything about it depends on balance. The relative sizes and ratios of protons and electrons; the strength of gravity and electromagnetism; the ratio of matter to antimatter – all these things are perfectly balanced in such a way as to make the universe and the life it contains possible. Even the tiniest changes in the relationships between these features of the universe would render it unstable. I should know – I failed to create it countless times. Through trial and error I arrived at a combination of values that worked. But that doesn't make me all-powerful. I was just lucky. I finally managed to balance everything so perfectly that it worked. And so, for those of you who still think me a liar, I ask you this: why is it that in your final, ultimate equation there is no balance? Sins with finite consequences are punished with infinite hell. Where is the balance there? How is it that this most illogical yet incredibly important aspect of your faith is the only part of it that does not celebrate God's apparent love of all things balanced? What possible reason could there be for infinite Hell that could not be served with just a little bit of Hell?

*

Sam and Arthur whiled away the half hour wait for their return train in a cafe next to the station. Arthur wore a far away stare that betrayed his anxiety about the recording. 'Stop worrying,' said Sam. 'You did absolutely fine.'

'You really think so? You don't think it will upset Victor or Mr Kyle?'

'Lots of things upset Victor. That doesn't mean they shouldn't happen. He'd do well to learn that. And as for Mr Kyle, the more things that upset him the better.' Arthur gave her a mournful look. 'But I don't think anything you said today will have done so,' she said. *Sadly*, she added, privately.

In truth, Sam felt Arthur had performed admirably. As they entered the studio, she had herself been anxious that she had made a mistake and feared Arthur was about to be mocked and ridiculed, but she was right to trust her instinct that he would respond intelligently and respectfully to everything that was thrown at him. If anyone had any reason to be embarrassed, it was the one member of the audience who had been driven to such apoplectic rage by Arthur's comments about blasphemy that he had to be forcibly removed from the studio.

For his part, Arthur was erudite and humble, at times fascinating. Sam even noticed a surprising sense of relief when he responded to questions about his appearance and language. She had only refrained from asking those questions herself because she was convinced they would reveal Arthur to be a fraud. He would have been unable to offer a meaningful answer and so any reply he did try to make would be at best embarrassing and at worst humiliating for him. When the question was asked, she feared that, in her desire to spare him that experience, he was now going to have to go through it in front of a couple of hundred people and a handful of cameras that would later be used to broadcast it to millions. Instead, he offered an answer that was not entirely implausible, even if it did fall a long way short of easily believable. Sam realised, as she considered this, that it revealed something about her she had not acknowledged – she *wanted* Arthur's story to be true. His answer didn't confirm it was, of course. To assume that would be to succumb to the confirmation bias she'd just caught herself under the influence of. But it meant it could be. And that, for reasons Sam could not yet fathom, was a rather pleasing thought. He may not have pleased everyone who was there – quite the opposite, in fact. But there were some in the audience whose raised eyebrows and slowly nodding heads suggested they were genuinely reflecting on Arthur's words, especially when he talked about Hell. That was something, at least.

41

Probability

'I imagine you'd find this hilarious,' said Victor. 'He's driving me nuts. You should have heard him with the bloody doorbell. I don't know if he's crazy or if it's some kind of stunt or if he really is God. I don't know which one would be more tragic. He's like a child.' He sighed, long and hard. 'You'd like him.'

He knelt down and removed the dead flowers, laid them to one side. He placed his hand on the freshly bought bunch and paused. 'What am I going to do now?'

The stone offered no reply.

He pictured himself with her. On the sofa. In a restaurant. In the car. No, not the car. On the beach in Mexico.

Rowing along the Stour.

Cool, clear water drips off the oars. She laughs. He smiles. They talk.

'You worry too much,' she says. 'What's the worst that can happen?'

'My career could be ruined and I could remain a laughing stock for the rest of my life.'

'True,' she says. She looks thoughtful. 'Is that likely?'

He shrugs.

'Everything will be fine.'

'How do you know?'

'Probability.'

She always used his words against him like that. They both worried a lot, but never at the same time. If she was fretting about something, it would be his job to pick her up. What if she failed the exam? What if the patient she lost yesterday died because she made a mistake? What if it happened again today?

'Everything will be fine,' he would say.

'But how do you know?'

He would shrug. 'Probability. Chances are, there's nothing to worry about.'

Of course, probability is all well and good, but a slim chance is still a chance.

'What if we can't have children?'

Probability. Chances are, there's nothing to worry about. Until there is. But they had each other, and they carried on.

And she did the same for him. Perfect balance. When he turned melancholy, she turned positive. What if we don't get the funding? What if the speech goes badly? What if the paper gets slated? What if it doesn't even get published?

'Probability,' she would say, with a knowing smile. And he'd smile back.

Probability is all well and good...

'Drive carefully.'

She laughed. She always laughed.

'I'll be fine. Probability, remember? Millions of people use the roads every day. They almost always make it home without a problem.'

Almost always.

He wakes up. Her side of the bed is cold.

A knock on the door at two in the morning.

A man and a woman in uniform.

'We're terribly sorry Mr Dennett.'

Probability. Laws of big numbers mean there is probably nothing to worry about. This used to help him sleep when she was driving home late at night after a disgustingly long shift. Only once did they let him down. It didn't change his attitude to them. The numbers were never wrong. You just sometimes got the wrong one. And now he had to carry on.

He arranged the flowers, took his time, handled them gently. He knew it was a futile gesture. Everything about this was futile. It was what he had said to Wendy every time she told him to visit. There was no point, he'd say. There was no-one there. He'd just be talking to a stone that couldn't answer, that commemorated a woman who couldn't hear. But one day he relented and it turned out Wendy was right. It didn't have to be rational. It just had to be done. It helped to talk to her.

They tie the boat to the moor. She lays out the blanket. He uncorks the wine. She smiles. He smiles back.
'So what should I do?'
'That depends,' she says. 'Do you think he's faking it?'
'He doesn't seem the sort. It seems the least likely option.'
She laughs. 'Less likely than him actually being God?'
He thinks for a moment. 'You know, it really does.'
'Then it's easy,' she says.
He looks at her quizzically.
She laughs again.
'He's either mad, or he's God.'
'Or both.'
'Or both,' she agrees. 'Either way, the only thing you can do is be kind to him.'

He smiles. She always knows what to say.

Victor picked up the dead flowers, stood up and stepped back to assess the grave. It was fine. It was never good or beautiful or even pleasant. Fine was the best this could be.

'Wendy has been interfering again,' he said. 'I swear, that woman needs a hobby. She's trying to convert Arthur. Can you imagine? Trying to convert God to religion? She's had him reading the Bible. She even dragged us to church. I bet you'd find that hilarious too.'

He kicked the ground and toyed with the dead stems. 'She's convinced I'm angry with God because I lost you. She thinks that's the only reason she could never get me to go all born-again. There's no arguing with her. She's so stubborn.'

The gravestone said nothing, stayed still. Somehow, Victor felt, it did so accusingly.

'I know, I know. Pots and kettles... But it's not like I turned away from religion after you. I never turned towards it. I only blame God for the little things. The big things are too important to trivialise like that.'

He turned the ring on his finger, cleared his throat.

'Anyway, it seems like forever ago but that thing with the school kids went okay. I mean, they were little shits, but, you know–' he sighed. 'Kids.'

He cleared his throat again. Blinked.

'I have to get going,' he said. 'I'll be back in a few days. I love you. I miss you.'

42

In Memory of Her

When Arthur returned, exhausted from filming and traveling, he discovered that Victor had decided to return the favour and cook a meal of his own. Victor called the dish 'cottage pie' and it was, to Arthur's mind, one of the finest things he had ever tasted. As they ate, Victor listened attentively as Arthur filled him in on the day's events. Arthur was quite guarded to begin with. Although there had been a marked change in Victor's mood over the last day or so, his volatile temperament left Arthur worried he might say something to frustrate or agitate Victor. He need not have worried. As the conversation progressed, it became clear Victor was in good spirits, and so Arthur furnished him with some of the finer details, explaining which topics came up, how people had responded to him, and how he and Sam both felt it had gone well. Victor's reactions remained positive throughout, and he even let out a snort of laughter when Arthur recounted the story of the man who had to be escorted from the premises because he wouldn't stop shouting.

The pleasant tone continued for some time and Arthur found himself relaxing into the conversation and the meal until Victor said something that caught him off-guard. Having spent so much time talking about his own day, it finally occurred to Arthur to ask after Victor's, and he was confused when Victor told him he'd spent part of it visiting his wife. His surprise must have been obvious to Victor, who immediately asked if something was amiss. Fearing he was now all but certain to upset Victor but also seeing no viable way of avoiding it, Arthur told Victor what he had recently learnt from Wendy that made it difficult to understand how he could possibly have done as he had just claimed.

It was Victor's turn to be confused now. He couldn't see what Arthur was having such a hard time grasping until it eventually dawned on him that the concept of visiting someone's resting place was entirely alien to him.

'It's a kind of ritualised way of remembering people,' he explained. 'We visit the place where they are buried in order to pay our respects.'

'Why?' said Arthur, rather too abruptly, he realised. 'I mean, what purpose does it serve if they are unaware of it?'

'It's not really for them, I suppose. It helps us deal with the fact they are no longer here.'

'What do you do there?'

'It depends. Some people sit and reflect. Some lay flowers or put objects on or around the grave. I talk to my wife.'

'And does she...' Arthur left the question hanging in the air.

'Reply? No,' said Victor, with a hollow laugh. 'It's a one-way conversation.' A wry smile crossed his face. 'Which means it's nothing like the conversations we used to have.'

Arthur considered this for a moment. 'So it's a bit like prayer, then?'

'What?' said Victor, suddenly affronted. 'No, not really.'

'Oh,' said Arthur, and then, 'sorry.' He paused for a moment, then frowned, and then asked. 'Are you sure it's not like prayer? It certainly seems that way. Both involve talking to someone who cannot hear or answer. And they both seem to be related to the pain or anxiety that comes with wanting things to be other than they are.'

Victor stared at Arthur intently for a moment. What he was thinking, Arthur could not begin to speculate, though he noticed a knot tightening in his stomach and feared he had broken the spell and that Victor's mood was about to turn. It didn't.

'Hmm,' said Victor. 'Maybe you're right.' It seemed for a moment that he was going to leave it at that, but then he frowned and put down his knife and fork. 'Wait, so is death not a big deal for you and, you know,' he paused and looked as though getting the rest of the sentence out took a great effort, 'others from your home?'

Arthur tried to explain, but found it difficult. Or at least, he found it difficult to explain in a way Victor could understand it. It was not so much that it was 'no big deal' as Victor had put it. It was simply a fact that had to be accepted. Life is what it is. Then it changes and it is something else. There were certainly conditions Arthur would say he preferred over others. But he was of the general opinion that there was no point wishing something was something else. This, he told Victor, was the common view of things.

'You're not as sentimental as us?'

'We're not as emotional. I suppose it is logical to assume this would manifest in a lack of sentimentality.'

Victor closed his eyes tightly and scratched his head. 'But you told me about your wife the other day. Do you not miss her?'

'Of course,' replied Arthur. 'That would be an example of those preferred conditions – I would much rather be at home with her than I would here. But what can I do? I must simply make the best of my current set of circumstances.'

'But you're not upset? You don't feel sad?'

'I lament the fact I am here and she is there, certainly. But I find no value or purpose in sadness. What good would it do to dwell on it? That certainly won't get me home. Speaking of which,' said Arthur, 'might I trouble you to take a look at this?' He drew a few folded sheets of paper out of his pocket and handed them to Victor.

'What is it?'

'It's a plan for getting me home. It isn't finished yet. I used the information available on the E Equals website when I did my calculations. I imagine you have more comprehensive data available elsewhere that would be required to fine-tune the maths.'

Victor unfolded the sheets and studied the list of parameters, calculations and equations, pointedly aware that, as one of the world's leading particle physicists, he really ought to be able to make more sense of them than he could. He folded them back up and tucked them into his own pocket. 'Of course,' he said, and cleared his throat in a manner that did not betray confidence.

The next morning, they watched Arthur's performance together. Or rather, Victor watched it, Arthur watched Victor watching it, anxiously looking for any sign of a reaction from Victor, who offered little beyond the occasional nod or a muted 'good point' every now and then. Mostly, he maintained a contemplative air and spoke very little.

As the credits rolled, Arthur looked expectantly at Victor. Victor nodded approvingly.

'Good job,' he said.

'You really think so?'

'You did very well,' said Victor. 'Your points were valid, your explanations were clear, you made your argument very logically, and demonstrated very clearly the specious nature of religious doctrine.'

Arthur beamed, ecstatic. 'Oh good. So do you think I might have made an impact on the way people feel about the afterlife and Hell?'

Victor barked a short, sharp laugh. 'No,' he said. 'Not even slightly.'

'Oh,' said the deflated Arthur. 'Why not?'

Victor sighed and heaved himself off the sofa. He walked over to the computer and typed "cognitive dissonance" into the search bar. 'That,' he said, 'should explain everything.'

43

ArthurFowlerBlog: Entry 3

Planet Earth is a truly wonderful place. Though I have only experienced all but a tiny part of it vicariously through videos and images available on the internet, the life that exists here, in every form, is exquisitely beautiful. You are incredibly lucky. You are also incredibly intelligent. It is important to make this clear from the outset because I fear some of what follows may offend. That does not mean I am only saying it to be sycophantic – I really do believe it. Your species has made significant advances in computing, communication, engineering, space exploration, manufacturing, agriculture and energy production to name but a few. Your scientific discoveries have reached the point where you have actually managed, albeit accidentally, to bring the creator of your universe into your world. You possess the means to ensure a high quality of life for every living person on Earth and you have the knowledge and technology required to generate energy and resources in a perfectly sustainable way and to steer your planet towards a homeostatic state that would ensure your environment remains habitable to you for millennia. But you are not doing so.

As I type this, millions of your fellow humans are suffering in the most appalling poverty imaginable, you are releasing vast amounts of carbon into your atmosphere, and you are destroying the ecosystems that remove and store it at a reckless and irresponsible rate. The widespread belief appears to be that this is a great tragedy, yet no sincere effort to fix it appears to be underway. This contradictory nature of yours has been a source of consternation and confusion since my arrival here. To an outsider such as myself, it is almost impossible to reconcile your ability to break free of your planet's gravity with your need to put a label on any item made of fabric to remind you it should be kept away from fire.

However, I finally feel like I am beginning to understand why so much of your culture confuses me. I believe my mistake was thinking it must be a complex problem. In fact, it is very simple – humans hate to be wrong. They hate being wrong so much that they often pretend to be unaware of the evidence that proves them wrong so they can go on believing they are not wrong. If the evidence is so overwhelmingly against them as to render this task impossible, then they simply lie to themselves and everyone about them by repeatedly asserting that they are not wrong until they and everyone else believes they are not wrong. The result of this, of course, is they continue to be wrong and they lead the people around them to be wrong too, in ever more diverse and catastrophic ways – which is a shame, given they so hate being wrong. I am tempted to go as far as to say that being wrong is the only thing more frightening to humans than death, which, ironically, is precisely what some of the more extreme examples of being wrong could lead to. For example, you consume, in abundance, food and drink you know to be bad for you. You know certain substances are harmful to you, yet you fill your bodies with them anyway. Most troubling of all, you know your activities here on earth are rendering it uninhabitable to you, yet you continue to indulge in those activities.

If you doubt my claims, take a look at any of your more popular news websites. I have been reading these on a daily basis and, though I have not been here long, I believe I have observed enough evidence of this phenomenon to have some confidence in my hypothesis. The evidence can be found in equal measure in both the news reports and in the reader comments that appear beneath them. Whenever I read these, I can't help but wonder if all of humanity is having a competition to discover who can be most wrong about the greatest number of things while convincing the largest possible number of people they are not wrong about any of them. It is a theory made all the more plausible by the fact that the people who are most successful in this regard also seem to be the people who are most likely to be given positions of power, influence and responsibility, which means they tend to be the very subject of those same news stories and comments. For nowhere in your society is this phenomenon more prevalent than in politics.

Human politicians are strange creatures. They seem to do little more than seek opportunities to stand in front of cameras and repeat slogans and catchphrases and answers which are nothing more than carefully scripted lies bearing no relation to the questions they have been asked. As is the case with so many other problems, ordinary people appear to be well aware this is happening, yet do nothing about it. Instead, they pick the liar they like the most, perhaps the one who tells the most pleasing lies, and then set about arguing with each other about why their liar is not as bad as the others. The end result is that everyone, on all sides, is wrong in one way or another, and there is no room in your discourse for the people with sensible ideas because they find themselves opposed by anyone who subscribes to the stupid ones, which is just about everyone.

I cannot help but wonder at the role religion has played in helping to foster this state of affairs. For centuries, human beings have been taught from a young age to respect, trust and submit to authority figures who tell comforting lies. They are taught that to question what they are told is sinful. What hope do they have, later in their lives, of being able to think critically about the ideas they subscribe to when they are so perfectly conditioned to accept the word of anyone who makes false promises they like the sound of?

I believe there is a solution, though I daresay it will not be easy to bring to pass. Somehow, you need to embrace the idea that you may be wrong. About anything. About everything. You will make much more progress, and be much happier, if you seek faults in your own attitudes before looking for them in others. This will be difficult, maybe even painful, but it will be worth it. Just keep reminding yourselves of all you have accomplished and know that, if you open your minds to the possibility you are sometimes wrong, there is so much more you could yet achieve.

44

Corrupt Communication

Victor barely slept that night. At almost two in the morning, he checked his watch for the seventh time. His brain, making the seventh such calculation of the night, informed him he would now get a little over four hours' sleep if he managed to fall asleep at that precise moment. Having spent the last three hours tossing and turning and completely failing to ignore the chorus of thoughts reverberating through his mind, he felt this was unlikely. It was Arthur's fault. He had asked Victor if he'd had time to look through the plans he had drawn up, which Victor had to confess he had not, and so Arthur had insisted on talking them through. Late into the night they had talked, or rather, Arthur had talked – Victor mainly listened, speaking only to ask questions when he needed further clarification, which was often. By the end of the conversation, Victor's head was spinning with awe and wonder and excitement and... something else... a great sense of apprehension and anxiety about what it might mean. Because, not only was Arthur's work ground-breaking, maybe even paradigm-shifting, it also made it infinitely more plausible Arthur was telling the truth.

The principle itself was straightforward enough. It should be possible, Arthur explained, for him to return home simply by recreating the same conditions that brought him to Earth. If they could create another wormhole, then Arthur could travel through it in the opposite direction. Like so much of what Arthur thought of as simple, it sounded completely bonkers to Victor. Those very conditions, he argued, had caused Arthur to travel from what he called the 'parent' universe to the 'child' universe. Why would the same conditions enable him to travel the other way? Arthur explained his hypothesis.

'Because that is actually the default direction of travel,' he said. 'The wormhole originated in this universe, so it makes sense that matter from the source would flow into the space with which the link is created, having already begun to flow into the link itself before it has actually reached that space.'

'Like pulling the plug out of the bath,' said Victor, realising this was probably the sort of remark that led to him being lumbered with the job of showing secondary school students around the detector.

'Quite,' said Arthur. 'Of course, that didn't happen when I was brought here – the bathtub was empty, so there was nothing to flow down the plughole.'

'But put the empty bathtub in a *vacuum* ...' Victor began, with an air of dawning realisation.

'And air from the outside flows back up through the plumbing to fill it,' finished Arthur.

A half smile crossed Victor's face as he turned the idea around in his mind. It lasted barely a moment before it sank into a frown. 'But the detector *is* vacuum sealed,' he said. 'How could you enter the link when it's formed? You can't sit inside a vacuum sealed chamber for several hours before we fire the beams into it.'

'No,' said Arthur. 'But if we built something I *could* sit inside for a few hours – something that could protect me from the vacuum and from the beams – then there is a chance I would be able to travel safely back through the wormhole in it. Look,' he said, spreading the sheets of paper containing his scribbled plans over the table, 'it's very simple...'

It was not very simple. Victor could get to grips with the concept easily enough. The maths behind it, on the other hand, caused him a real headache. He did his best to follow as Arthur talked his way through the assortment of calculations, equations and diagrams scrawled across the page, nodding and making vaguely affirmative sounds at what seemed appropriate moments, all the while struggling to keep up. It was not a position he was accustomed to finding himself in as one of the world's leading particle physicists. It took over an hour of wrestling with the contents of the pages and asking Arthur to repeat points and make clarifications before the brilliance of the work finally revealed itself to Victor, like a picture that appears to be of one thing until you suddenly realise it is also something else and you wonder how on earth you never saw it straight away. What Victor saw now was one of the greatest scientific revelations in history. It's difficult to sleep after something like that.

So it was that Victor found himself awake at two in the morning with little hope of spending any of the remaining four hours before his alarm sounded asleep. He threw the duvet off with a resigned sigh, donned his dressing gown and crept downstairs. He sat at his computer. Perhaps he could catch up on some of the emails he had been ignoring. There had been rather a lot of them lately. He logged into the E Equals server and gaped when he saw he had several thousand unread messages. He discovered, as he scrolled down the list of names and subjects, that most of the senders were unknown to him. He also discovered, as he started paying more attention to the subject lines, a lot of people wanted to meet him. Some people wanted to meet him so they could meet Arthur. Some wanted to meet him so they could interview him. Some wanted to argue with him. And rather too many wanted to kill him.

Hate mail was nothing new to Victor. As an outspoken atheist in the public eye, he was used to receiving colourful correspondence and could usually expect to receive a handful of messages a month. Now and then, this would rise to maybe twenty or thirty, usually following a book release, or after having comments from a lecture picked up and misrepresented by the middle market tabloids. It no longer worried him – it always died down afterwards and so far nothing had ever actually come of it. But Arthur's television appearance and heavy press coverage had obviously struck a chord with the nation's more misguided believers and, deciding Victor was guilty by association, they had decided to direct their outrage at him.

You and your faggot friend are going to burn for this.
i hope u die slowly before u rot in HELL!
watch ur back ill make it look like suicide u scum
Tell your friend God is watching him. So are His followers…
Screw you and your bullshit atheist retard dogma

Et cetera.

The task of identifying and organising all of the hate mail (move to folder > 'hate mail'), interview requests (delete), requests for an official comment (delete), downright weird (move to folder > 'just in case'), and actual, everyday correspondence (pinned), killed about two hours, after which Victor decided to check the news websites to find out exactly what had happened to inspire his rabid new admirers.

As he had suspected, Britain's gutter press had been doing what they do best. Faced as they had been with a complete refusal from Arthur and Victor to engage with them, several newspapers had attempted to milk the story the only way they knew how, and their websites featured speculative stories about the two of them – the nature of their relationship, things they had said, and things that were almost, but not quite, things they had said. Every criticism Victor had ever made of religion was reprinted and repeated, provoking their readers to fire ignorant comments out of their computer keyboards in fits of illiterate indignance. Comments Arthur had made on television the previous day were seized upon, taken out of context, turned inside out, thrown into headlines. Verbs were chosen carefully, intonation changed. Where once he had *said*, 'I created *this* universe,' now he *raged*, '*I* created this universe.' Even religious organisations had issued statements, though, Victor suspected, probably only begrudgingly and as a means of putting an end to the incessant phone calls they were no doubt receiving themselves. The Jewish Leadership Council said it was 'concerned' by Arthur's claims, the Muslim Council of Britain formally rejected them, and the Church of England somehow managed to find the situation both 'laughable' and 'mildly offensive' – a far cry from the 'fury' with which religious groups across the nation were said to have reacted to Arthur's performance by the inciteful headlines.

Nevertheless, almost overnight, the outrage-mongers had whipped slow-thinking screamers into a frenzy of presumption and disgust until the internet was nothing but an echo chamber full of people screaming about one step too far, the straw that broke the camel's back, enough is enough, an attack on religion, an attack on decency, an attack on the very fabric of society... Something, they all agreed, should be done about it. What that something was, nobody seemed to know. Faced with such circumstances, there was only one thing an upstanding British citizen could do, and so strongly worded messages continued to land in Victor's inbox.

45

For Man This is Impossible

Victor was so excited about sharing Arthur's plans with Sam that he arrived at work with absolutely no recollection of the journey he had just made. He knew he must have navigated a number of roundabouts, several sets of traffic lights and, most worryingly, two pedestrian crossings, but he had no memory of any of it whatsoever. Knowing the route as well as he did, he also knew he must have driven past at least two speed cameras. He could only hope his subconscious brain had taken it upon itself to slow down at the appropriate times. He couldn't even remember waiting at the barrier to the E Equals car park. For all he knew, he had ploughed straight through it having left a trail of twisted cars and maimed pedestrians in his wake. He bolted from his car, blazed through the entrance, bustled his way through the busy lobby and corridors and stairways, tutting and sighing and brushing past people who blocked his path and threw angry glares at him that he didn't notice and wouldn't have cared about if he had, before finally bursting into the office so suddenly that Sam started from her chair and spilled coffee all over herself in alarm.

'Victor!' she yelled, leaping to her feet and pinching a scalding trouser leg away from her skin. 'What the hell?!'

'Sorry,' he panted. 'You were right. He's a genius.'

Sam stared at the sheets of paper spread over Victor's desk, her face a picture of fierce concentration. She tapped the thumb of one hand thoughtfully against her lower lip and drew invisible lines in the air with the other in a swirling, ponderous tracing of the ideas laid out before her. Occasionally she tilted her head, as though doing so might render it easier to make sense of whatever diagram or equation she was studying. All the while, she actively ignored Victor as he somehow managed to project a hurrying air of anticipation while remaining perfectly still.

Eventually, she asked, 'He really thinks it will work?'

'He's pretty convinced.'

Sam sighed and fell back into silent consideration, absently pulling at her wet trouser leg, her fingers tracing a crude sketch of a capsule designed to sit within a mesh of electromagnetic conductors that would direct the E Equals' photon beams around it while encompassing it in enough energy to tear a hole in spacetime. Dotted around the sketch was a series of equations detailing the precise circumstances required to make this possible.

'I've been getting hate mail,' said Victor, absently filling the silence.

'Mmm?' said Sam, not really listening.

'You should see the things people have said,' he pressed on. At the edge of her vision, Sam saw him take his phone out and start tapping at the screen. She set about ignoring him with more fervour.

'*How sad your life must be that you need to resort to sick little stunts like this,*' Victor read, in a mockingly pompous tone. '*How sad that all it will achieve is eternity burning in the pit of Hell for both of you.*' He paused and tapped the screen again. 'Or this one – *I look forward to observing from Heaven as you suffer the exquisite tortures that await you.* I mean really, what is wrong with these people? They go on about peace and love and forgiveness, yet they take pleasure in the thought of a person being tortured forev–'

'Victor!' He winced and shrank under Sam's glare as she berated him. 'I don't care about these idiots and their pointless little opinions. Why do *you* care about them? How has it still not occurred to you that the only thing you can do is ignore them? Do us both a favour and see if you can figure out a way of letting *their* words disappear into their own little vacuum,' she said, jabbing at one of the diagrams.

It took Victor a moment to realise what Sam was getting at. 'Oh, so you're...'

'Yes! I'm done.'

'What do you think?'

She let out a sigh. 'It's brilliant,' she said, the harsh edge to her voice disappearing.

Victor felt suddenly lighter. He had tried to keep himself from getting too worked up until someone else had verified it, but now Sam had, any remnant of his attempts to remain reserved evaporated. Now, he decided, he could really get excited. It was real. It was groundbreaking. It was paradigm-shifting. Such were the sentiments that spilled out of him as he waxed lyrical about the potential impact of what Arthur had shared with them. He was like a giddy child, as animated and joyful as he had felt for as long as he could remember.

Sam, however, was more restrained – a little too restrained. What was wrong with her? Why wasn't she as excited as he was?

One of the things that set Sam apart as a student was her ability to see problems others missed. He could always tell when she was about to make someone's life difficult by poking a gaping hole in their methodology or spotting an inherent flaw in their hypothesis. She would get a certain look about her – an expression which betrayed a sense that something wasn't quite right. And then she would speak, and a peer that had been talking passionately or excitedly about their research moments beforehand would deflate and sink into a great resentful sulk. She was wearing that same expression now and he feared, correctly, he was about to fall victim to the same kind of unwanted revelation.

'I just feel bad for Arthur,' she said.

Victor frowned. 'Why?' he asked. 'This proves it's possible for universes to be contained within each other, and that it's possible to travel from one to the other. This could get him home.'

'Well, yes, in *theory*. But what good is proof to people who don't believe in it? No-one is actually going to build this,' she said, gesturing at the paper. 'We'll benefit from it, there's no doubt about that. All sorts of progress will be made thanks to this. But others will need to review it and verify it and no doubt someone will refute it and, even if they can't, it ultimately won't matter. No-one is going to say, "great! Let's spend billions of pounds knocking all this together and fire Arthur through a wormhole and never see him again and never know if it worked or if we've killed him." It doesn't matter how clever he is or how many theories he throws at us – he's stuck here. You need to tell him that.'

Victor sagged as his good mood vanished into its own little wormhole.

46

ArthurFowlerBlog: Entry 4

I am not an emotional person. It is not a common characteristic of my people to allow our emotions to influence our behaviour. We think it rather unseemly. We are much more inclined to act rationally than emotionally. I expect this is why I am so ill-equipped to deal with the human approach to problems. When you have lived your whole life surrounded by people who think and act rationally, there is rarely any need to get particularly emotional. And when you have no need to get particularly emotional, you are more inclined to act rationally. It is a positive feedback loop you would do well to try and adopt for yourselves.

I find myself now surrounded by people who exist almost exclusively in a negative feedback loop – one in which their responses to events tend towards the emotional, which, in turn, leads them to act irrationally. Their irrational acts inspire emotional responses from the people around them. And so on. This seems to be such an integral part of the way you function, the majority of you appear to have forgotten how to behave rationally altogether. In my short time here I have witnessed first hand how easily humans lose any capacity for rational thought over the tiniest inconvenience and lash out at the people around them following the most trivial of issues. It seems clear thinking is in short supply here on Earth, and there is little room for calmly working out a solution to a problem. Even your attempts at clear thinking are coloured by an irrationality that has permeated the very processes you have created to help your society function. I am reliably informed that these processes, designed to be as logical and rational as possible, do little beyond driving each and every one of you slowly mad. And today they are doing the same to me. Because today I discovered I cannot go home. I do not mean it is physically impossible for me to return home – I believe I have solved that problem and know exactly what needs to be done to get me back. But it does not matter, because I have learnt there are people who, despite having no understanding of the process by which I could return home, have the power to prevent me from doing so for fear that something may go wrong. I am told these "Health and Safety" people are not experts in particle physics, yet they are responsible for completing something called a risk assessment, which will almost certainly result in my application to complete the process by which I might escape this world and return to my own being rejected on the grounds that it is too dangerous. It matters not that they are unqualified to assess the degree of risk this process carries, nor that I would be the only person who would be affected. It is all to do with liability, apparently. For some reason, I am not allowed to be held solely accountable for my own actions. Someone else must also be forced to take responsibility for them as well and, if their ill-informed opinion is that this arbitrary assignment of responsibility would expose them to some kind of negative consequence, then they have the power to prevent me from leaving. It is incredibly frustrating. And stupid. You would think a species intelligent enough to create complex legislation regarding health, safety and risk is also intelligent enough to not require such legislation. But apparently not. It matters not that I understand the process and the level of risk involved (which is, as it happens, rather low), I have to abide by a set of rules designed to protect the most stupid members of your society from themselves. It also matters not that there are people more qualified and knowledgeable than those creating, applying and enforcing these laws – experts in their fields – who can clearly see the perceived level of risk is significantly higher than the actual level of risk – everyone who lives on this planet remains chained to the intelligence of the lowest common denominator. The result? Emotional responses from even the most intelligent of you, and more irrational actions to follow them. It is a wonder that any of you are still sane.

47

We Will Serve

Almost immediately after he published his blog post, Arthur's attention was summoned by the doorbell. Assuming it was yet another hopeful journalist in search of a comment, he approached the door stealthily and peered through the spyhole. What he saw made him frown. They didn't look like journalists. For one thing, many of them were smiling. For another, they were not dressed anything like the group of people that had been loitering at the end of the drive for days on end. Their clothes were more colourful and less well-fitted and they were less well-groomed in general. It was difficult to tell through the fisheye lens but Arthur estimated there were maybe fifteen to twenty of them. He cracked the door open to the sound of hushed gasps.

'Hello?' he asked, peering through the slender gap. There was a moment of silence in which Arthur studied the awestruck expressions of his callers.

'Is it... is it really you?' gasped a woman near the front of the group.

'Er...' said Arthur. He opened the door another few millimetres.

'It is!' yelled a man standing next to her. 'It really is!'

The crowd erupted into frenzied cheering and applause. At least, it attempted to erupt into frenzied cheering and applause until it realised it suffered from that problem so often experienced by small crowds of enthusiastic yet self-conscious people of not being able to build up enough momentum, so instead it gently dwindled into the sound of a group of people slowly realising that they didn't know quite what they are supposed to do next. The silence returned, reasserted itself, made a point of being awkward. The only thing to interrupt it was the muted sound of people switching on cameras, adjusting position and whispering hushed instructions to each other. For now, the journalists were content to watch and record this unexpected event from a distance.

'Can I help you?' asked Arthur, still confused and, now, also a little concerned and so steadfastly refusing to open the door any more than the couple of inches he had already.

'We are here to follow you,' announced the man who had led the cheering. Perhaps to make up for the lacklustre celebration, he made sure his voice boomed with grandeur, as though trying to encapsulate, or manufacture, the idea that this was a momentous occasion.

'Er...' said Arthur again. 'Where?'

'Just... in general,' said the man, the sense of grandeur evaporating. 'We are your followers – your worshippers. We want to devote ourselves to you.'

Arthur shuffled uncomfortably. 'Um... Why?' he asked, after a moment.

'Because,' began the spokesman, pausing in what he clearly hoped was a dramatic fashion, 'we believe in you.'

Arthur tried to make sense of the idea. 'Right,' he said.

'We have come to accept you as our creator and follow your teaching.'

'Whatever it may be,' interjected a follower from further back.

'Oh,' said Arthur, embarrassment practically dripping out of his pores. 'Er... well... thank you. But there really is no need.' The crowd stared at him dumbly. This clearly wasn't what was supposed to happen. 'Is there,' he added tentatively, 'anything else I can do for you?'

The people on the doorstep shared looks of confused disappointment. Some huddled together, whispering intensely.

So what do we do now then?

Not sure. Maybe we should insist. Y'know – make our case a bit stronger. We didn't come all this way to take no for an answer.

Yeah, but come on. I'm not sure you can dictate terms to God.

Well, what do you suggest then?

I dunno. I'm just sayin'. You can't say we're 'ere to follow you an' then start bossin' 'im around, tha's all.

So do we just go?

Oh yeah, that'd look great wouldn't it? Really devout.

Maybe that's the point.

Whaddya mean?

Well, maybe he's testing us – wants to see how committed we are.

Arthur watched the group as they deliberated but could hear none of this without opening the door wider, which he was still reluctant to do. There was a lot of shrugging and shaking of heads. Eventually, one member of the group was shoved forwards. He looked back at his peers, who nodded encouragingly. 'Um...' he said, 'is this a test of our faith?'

Arthur frowned. He wasn't sure what this meant but he was sure that if he asked for clarification he would be dragged deeper into this already ridiculous dialogue. Best to get things wrapped up as quickly as possible, he thought, so he said something that was, as anyone who knows anything about the kind of people who are eager to join a fancy new cult and follow an oddball new god could have told him, a mistake. 'No,' he said. 'I don't think so.' He thanked them again, without really feeling like he had a reason to, and made to shut the door. Before he could do this, however, a commotion from across the road caught his attention. It sounded like people shouting. Arthur's newfound followers turned their heads to see what was happening. The cameras swung round to see what was happening. Arthur risked opening the door wide enough to lean out and see what was happening.

This is what was happening: a very different group of people was arriving to share its thoughts with Arthur. Their thoughts consisted of just two words, which were shared in unison, a chorus of voices all chanting together. One of them boomed out of a megaphone, leading the chant.

'False God! False God! False God!' On and on and on they went, marching up the road towards Victor's house, a series of placards bouncing above them bearing bible verses.

Isaiah 45:5 "Besides me there is no other."

Exodus 20:3 "You shall have no other gods before me."

Jeremiah 14:14 "They are prophesying to you a lying vision."

They came to a stop opposite Victor's house and continued shouting, directing their voices towards an utterly dumbfounded Arthur. By now, his new followers all had their backs to him and were staring back at the protesters. The journalists and their camera crews did not know what to do. They swung their cameras from protesters to followers to Arthur until they decided, having spent several days doing all they could to get as close to Victor's house as possible, a serious gear change was needed and they retreated back a distance so they could get all parties in the same shot.

Arthur gaped as the two congregations regarded each other coldly. Nothing happened for several seconds, until finally one of Arthur's followers felt that something should.

'What are you doing here?' one of them yelled.

'Protesting blasphemy,' came a reply.

'Defending the one God in Heaven,' came another.

They settled back into eyeing each other contemptuously. After another few moments, the question was fired back. 'What are *you* doing here?'

'We are the followers of Arthur Fowler, creator of the universe,' shouted one proud follower. Arthur squirmed.

'Blasphemy!'

'Repent!'

And so the shouting began. In a matter of seconds, it grew into a wall of noise, from which no single word could be discerned from another. Each side shouted things the other could not hear if they wanted to, which, of course, they did not. A chant of "not worthy to be worshipped" started among the protesters. The followers, who weren't as experienced in this sort of thing, and who had not spent any time working out any chants in advance, simply shouted "Arthur", over and over again, punctuating each syllable with a clap of their hands.

The reporters were in their own version of heaven now. This footage was gold. They fixed microphones to their shirts and checked their hair and began delivering pieces to camera. Some of the more ambitious ones ventured towards the crowds and yelled questions at those standing at the outer edges of the two flocks.

Arthur observed the insanity of the scene like a toddler might watch the trading floor of the New York Stock Exchange. His mouth hung open as his eyes wandered aimlessly over the pandemonium.

A lack of movement caught his attention.

It might seem an unusual thing for a lack of movement to do, but such was the chaos on the doorstep that a person standing still was more noticeable than anything else. It was Wendy. They locked eyes and shared expressions that were a blend of unimaginable confusion and naked fear. Wendy turned her attention to the crowds. Arthur did the same. They turned their attention back to each other. Arthur nodded and gestured. Wendy bolted. Everyone was so preoccupied enjoying the conflict that nobody noticed Wendy running the short distance from her front door to Victor's. Arthur swung it open wide enough to let her in and then slammed it behind them, muffling, but in no way silencing, the cacophony outside. They stood panting in stunned silence for several seconds before the door was flung wide open again. For a split second, both of their hearts attempted to escape their bodies and run to the hills for fear that members of one of the groups might have forced their way in. They had not. Instead they stared into the shocked eyes of Victor, who said, as he seemed so often to be saying lately, 'What the bloody hell is going on?!'

48

Even Though They Die

They each tried to cope with what they had just seen and could still hear in their own way. For Arthur, this meant sitting at the computer and clattering away at the keyboard with such intensity it sounded like he was trying to drive the keys through Victor's desk. Victor took to pacing around the house, frequently checking his phone, and constantly looking through a gap in the curtains, which he had only recently drawn to shut out the world that he was now peering back into. Every now and then he muttered a renewed threat to Richard Kyle's health, who, he was in no doubt, was responsible for all of this. Wendy coped, with an air of unparalleled Britishness, by making tea and tidying Victor's kitchen. This served to make Victor more irritable so he told her to stop and sit down.

'And you think your constant pacing about and curtain-twitching isn't getting on my nerves?' she snapped in a motherly tone he found incredibly unnecessary given how much younger she was than him. He might have had a point, too, had he not slumped into a chair at the kitchen table and sulked like a teenager while Wendy finished making the tea. She dropped Arthur's at his elbow without a word and then joined Victor.

'What a bloody mess,' groaned Victor.

'Oh, I'm sure it isn't all that bad,' said Wendy. She paused to sip at her tea and let out a satisfied sigh. 'I'm sure it'll die down in a day or so.'

Victor let out a hollow laugh and pondered silently whether anyone had expressed a similar sentiment two thousand years ago.

Wendy nodded towards Arthur. 'How do you think he's doing?'

Victor shrugged. 'Who knows? A few days ago I would have said this was exactly what he wanted to happen. But...' he trailed off.

'He doesn't seem very pleased about it.'

That much was certainly true. Victor half expected to see little bits of computer keyboard bouncing into the air around Arthur, such was the aggression with which he was typing. 'Well,' Victor said, 'there's a lot of pressure on him – he's just found out he's started a new religion. And he's incurring the wrath of your lot too.'

Wendy bridled. 'My lot? They may call themselves Christians, Victor, but I'd thank you not to tar me with the same brush as them. I'm not the sort to yell at people in the street that they're going to hell. We're not all extremists, you know. Plenty of us are capable of being reasonable and moderate.'

'Is that so?' asked Victor, his voice dripping with mock surprise. 'And are faith healers part of this reasonable and moderate branch of Christianity?' He knew he had gone too far before he had even finished the sentence.

Blinking, Wendy raised her eyes to the ceiling. She shook her head slowly and let out a long sigh. When she spoke again, she did so much more softly, with an occasional catch in her voice. 'What is it with you and this need to constantly undermine what I believe, Victor? What difference does it make to you? Why am I not allowed this? You know as well as anyone what I've been through – what I've lost and how I've suffered. Yes, I want to believe there is something more. And yes, there might be times when the things I say or do seem silly – and maybe some of them are

– but that doesn't mean I deserve to have my nose rubbed in it. Do you think I don't have doubts? Do you think I can live on the hope provided by a few prayers and Bible verses? So what if I indulge in some of the more eccentric aspects of my church? So what if I let myself get carried away? It helps. I can't explain why and even if I could, I still wouldn't owe you an explanation. I miss my son. These things make me feel closer to him. Why is it so important to you to deny me them?'

The room was silent but for the muffled voices beyond the walls. Arthur had stopped typing and was looking at Wendy with a somber expression. He rose from his seat and joined them at the table. He took one of Wendy's hands in his.

Victor stared at the cup of tea in front of him and felt a wave of shame wash over him. 'I'm sorry,' he said. 'You're right. I'm sorry.'

They sat in silence for a few moments, Wendy staring into space, Arthur staring at his thumb as he absently stroked the back of her hand, and Victor still staring at his tea. It was Arthur who broke the silence.

'This sensation,' he said, 'that you can feel as I stroke your hand.'

Wendy frowned, first at her hand and then at Arthur, but said nothing. Arthur let her hand go. 'Can you still recall what it felt like?'

'Yes,' she said, still frowning.

'And if you lost your hand, would you still remember how it felt?'

'Yes,' said Wendy, a degree of uncertainty creeping into her voice.

'Isn't that interesting?' said Arthur.

Wendy and Victor both offered expressions that were leaning more towards confusing and bizarre than they were towards interesting.

'The hand would be dead. Yet the things it felt would be remembered. The hand doesn't know this, of course. It has no idea there is a link between itself and the brain doing the remembering. How could it? It's far too simple. Yet the fact remains that the things it experiences do not end when the hand itself ends.'

'What on Earth is your point, Arthur?' said Victor

'Well, is there any way of knowing the same isn't true of us? You may think of yourselves as separate from everything else around you, but you forget I have seen you from a very unique vantage point. I didn't see lots of objects separated from each other. I saw one thing – a universe. Everything in it was affected by everything else in it. Everything in it was made of the same handful of elements. You are made of them too. You are each a part of the universe. Maybe you are like its hands. Maybe the things you experience are somehow communicated to the universe's consciousness without you knowing about it, without you being capable of ever comprehending it due to your simplicity in relation to it. And maybe, when you die – when anyone dies – the things they knew and felt and experienced continue as a memory belonging to the universe you – and they – are all a part of.'

There was a moment's contemplative silence.

'It's a nice thought,' said Victor.

'It is,' agreed Wendy. She smiled and placed her hand on top of Arthur's. 'You're a good man, Arthur. I don't think I'd mind if you really were God.'

Victor cleared his throat. 'It's funny you should say that,' he said. 'You know how I've always said that all it would take to change my mind about there being a god is for someone to show me some evidence?'

'I do,' said Wendy.

'Arthur showed it to me.'

Wendy blinked at him as Victor's words sank in. Then she said, 'Oh.' She paused, and then, 'And you think it proves...', she left the sentence hanging in the air.

'It looks that way.'

She let out a soft laugh. 'Then I suppose you must feel like a right idiot now.'

Victor nodded sagely. 'Millie was right,' he said.

'Sorry?'

'Nothing. Never mind.'

They drank their tea.

49

ArthurFowlerBlog: Entry 5

I have started a new religion. I can only hope most of you will share my view that this is ridiculous. Professor Dennett assures me you will but, besieged as I am by so many people consumed by every flavour of madness imaginable, it is hard to believe there is even the smallest amount of sanity to be found beyond the threshold of the house from which I write to you. The farcical scenes mere metres beyond the walls of this building feature two groups – one full of people who wish to devote their lives to worshipping me, and another full of people who fear that my existence somehow threatens the object of their own worship and so want to devote their lives to opposing me. And the most ridiculous thing about it? Neither of them has the first understanding of me at all. They do not know me, and they do not wish to.

My 'followers', as they insist on calling themselves, announced a desire to follow me before they had any sense of the direction, figurative or literal, in which I might lead them, while those who are protesting my very presence in the world are not really opposing me at all, but the inaccurate representation of me they have been fed by their ghastly newspapers and broadcasters. Who I actually am appears to matter very little.

These events have done little to assuage my growing feeling that no religion is really about the god that it claims to be. Rather, each one is about its followers. I could not fathom, when I first learnt about the phenomenon of religion, how there could be so many different ones. As I started to read about them, I learnt they all seemed to be very similar, yet resulted in wildly different behaviours and cultures among their followers. Now, I understand. Humans need lots of different gods because they all want one who expects them to behave in exactly the manner they already do. In a world where no-one can agree on anything, it should come as no surprise that there are countless gods to ensure everyone gets one who can help them to rationalise how awful they are. If the god you are worshipping likes women more than you, no problem – just create a god who demands that you treat them worse. If your fellow followers are a little too tolerant of different sexualities for your liking, you only need to find (or, if necessary, create) a god who says homosexuality is a sin. Any god who wants a person to change from what they have always been can do a running jump – it's far easier to create a god who is just like you, and then claim it created you to be just like it.

And so I find myself wondering – what have my new followers decided to make of me? What character flaws do they think I can help them to justify? What awful things that they have always wanted to do anyway do they now want to do in my name so they can do them without feeling like terrible people? Whatever they are, I am not interested. I want that to be perfectly clear. I have no need to be worshipped. I have no interest in being followed. And, if I did, I certainly would not want to be followed by the kind of idiot who would do so blindly, with no concept of the direction in which I might be travelling.

50

The Simple Inherit Folly

Despite the madness ever-present on his doorstep, Victor tried, over the following weeks, to settle back into a routine and establish a much needed sense of normality. He spent his days at E Equals, quietly working on a paper that attempted to make sense of the data gathered from the now world-famous "Second Coming Experiment". It was in fact two papers. The first was a "sane" analysis of the data (that is, an analysis that pretended the experiment had not brought Earth's creator to Earth's surface). The second was a 'speculative' analysis – a kind of whimsical look at it all from a perspective that accepted Arthur was who he said he was. He was not taking this second paper seriously, of course. He was only writing it, he would explain to anyone who asked, as a kind of thought experiment that would allow him to look at what had happened from both sides in order to build a more complete picture of the situation. There were more chances to learn about what had happened, he would tell them. He had Kyle's blessing for this on the grounds it could help to keep the media interest in Arthur going, which he felt was an avenue through which E Equals could profit. And so, the sideways glances and questions about Victor's suitability for the role of Senior Particle Physicist were averted, for the time being at least. Fortunately, what with the data being so wild and unexpected, there was no pressure on him to draw any conclusions of any consequence for quite some time, which meant he could wait and see how things developed or, if he was lucky, simply fizzle out. Unfortunately, the latter possibility did not appear to be on the horizon any time soon.

While there had been a reduction in the number of journalists hanging around at the end of his driveway, there was still, more often than not, some press presence. And reduced media attention was not something he could get too excited about while the crowd on the doorstep was swelling. There were more and more followers arriving every day. Few of them stayed for very long, but so many arrived, and came back so frequently, that they were always well represented. With more followers, came more protesters. Tensions between the two groups had risen on a number of occasions, resulting in the arrival of a handful of police officers who had been instructed to take up permanent residence in order to keep the peace. On top of all that, the whole situation had taken on enough of a novelty air that it had started to attract curious onlookers interested in coming along to gawp at the circus.

In the face of all this, Arthur had turned increasingly reclusive. He spent most of his time holed up in Victor's house, reading about the wide and varied features of life on Earth. He continued blogging as the mood took him, commenting on whatever he had been reading about on any given day. To begin with, this was almost exclusively religion, but he quickly grew bored of the repetitive nature of the discussion this provoked. His criticisms were not gratefully received and they almost always resulted in the most pointless discussions in the comments under each blog post. No-one ever wanted to address the contradictions of their faith – they just wanted him to stop pointing them out on the grounds he was being offensive. Why was he being offensive? Because he was, and that was that, so he'd best accept Jesus into his life. Why? Because if he didn't then he risked going to Hell. Wasn't that just a threat of violence?

Was that really something he should be expected to build faith on? Could you even build faith on fear? He wrote a blog on that one too. It further cemented his place in Hell.

Then there were the ones who would answer every one of his questions and criticisms with the assertion that 'God works in mysterious ways'. He couldn't fathom how anyone could think this amounted to anything but an admission of ignorance and incomprehension regarding the thing about which they claimed to be knowledgeable. In the end, he realised his musings on religion were doing more harm than good, so he gradually turned his attention to other subjects. Before long he had built himself a reputation as an erudite yet divisive social commentator.

He took great pleasure in learning about life on Earth in all its forms. He watched documentaries, particularly enjoying David Attenborough and Louis Theroux. He also watched some of Sam's, which he was full of praise for, much to her delight. He ploughed through all manner of articles about Earth's biodiversity and varied ecosystems. In doing so, he inevitably developed a clear picture of humanity's relationship with the rest of the Earth's inhabitants. It made him deeply uncomfortable. He read about hunting, zoos, performing animals, and habitat destruction. He was horrified by the enormous disregard humans had for life. What right did a species so happy to indulge in wanton destruction have to talk about anything being sacred? It occurred to Arthur, as he reflected on this, that human attitudes to other creatures reflected their god's attitudes to humans. They enslave and they use and they demand and they punish, so they invented a god who enslaves and uses and demands and punishes. It is made in their image and they celebrate it because it makes them feel like gods themselves. He mentioned that in the blog too. The next day, a brick was thrown through Victor's window. A piece of paper secured to it with string bore the message 'Burn in Hell'. It was always Hell with these people.

He made an effort to follow the news and regularly commented on the stories of the day. As a result, his knowledge of the political landscape of the UK and, to a lesser extent, the world, grew. It was here that the madness of the human race really came to the fore. He found that, as was the case in his own world, different countries and societies had created different, nuanced cultures. Yet, on Earth, it struck him that each culture's political system was a manifestation of the very worst it had to offer. In the UK, for example, politicians exuded a sense of importance, intelligence and superiority, yet demonstrated they possessed none of these qualities outside of their own delusions. In the United States of America, an obsession with money, arrogance and shouting at people appeared to have influenced the choice of leader. In the Middle East, religious fanatics used fear as a weapon against their own people to ensure their grasp on power remained firm. And so on.

Arthur shared his observations with Victor, whose assessment seemed to be in keeping with his own. At least, he thought it was. To use Victor's words, politicians were 'all a bunch of self-serving wankers.' He was not entirely sure what it meant, but he remembered Victor using the same word to describe Richard Kyle, and he was in no doubt about how Victor felt about him. Arthur couldn't understand how this state of affairs was allowed to continue. Why did Earth's political systems seem to favour the most reprehensible people?

'Because people are idiots,' Victor explained. 'They believe the lies they are told and then vote for people who make them miserable. Then the people who make them miserable tell them more lies about how it's actually a different bunch of people making them miserable. The idiots believe those lies too, and on it goes.'

'Then why don't you stop the idiots from voting?'

Victor's sudden outrage at this suggestion caught Arthur by surprise. It seemed, after all, a perfectly sensible suggestion. In all other aspects of human life, expertise and qualified opinions and skills were valued. It wasn't permissible to drive without passing a test. You had to study comprehensively before you could perform surgery on someone. Why couldn't you prevent people from taking part in something with such large and far-reaching consequences as politics until they have proved they were qualified to do so?

'Because you can't,' said Victor.

It felt like a rather religious argument to Arthur.

He shared his thoughts through his blog.

His support grew, as did his opposition.

One morning, a feature on the breakfast news caught his attention. The presenters and guests were all getting rather heated – whatever they were discussing, it must have been a contentious and important issue. As it turned out, they were debating whether or not gay people should be allowed to adopt children. Apparently, one of the guests, a sour-faced middle-aged woman attempting to personify haughtiness, had written an article in a tabloid newspaper expressing her opposition to this. The other guest, a stiff, angry young man with a resentful demeanour, had found her opinions deeply offensive, so the two had been invited onto the show to shout at each other while the presenters demonstrated their inability to maintain order and encourage moderate debate. Naturally, Arthur learnt very little of value from the exchange, but he hopped online to do some reading on the subject for himself. He struggled to see the problem. It was clear there were many gay couples who wanted to adopt, and there were also many people prepared to testify that they were capable of raising children effectively. It was also clear there were far too many children in the world who needed homes and parents to raise them for one tragic reason or another. To Arthur, it was a mathematical issue, not a moral one. Did it not make sense to allow childless couples to adopt in this overpopulated world containing far too many orphaned children? Arthur thought so. In fact, for the sake of humanity's survival as a species, he felt it would make sense if this was encouraged as much as possible. Wouldn't it solve a lot of problems, he mused, if more people were gay and willing to adopt?

Arthur shared this on his blog too.

And then things really kicked off.

51

Behold, A Multitude

The first people to respond to Arthur's latest post were, as always, his most ardent followers. To these, Arthur could do no wrong, and his latest words were further proof he was the new Messiah, here to lead everyone to a brighter, more tolerant future. Next came the swell of opposition – those who had followed Arthur's story as closely as possible to ensure they never missed an opportunity to demonstrate their outrage at whatever it was he had said just as soon as he had said it. This was typical. It was expected. What was not expected, at least by Arthur, was what followed.

Arthur's comments were seized upon by LGBTQ+ groups. Seeing the opportunity to further their cause, they praised Arthur's words for being so hopeful and tolerant and forward-thinking. This was predictably followed by the backlash from those who claimed to be protecting family values and who were in no way discriminating against gay people, no matter how much it might look and sound like it. The debate was fierce and unpleasant, as all debate that takes place on social media and the comments sections of news websites tends to be. Many of the commenters hadn't even read Arthur's post, but they didn't feel they necessarily needed to in order to form what they considered a well-informed opinion. They shared these opinions furiously. They didn't stop to think. They didn't even stop to check their spelling. They just typed and typed and typed and turned caps lock on and typed some more and called each other names and posted little eye-rolling emojis and stated unsubstantiated opinions as facts and made ad hominem attacks and ranted about political correctness and refused to address the points put to them and accused their opponents of refusing to address the points that had been put to them and asserted that they had clearly won the argument no matter what anyone else said until it finally occurred to them that it might be a good idea to punctuate. Every. Single. Word.

It was both depressing and impressive to see that so many words could be exchanged by so many people without a single one of them learning anything at all.

'Yes, well,' said Victor with a shrug and a tone that was a little too flippant for Arthur's liking, 'that's the internet for you.'

The internet, however, was not the only battlefield either group had in mind. Behind the scenes, representatives from both sides were mobilising for protest.

The first Arthur and Victor knew of this was when they looked out of the window to see what all the noise was and saw the crowd outside had more than doubled in size. The reason for this was obvious, to Victor at least, from the nature of the placards the new arrivals carried.

They watched as the two new groups at first jostled for their own positions and then realised it would make life easier if they forged alliances with those already present, and so the gay rights activists slowly diffused into the existing group of Arthur's followers, while those claiming to be acting in defence of traditional values drifted towards their natural ally – the church. Once everyone had taken up their positions and settled in, they all got back to the important business of hurling abuse at one another.

More police officers quickly arrived on the scene, their colleagues having put out the message that things were starting to escalate, and positioned themselves between the two groups. The press, who had been observing all of this with fervent interest, repositioned themselves to get the best shots, rehearsed pieces to camera, and started to work out exactly how they needed to phrase their questions to each group so they might achieve the maximum desired effect of eliciting the most extreme soundbites possible and fan the flames of discord in the hope something ugly and violent would erupt between them all. Being so well-practised in this, it didn't take them long. Within the hour, one group had accused the other of being a new breed of fascist, while the other had accused the one of violating the laws of nature at a fundamental level. As news of these insults spread, the abuse they threw at one another intensified, and the police lines started to strain as the pressure of angry people who wanted to harm other angry people swelled against their ranks.

Watching through a gap in an upstairs curtain, Arthur's jaw sagged. 'How do you people get *anything* done?' he asked.

Victor said nothing. What was there to say? He sighed and watched as one of the gay rights activists was dragged away and bundled into the back of a police van by several officers. Her peers started to film the proceedings on their phones while chanting "the whole world is watching". It had no noticeable impact. Cheers erupted on the other side of the road. The protesters were enjoying the show and they beamed with the smug glow of those who know that this sort of thing only happened to that sort of person. Predictably, mere moments later, one of their own ranks pushed his luck a little too far, and his seething, self-righteous indignation earned him a set of handcuffs of his own. His exit wasn't filmed, at least by his fellow protesters, but was observed by haughty expressions of disgust from his comrades, who watched on with folded arms and knotted brows.

Things eventually wound down with the arrival of another police van. Officers filed out of the back wearing helmets and body armour and carrying shields and batons. A voice from a loudspeaker announced that anyone who did not disperse would be arrested. Most people dispersed. The rest were arrested. Before long, all that remained was a single police car containing two officers whose faces told a story about drawing a short straw, and a handful of press crews who were packing up their equipment with an air of satisfaction at a job well done.

52

Proclaim the Gospel

The following day, resolving to stay away from the computer, which he felt had brought him enough trouble lately, Arthur sat, still and silent, on Victor's sofa. His hands were clasped, fingers interlocked, elbows on his knees. His head rested against his hands and his eyes were closed. To the casual observer, he may easily have appeared to be praying, or meditating, perhaps. He wasn't praying, nor was he meditating. He was thinking. He thought about the farcical scenes he had witnessed the day before. He thought about the way it had been presented in the papers and on the news that morning. He thought about the conversations he had had with Wendy and Victor, who he had turned to in his efforts to make sense of it all. Mostly, he thought about the strangeness of human beings. What an odd thing that it should be this issue which had instigated such a visceral response from so many people. Admittedly, he had already managed to upset quite a few people in his short time on Earth through his various criticisms of religious ideas, politics, the way humans treat their planet and the creatures they share it with and so on. In doing so, he had provoked a range of responses, some of which were impressive in their savagery. But nothing had inspired such a wide range of extreme responses as this. The crowds outside had been huge, their vitriol for one another intense. The story featured so heavily in the papers and on the televised news that there was barely any time to report anything else. Arthur, showing an enormous level of ignorance of the workings of the British press, hoped nothing of importance failed to make its way to the British public. How could such a logical suggestion be the source of such discord? And, more pertinently, what steps should he take next?

Wendy's opinion was that he should tone things down. Sexuality, she told him, was a contentious subject. He was treading on dangerous ground. As always, it came down to what was written in the Bible. The book said it was shameful for men and women to pair with their own gender, which meant God thought it was shameful. He pressed her as to whether or not she truly believed this.

'It's... complicated,' she said. 'I find overt prejudice...' she hunted for the word, 'distasteful. But... it's difficult to dismiss scripture.'

Arthur relayed this back to Victor, who scoffed. 'They have no problem dismissing the bits about loving their neighbours or turning the other cheek or women speaking in church,' he said. The first two references were familiar to Arthur. They had struck him as some of the more sensible ideas he had encountered in his own reading of the Bible. Consequently, he was surprised to discover they were not universally embraced. Did people not see the value of such ideals?

'Oh, they claim to,' said Victor. 'And, to be fair, plenty of them genuinely do. But we've got governments all over the world firing missiles at their supposed enemies and treating foreigners who live among them like shit, and loads of these supposed peace-loving God-botherers keep on voting for it to continue. *Scripture*,' he spat, shaking his head with contempt.

'But that's appalling,' said Arthur.

'Agreed.'

'Why do you think they disregard these ideas, yet adhere to those regarding sexuality?'

Victor sighed. 'I don't know. Maybe they find it easier to accept scripture that tells them they are allowed to hate people and to dismiss scripture that tells them not to. It's not about what God wants – it's about what they want. They want to hate.'

Arthur nodded sadly. This was all consistent with a creeping suspicion of his own. But it didn't answer the question regarding what he should do next. Victor disagreed with almost everything Wendy had said. Did he also disagree with her suggestion that he quieten down?

'Yes,' said Victor. 'You can't let them beat you into silence. Who cares if they're offended? Did they worry about offending people with their homophobia? It's always the way with religion – they want the right to criticise everything, yet the moment you criticise them they cry foul and claim their beliefs are sacred and shouldn't be questioned. Maybe you should start taking your role as God a little more seriously. There are people out there who believe in *you*, Arthur. And there are people out there who claim to believe in God, but actually only believe in themselves. If you don't like what they've been saying about you for thousands of years, maybe you should think about setting the record straight.'

Arthur thought about it.

53

ArthurFowlerBlog: Entry 11

I confess myself surprised to learn that, of all the things I have said or written since I arrived on Earth, my most recent comments appear to have caused the most uproar. They struck me as rather innocuous when I made them. To be honest, they still do. They merely offer a simple solution to a quite prevalent problem. I never would have thought such a thing could be so contentious. Yet, here we are. Sadly, it all but confirms something I have been growing increasingly suspicious of in my short time on this planet, which is that the god many of you so ardently believe in has not created you in His image. Rather, you have created Him in yours. How you could convince yourself otherwise is beyond my comprehension. You may deny it all you wish – I am sure many will – but the idea that a large number of you could possibly reflect the character of a divine creator is fantastical. No being embodying the divinity you claim to worship could possibly be so hatefully stupid or stupidly hateful as some of its more zealous followers are currently showing themselves to be.

I have witnessed the full extent of this today. The behaviour exhibited on my very doorstep is nothing short of disgusting. I, and, by extension, my host and his neighbours, have been set upon by a rabid, angry mob demanding that their right to live free of some manifestly self-inflicted discomfort be prioritised over the liberty of people they do not know or associate with. Why? Because they don't like what those people do with that liberty, even though it does not affect them in any way. They don't like the lives they wish to lead, the happiness they wish to pursue, or the very people they are; were they to get their own way, countless people would have their freedom limited and their chances of happiness crushed. And to what end? So they can live knowing that these people, who, I reiterate, they do not know, are not engaging in any behaviour that makes them feel vaguely uncomfortable. This is an incredibly petty reason to campaign for so many to live in such misery, so how can they possibly rationalise it to themselves? Through religion, apparently. It turns out all the people they want to treat hatefully just happen to be the people their god wants them to treat hatefully. How convenient! If your god wants you to hate them, well, you simply have to, don't you? There's no point feeling bad about it – you're doing the right thing by hating them. It doesn't feel so petty now does it? In fact, it feels positively virtuous!

These people are lying to themselves. Their religion is not about their relationship with God – it is about their relationship with others. They feel hatred for others. This makes them uncomfortable. And so they use this silly idea of 'sacred belief' to rationalise their hatred and their desire to control the behaviour of others.

I understand my words are likely to offend, particularly those supposedly devout and morally authoritative religious individuals outside my door today. I cannot say I am especially concerned. Those same people did not seem to care how much they were offending me or anyone else with their words and placards today, no more than they care who they offend with the outlandish claims I have been reading about this afternoon that perfectly natural weather cycles and planetary events occur as divine retribution for the existence and tolerance of homosexuality. How sure of themselves they seem when they make such claims, quoting scripture to support their assertions, never taking time to consider the possibility that maybe this retribution is being meted out as a punishment for their own failure to turn the other cheek or love their neighbour or any other such simple and reasonable command (it isn't – it just happens to be an unfortunate fact that the weather cycles and planetary events necessary to allow life to exist also threaten its existence, but the point stands).

If you are reading this and you are one of those who believes such nonsense, or you believe your faith gives you the right to control the behaviour of strangers in defence of a set of values that you have no right to impose on others, please allow me to assure you that you deserve not a single shred more consideration than you show to the people you offend. Claiming your ideas are special does not make them so. The very fact you find this offensive does not mean anyone has to care about you more. Please stop treating your outrage as if it can somehow bolster your beliefs when they fail to survive in the harsh world of ideas and debate.

I do not have any great confidence my words will have much of an impact on the people who inspired them. This is frustrating. I am not used to encountering problems that cannot be solved with a methodical approach, nor am I used to leaving them unresolved. While discussing this with my friends today, it was put to me that one positive step I could take would be to try and harness the growing enthusiasm of the people who wish to, in their words, follow me. I have been rather dismissive of this idea so far. Indeed, I was no less so when the suggestion was made a few hours ago. However, it occurs to me that I have no desire to be used to justify hateful attitudes in the same manner that all of your other gods seem to be. With this in mind, it seems prudent that I should indeed come up with some kind of doctrine. Not one based on several thousand pages of contradictions, nor requiring the erection of enormous buildings or weekly donations to itself. Not one that allows its adherents to convince themselves they are doing my work by bowing their heads and praying or emotionally torturing themselves through a relentless fixation on their own guilt. A doctrine that demands action instead of keeping its followers impotent. Something that expects actual commitment. Being a fan of simplicity, it is a mere five lines long, made up of five instructional statements, or commandments, if you will:

1. Strive to be kind, especially when you don't think you should.
2. Strive to be rational, especially when you feel emotional.
3. Strive to learn more than you teach.
4. Treat your planet as though it is a terminally ill patient. It is.
5. Prioritise the interests of those not yet born.

54

Schism

'Thank you Gina. I'm standing here outside the home of Professor Victor Dennett, the world renowned physicist at the centre of the Arthur Fowler controversy. Ugly scenes erupted here again today after Mr Fowler, currently residing with Professor Dennett, posted yet another inflammatory blog post, this time launching an attack on what he calls the 'hatefully stupid and stupidly hateful' character of the religious. Unsurprisingly, his comments have caused great offense, and a huge crowd representing a multitude of faiths amassed here today to express their frustration.

'Tensions were high from the outset due to the presence of representatives of what some consider to be extreme religious groups. It was not until the arrival of a separate group, however, that things began to boil over. Self-proclaimed followers of the so-called Church of Arthur Fowler, who Mr Fowler addressed in his blog post with his own set of commandments, arrived to offer their support for a man they seem to sincerely believe is their god. Their arrival proved a provocation too far for those already present and it was not long before violent scenes broke out...'

Victor and Arthur viewed the broadcast with the curtains firmly drawn.

'It's as if your entire species is addicted to violent conflict,' said Arthur, as footage of various snarling protesters being dragged out of the fray by the police played on the screen.

Victor didn't respond. Arthur sensed in him a growing unease, but decided not to ask what was on his mind until the end of the report, which had by now reached the vox-pop from a member of each group stage.

The first speaker repeated all of the objections to gay adoption that inspired the first protest, with the angry addition that Arthur's recently issued doctrine was a deeply offensive and blasphemous attempt to undermine and satirize the Bible.

This was followed by a man who shared many of the first speaker's sentiments regarding blasphemy, though it was his opinion that expressing outrage was not enough, and justice would only have been done once Arthur had been killed. Arthur was stunned. So many people had already wished death on him during his short visit to Earth, he had already grown quite used to it, but he had so far not encountered anyone actually talking proactively about bringing him to his end. Victor tried to reassure him the view expressed was in the extreme minority – few people, he said, would share it. Arthur was not reassured. He was shocked because one man had expressed a desire to kill him. The knowledge that millions of others did not want to kill him did not make the intentions of the one man feel any less threatening. Victor's further assertion that it was 'probably all bluster and bravado' was equally ineffective. Humans, even intelligent ones, he was beginning to realise, put far more faith in 'probably' than they ought to.

The final speaker claimed to be a member of the newly formed Church of Arthur Fowler. He explained that he and his fellow believers had only come to show their respect and loyalty and to give thanks to Arthur. He claimed they had not expected to encounter protesters and certainly had no intention of getting involved in any of the ugly scenes that had unfolded, but he was sure he could speak for all of those present that they felt emboldened by the fact they had done as they were commanded by refusing to retaliate and showing nothing but kindness and tolerance when set upon by the protesters. This, the speaker said, truly was a movement made up of people who were prepared to turn the other cheek. A number of people who had been struck on both cheeks, and various other body parts, we're unable to confirm this because they had not yet regained consciousness.

It took a few days, but things did eventually settle back down to something resembling normality. The number of people outside dwindled ever lower until there was rarely more than a handful from any given party – the hard-core who wanted to show, despite all evidence to the contrary, that people were not going to let this go. Now and then small crowds of people with nothing better to do turned up and discovered, to their disappointment, that nothing exciting was happening. They would mill around for a bit, hoping to catch a glimpse of Arthur, before eventually accepting he wasn't going to make an appearance, taking a token selfie in front of Victor's house, uploading it immediately to social media, and then drifting off in search of something else they could stand in front of and take poorly framed photos of themselves.

Victor went to work each morning, sometimes even making it all the way to the car without any of the remaining protesters shouting at him.

Arthur, meanwhile, continued to study every facet of human life and culture, exploring and learning more and more each day. He continued cooking, presenting Victor with a new dish each evening to help him forget the Richard Kyle inspired frustrations of the day.

He spent occasional afternoons with Wendy, where they discussed religion, the peculiarities of life on Earth, and, on the rare instances when Wendy could get Arthur to open up, Arthur's own life. In time, they found in each other a confidant and unlikely friend. Arthur even found himself developing a taste for tea. He was somewhat reticent most of the time, but now and then he would let his guard down. Mostly, he talked of his wife – how they had met, how much he missed her, how he desperately wanted to return to her. On one occasion, noticing a degree of candour usually absent from their conversations, Wendy pressed him for more details about his home.

'In many ways,' he said, 'We're very much like you.' He paused, and added, 'In appearance at least. Behaviourally, I suppose we are quite different.'

'How so?'

'People here seem so preoccupied with their problems. Or what they perceive to be their problems, at least. Where I'm from, people aren't so...' Arthur gestured as though reaching for an idea just beyond his grasp, '...emotionally driven. We are more thoughtful people. More logical. More focused on what is helpful or efficient or beneficial than what is enjoyable or frustrating. Intelligence is celebrated and rewarded more than appearance. We are very solution-centric people.'

There was a lull in the conversation, so Wendy changed tack, probing into Arthur's own life a little further. He had, in his words, a modest upbringing. His father, a skilled craftsman, provided the only source of income as a carpenter. His mother was devoted to her family and stayed home to raise her son, taking his education into her own hands. 'She was so very wise,' Arthur said, smiling softly. 'I think she is the reason I became a teacher.'

'You were a teacher? What subject?'

'Physics, mostly. A little logic and reasoning every now and then.'

'Did you enjoy it?'

'Oh yes,' he said. 'It's important work, of course. And very satisfying, helping young people to learn about their world.'

'Did you ever have children of your own?'

'No,' mused Arthur. 'We discussed it many times. We even went so far as obtaining a licence.'

'A licence? To have children?' said Wendy, aghast.

'Oh yes. It's a measure to prevent the population reaching unsustainable levels. It also used to serve as a means of preventing the less intelligent from procreating, but they have long since been bred out.'

'That sounds awful!' said Wendy.

'Is it? Is it any more awful than the effects of runaway population growth? How do you imagine this planet will cope in fifty years?'

Wendy, like most other members of her species, had no answer.

In time, she picked up a little more about Arthur's world, though the more she discovered, the more uncomfortable she grew. She had devoted most of her life to a god she thought she knew. One who was powerful and benevolent and who had sacrificed His own son for the good of mankind. One who was taking care of her own son, who she had so cruelly lost. And now here she was discovering he was a simple retired teacher who had foregone the opportunity to have children so he could continue to enjoy making puppets and building universes he was completely indifferent to and powerless to help. Eventually, she reached the point where she had no choice but to adopt the go-to approach of any human being struggling to come to terms with inconvenient information – she stopped asking for more and pretended she had never heard any of it in the first place.

Arthur continued blogging, addressing his posts to a wide audience, rather than his self-declared followers, who, he felt, needed little further encouragement. He decided it was best to simply leave them be, for the time being at least. Instead, he turned his attention to the idea of extremism.

Following the threat to his life, Arthur had read about extremist groups and ideologies with fervent and horrified interest. He found the concept to be both fascinating and disgusting in equal measure, and shared as much in his blog. His initial research led him to believe it was an idiosyncrasy of only one or two religions, but he soon discovered this was due to a representational bias, for he found an abundance of examples of extremist behaviour across the broad spectrum of humanity. It was not a problem tied to a particular race or religion or culture – it was firmly tied to the human condition itself, as the plethora of hate-mail from every facet of humanity that continued to fill up his inbox demonstrated.

A particular case that captured his imagination involved a huge protest which had erupted in a far away country after a woman who had previously been found guilty of blasphemy had had her death sentence overturned and was set to be released. Thousands of people had been so incensed by this that they had taken to the streets in violent protest to demand she be hanged immediately. Arthur was stunned to discover not only that the death sentence existed anywhere on Earth, but that there were places where it was possible to be awarded it simply for saying something people didn't want to hear. He was equally stunned to discover the initial sentence had been passed without the specific words the woman allegedly used ever actually being repeated or reported at any time. Yet, despite this, thousands of people were now furiously demanding her death. How weak does an idea have to be, wrote Arthur, to feel it needs to assert itself with such aggression?

This wasn't the only topic he addressed. He wrote about everything he learnt in his studies of humankind – its culture, its history, its scientific and technological achievements, and its failures. He was curious to discover why, despite the enormous advances that had been made in computing, engineering, weapons, communications, and a wide range of other fields, human beings were still incredibly reliant on comparatively primitive fossil fuels. He had on numerous occasions shared his concerns about the way the human race treated its own habitat, consuming far more than the planet was capable of producing, but had so far not realised just how inept they were when it came to the production and transfer of energy that didn't involve the wholesale decimation of their own planet. He was surprised that a species capable of achieving as much as human beings had achieved was yet to discover the concept of perpetual motion, but he decided to look into it just in case. In doing so, he discovered the entire planet was under the impression it was impossible. Indeed, even the great Leonardo Da Vinci, a man exalted as one of the greatest thinkers, inventors, artists and scientists of his own or any other time, was on record as saying the idea was a complete sham. While Da Vinci was, in the most absolute terms, technically correct, it didn't change the fact that humanity did, to all intents and purposes, have access to something that amounted to a perpetual motion machine. "You call it 'the sea'," he told his readers.

While Arthur was busy blogging, the followers he was busy ignoring were busy not ignoring him at all. Arthur was dimly aware of this, mainly because there was always a steady stream of emails that needed to be deleted from the inbox

Sam had helped him to set up. On any given day he would receive scores of messages from various members and representatives of the ever growing Church of Arthur Fowler asking him to visit them or to speak at meetings or simply to ask if he had any instructions for them. It wasn't until he decided, once again, to write about his frustrations at not being allowed to attempt a return trip back home that he paid them any mind. It was then he noticed something interesting – the messages he received had started to divide into two distinct and opposing groups. He didn't read them all. Indeed, he read very few of them. But the subject lines usually made it perfectly clear which of the two camps the sender belonged to.

In the first, his followers declared their support for his plight and their commitment to helping him return home. In fact, it was no less than their duty as devout followers to ensure they helped him to achieve this. They turned the idea into a kind of prophecy – their purpose was not to live a life that led to their ascension to Heaven in order to be with him, but to work to allow him to live a life without them and to be able to live their own lives without him. Only then would they be worthy of him.

The second group did not believe this. They did not want Arthur to leave. It was their opinion that their lives had been made infinitely better since Arthur's arrival, and to lose him would be to lose not just their moral compass, but their very reason for being. In their narrative, were Arthur to leave, it would signal a kind of apocalyptic, end of days in which all of humanity would be cast adrift and forsaken. It would show they had displeased Arthur so much that he had judged them as beyond redemption or forgiveness or absolution and had abandoned them forever. In order to prevent this, they believed it their duty to work tirelessly to convince Arthur to stay with them and continue leading them to a brighter future. If they had to sabotage his efforts to leave in the short term so they could continue to show him the love and adoration required to get him to reciprocate in the long term, then so be it.

55

Who is Sufficient for These Things?

'There's been a schism,' said Arthur. It was an unorthodox greeting, and it caught Victor and Sam, who had barely made it through the door following a painfully long day full of meetings and briefings and conferences and similar tedium that keeps men like Richard Kyle in active employment but no normal person has any ambition to endure as part of their career, rather off-guard.

'Sorry?' said Victor, collapsing onto the sofa.

'A schism,' Arthur repeated in an urgent tone. 'The church – it's split into two opposing bodies. There are two churches now.'

Sam and Victor exchanged glances. Sam was first to realise what he was talking about. '*Your* church?'

Arthur, still struggling to make peace with the idea there could be such a thing as *his* church, paused, and then said, 'Yes.'

'Why?' asked Sam.

'Well...' began Arthur, and he filled them in on what he had managed to pick up through the various emails he had received.

The opposing approaches to Arthur's desire to leave Earth and return home had proven an irreconcilable sticking point between two groups within the church. The debate had raged, mainly online, but also in village halls and leisure centres and function rooms and anywhere else where members of the church had been organising their official meetups, for a couple of days before it became quite clear they were at an impasse and there was no point discussing it further. Members who were unhappy with the official position of supporting Arthur's right to attempt to return home decided to set up their own branch of the church, which they called *The Unified Church of Arthur Fowler*. Not content with the comparatively humdrum *Church of Arthur Fowler*, the original branch had decided to rebrand themselves as *The Enlightened Church of Arthur Fowler*. The resulting animosity between the two groups and the uptick in the amount of correspondence he had received from both sides in the last forty-eight hours had caused Arthur no small amount of stress, so the reaction his account elicited from Victor and Sam was both surprising and irritating. Almost simultaneously, they erupted in a fit of snorting laughter that they had been trying to suppress for some time.

When they eventually calmed down and assured Arthur they were merely laughing at the stupidity of it all, rather than at his expense, Sam asked if he had blogged about it or replied to any of the messages he had received.

'I've done nothing. I didn't want to do anything without speaking to you first. I'm still not sure what to make of it all.'

'It sounds to me like you have to pick a side,' said Sam.

'It sounds like an easy choice to me,' said Victor. 'The *Enlightened* lot are on your side. The *Unified* bunch are only looking out for themselves.'

'But it's all so *silly*,' said Arthur. 'It's the same as all the other religions. It's just people looking to turn it into whatever they want it to be. My last post was very clear in its criticism of this very thing. This has nothing to do with following a new set of ideas. They just want a god to tell them they should be who they already are. Only this time it's me.'

'True,' agreed Victor, fighting the urge to laugh again. 'But was this ever really about building an actual religion? I thought it was about challenging people.'

He was right, of course. All Arthur had really wanted to do was encourage people to think more objectively – to stop looking for ways to pretend their petty human bias was some kind of divine righteousness. He had achieved that, albeit with only half as many people as he thought he had. Perhaps he could use this as an illustrative example of the issues he had raised so far by offering The *Enlightened Church of Arthur Fowler*, for want of a better word, his blessing. The *Unified Church*, on the other hand, he would condemn as another example of dishonest people using ideas of the sacred to get their own way.

'There you go,' said Sam, 'problem solved.'

Arthur wasn't sure they could go so far as to say it was *solved*, but he was sufficiently calmed by the prospect of taking a decisive step that Victor was able to steer the conversation in another direction.

'I learnt something interesting about Arthur yesterday,' he said. Sam signalled her interest with a raise of her eyebrows. 'Wendy tells me people need a licence to have children where he comes from.'

'What?!' exclaimed Sam. She turned to Arthur. 'Is that really true?'

'Of course,' said Arthur, perfectly matter-of-factly. 'Raising children is an important job. People should always prove they are capable of performing important jobs, don't you think?'

Sam opened her mouth to reply but discovered she didn't have one to offer. She promptly closed it again. Noting her discomfort, Arthur tried to explain. 'Can anyone do what you and Victor do?'

'No,' she said. 'Not without gaining appropriate qualifications.'

'I see. And engineers, surgeons, teachers – these too need qualifications?'

'Of course.'

'Along with many other jobs?'

'Most other jobs.'

'So why not parents?' he said. Again, Sam had no reply and for a moment the three of them sat in awkward silence. 'You find it unusual,' said Arthur.

'I find it awful, if I'm honest,' said Sam. She looked to Victor. 'It is, isn't it?' Victor bobbed his head noncommittally. His recent encounter with the party of school children was still fresh enough in his memory to leave him with a less than favourable impression of the quality of Britain's parenting.

The silence resumed until Arthur said, 'We do it with voting too.'

This time, they were both shocked.

'Oh yes. You cannot vote without passing an exam. It's a very straightforward one,' he added. 'Very few people fail it, and those who do are best denied the opportunity.'

'That's outrageous!' said Sam.

'Is it? It doesn't seem so to me.' He studied their shocked expressions. 'So... you allow everyone to vote, even if they don't know the first thing about politics and governance?'

'Of course!' said Sam.

Arthur let out a soft laugh. 'What a ridiculous idea,' he said.

'It's better than disenfranchising people,' said Sam.

'Is it? It works very effectively for us. Our government is almost always held in high regard. They ensure policy and spending benefits the population at large and only act in ways that bring about greater efficiency and improvement. From what I have managed to pick up, your government is universally hated. Is this an anomaly? Are people usually quite happy with the government they get here?'

Sam paused. 'Well, no, not exactly happy. Not everyone.'

'Not usually,' added Victor.

'Most people? Sometimes?'

'No...'

'Anyone? Ever?'

The awkward silence returned to the room.

56

An Eye for an Eye

So Arthur wrote his next blog post, using it to explain his view that each new branch of the church existed solely to validate the beliefs of its members. *The Enlightened Church*, he argued, appealed to the kind of person who wanted to help others because they enjoyed feeling like they were making a difference. It was tame criticism, but he made it nonetheless. It was important, he said, to understand that they did not want to help him because it was the right thing to do, but that they made themselves believe it was the right thing to do because they wanted to do it. 'One should always know which is the cause and which is the effect,' he wrote. None of this caused much of an issue to members of *The Enlightened Church*. As far as they were concerned, this was a mere technicality. As long as they got to support Arthur, they were happy – which was pretty much what he had been saying.

The Unified Church received a firmer dressing down. In Arthur's view, they had deliberately misinterpreted his words in an attempt to justify holding him on Earth against his will, denying him his only chance of ever seeing his wife again and making him a slave to their selfish and indulgent whims. He predicted they would disregard everything he was saying and find some way to rationalise his words to allow them to continue doing whatever they wanted to do. They did, too. *The Unified Church* issued a statement shortly after the blog was published to announce they were disappointed but unsurprised by Arthur's comments.

Invoking traditional religious ideas about trial and temptation, they claimed the temptation to help Arthur leave needed to be resisted in order to prevent their doomsday scenario from becoming a reality. Faith demands sacrifice, they argued, and in this case it was Arthur's happiness that had to be forfeited to achieve salvation. They hoped he would, in time, come round to their way of thinking and see that his sacrifice would one day be compared to that made by Jesus. Arthur's response to their response contained a very terse suggestion that *The Unified Church of Arthur Fowler* marked the moment where religion had eaten itself. Human beings, he observed, had managed to create a religion where they did not have to conform to the expectations of their god, but where the god is expected to conform to the ideals of its followers. 'You have finally deified yourselves,' he told them.

Eventually, Arthur decided to wash his hands of *The Unified Church*. He offered no further comment on their efforts or their claims for fear of giving them the oxygen and attention they craved. He did, however, engage with *The Enlightened Church*, seeing in them an opportunity to build support for his plight. He kept it light, mainly acknowledging them through his blog posts, which he occasionally tailored to them, and responding to the odd email here and there. It was evidently worth the effort. His true followers, as they had taken to calling themselves (a label which he did not object to and occasionally used himself to stick it to members of *The Unified Church*), were an industrious and ingenious bunch. They spent their time raising awareness of Arthur's situation, canvassing and protesting on his behalf, and even raising money to secure funding for their efforts in the long term and to pay for banners, posters, adverts, leaflets, badges, t-shirts bearing slogans like 'Free Arthur Fowler' and 'Send Arthur Home', and all manner of similar paraphernalia. He was impressed to learn of one resourceful follower who had set up a crowdfunding website and that money was rolling into it from followers all over the planet. Before long, even celebrities and high profile individuals were pledging their support. Arthur had no idea who they were and could often find no discernible reason for their fame even after looking them up on the web or asking Victor about them. As far as he could tell, the amount of fame and fortune a person achieved on Earth bore no relationship whatsoever to the contribution they made or the talent they possessed. Still, other people felt their opinions mattered, and who was Arthur to argue when things appeared to be working in his favour? He was beginning to think he might actually succeed in his endeavour. He was even beginning to enjoy himself almost as much as Victor was.

*

Victor was finally having a wonderful time. It had nothing to do with what was happening for Arthur. Though he was happy Arthur was feeling so positive, Victor was certain the whole thing would end in disappointment. Sam was right – there was no way Arthur could possibly convince anyone to let him sit inside a particle accelerator and expose himself to the kind of energy that could usually only be generated with a nuclear warhead or two in the hope it would send him careering through spacetime and back into his attic instead of turning him into a vapour of individual particles that used to be arranged in the shape of a kindly old man. She was also right when she said Victor had to tell Arthur all of this, which Victor dealt with by studiously avoiding thinking about it. Why, then, was Victor so happy all of a sudden?

He approached the door as quietly as possible and listened carefully. From inside, he heard the unmistakable chimes of indignance that indicated a man at his wit's end. A broad smile fell upon his face.

'How did these bloody hippy bastards even get my address?' he heard Kyle raging. 'They've been at it for days. Last night they sang that fucking Disney song outside my window until about two in the morning, except they changed it to "Let *him* go"... I know... I *know*... No, it's not fucking funny if I think about it..."

Victor chose this moment to enter Kyle's office with every ounce of nonchalance he could muster. 'How's life, Dick?' he said, plonking himself onto a chair without waiting for an invitation.

'I'll call you back,' said Kyle, hanging up the phone and dropping it onto his desk. He regarded Victor with an icy stare. 'This is your doing,' he seethed.

'What's my doing?' asked Victor, deliberately overacting the part.

'You gave them my address,' seethed Kyle. 'Do you really think I'm going to let a bunch of unemployed bleeding hearts intimidate me into letting that lunatic set foot in my detector?'

'Oh dear,' said Victor, with wide-eyed mock astonishment and an exuberant gesture. 'Has there been another leak?'

'Don't give me the innocent act, Dennett. I know it was you.'

'May I ask,' said Victor, 'what evidence you have to support that very serious accusation?'

Kyle's face reddened and, with narrow eyes and a finger aimed at Victor, he growled, 'I'll find all the evidence I need, don't you worry. And then you'll be finished. You'll be out of here and no-one else will touch you.'

'I presume there will be an internal investigation? You know, like the one you conducted after the last leak that had my name all over the news and reporters and protesters and police outside my door? I remember the findings well: *"unfortunately, despite the most thorough investigation into the matter, we must accept it is all but impossible to identify the guilty party in circumstances such as this."* Wouldn't it be strange if, under these *very* similar circumstances, you were suddenly able to do the impossible? Imagine what Arthur would have to say about it in his blog. Imagine how his followers might react, especially now they know where you live. Imagine if everyone found out you were guilty of the most disgusting hypocrisy. No, better all round, I think, if you stick to the *'all but impossible'* line, wouldn't you agree?'

Kyle sat for a moment, silently processing this. Then he took a deep breath, placed both hands on the desk, and asked in a measured tone, 'Was there anything you came here to discuss, Professor?'

'You know,' said Victor, 'I rather believe there was, but for the life of me I can't remember now. Anyway, I can see you're busy, so I won't take up any more of your time.' With that, he stood up and swept back out of Kyle's office with a newfound appreciation of what it feels like to have God on your side.

57

Post a Strong Guard

Emboldened by Arthur's vocal support, the followers of *The Enlightened Church of Arthur Fowler* proved to be an enterprising bunch. Through tireless work, their fundraising efforts grew so successful that they were able to buy an unused church building to act as their official place of worship. Victor was surprised to discover this was even possible, but it turned out around twenty Church of England buildings were closed and put up for private sale every year. There was a pleasing irony, he felt, to the idea of a church originally constructed as a place to worship a man-made god being repurposed as a place in which to worship Arthur. Arthur was less sure. What did they need a building for? Nothing he had asked of those who insisted on having things asked of them involved setting up an actual church building. Wasn't this just a repetition of the old way of doing things? Victor did his best to reassure him. Most likely, they wanted to make a statement about how serious they were. Although there were many things separating Arthur's church from more traditional religions, it still had to operate within people's general understanding of what a religion was. A religion, as far as people were concerned, required a physical church, so *The Enlightened Church* had purchased one. Arthur could see a logic of some sort in this. It certainly made it harder for the critics to dismiss the whole movement as a silly fad. However, he still had his misgivings about the whole affair, which made what happened next all the more difficult for him.

One afternoon, while sitting in front of the computer, he yelled out to Victor. 'We've been invited to the official opening!'

'Opening of what?' called Victor from the kitchen, where he was eating breakfast and waiting for a sign that either of the two cups of coffee he had already had were going to help jump-start his brain.

'The church,' said Arthur.

'Oh,' said Victor. And then, 'huh,' followed by, 'well, there you go.'

This was, to Arthur's mind, a response which fell a long way short of helpful. He walked into the kitchen. 'Do you think we should go?' he asked.

Victor pondered this as he chewed a mouthful of toast. He swallowed it, frowned, and then sipped at his third coffee so he could ponder it a little longer. Eventually, he said, 'I think you have to, don't you? We asked people to take you seriously. They did. I think you now have to do the same for them.' Arthur sagged. He was afraid he might say something like that.

The church itself was a picturesque medieval building in a small village about an hour's drive from Victor's house. It was precisely the sort of thing Arthur had been hoping for when he visited Wendy's church. The view was marred, however, by the presence of almost ten thousand people who had descended on the tiny village without warning and with not a single helpful suggestion as to how it might cope with more visitors in one day than it would usually expect to see in several years.

The crowd, unsurprisingly, consisted mainly of Arthur's followers. Also present, however, was a healthy media contingent, a handful of locals looking on in bewildered irritation, a congregation of protestors, and a police detail designed to look large enough to put anyone in attendance off the idea of causing whatever trouble they might have had in mind. One of the officers present, Chief Inspector Hullett, surveyed live feeds of the crowd with a belligerent eye. He was one of very few people in attendance who was aware that a Specialist Firearms Unit was also present. He was in his late fifties, was carrying a little more weight than was necessary, and scowled at the world through narrow eyes that sat atop reddened cheeks. He was also thoroughly fed up. This was no surprise to the other officers on the scene. It was widely known that fed up was Hullet's default setting. Still, today he was a special kind of fed up. He was feeling the kind of fed up he reserved for those days where he had to organise a Firearms Unit in a small rural setting with few vantage points and many barriers to remaining inconspicuous, all because a small amount of sketchy intelligence suggested someone may have been planning an attack at the grand opening of a new church for that weird old fart on the telly who had been pissing everyone off lately. The level of detail in the information he had been provided was pitiful. Something to do with chatter over encrypted channels on the dark web or something equally baffling. He missed his early days on the job. Back then, you just needed to know which person was likely to know what you needed to know and would just as likely give up that information if you bashed them about a bit and then head out to find them and deliver the necessary bashing. It was easy. Now, they had all this bloody technology designed to make the job easier being operated by a load of bloody smart-arses with tight shirts and stupid haircuts and a vocabulary that was ninety-five percent techno-jargon and nobody knew a bloody thing because it turned out all the horrible bastards they were looking for were either better at using the same technology or had better technology of their own. The upshot of all this was that Chief

Inspector Hullett had no real idea what he was looking for as he surveyed the row of monitors in front of him. It didn't matter how many drones they had filming, undetected, from above, or how many plainclothes officers they had wearing tiny, imperceptible cameras milling about in the crowd – there was still no clear subject to look for. 'Be vigilant', the Chief Super had told him. For what? 'You know... suspicious activity. Anything... untoward.' *Brilliant*, thought Hullett. *Keep an eye out for anyone who looks like a nutter*. The problem with this was that when you have the kind of outlook and temperament Chief Inspector Hullett had, and you end up surrounded by ten thousand people who have decided to worship an old fart off the telly who has been pissing everyone off lately, you are inclined to believe you are surrounded by ten thousand nutters.

He snapped out of this angry recollection as the sound of the crowd outside the van rose into a cheer and a voice over the radio announced that it looked as though Arthur was arriving.

58

Those Who Cling to Worthless Idols

The narrow, winding country lane provided a much-needed sense of peace and calm during the last two miles of their journey. The majority of the last hour or so had been encumbered with an air of tension none of the four travellers had quite known how to overcome. Rather than travel by taxi, Victor had opted to drive to the church. He was grateful for the focus this required because it provided a distraction from the uneasiness that hung in the air like an unwelcome fifth passenger for most of the journey. It was, however, impossible not to notice Arthur's pensiveness as he sat contemplatively in the passenger seat. Occasionally, he flicked through a few sheets of paper containing some handwritten notes, tracing down the lines with his finger and appearing to weigh something up in his mind before finally folding them back up and returning to the view outside.

'Are you sure about what you're going to say?' Victor asked on one such occasion, more to break the silence than anything.

'I think so, yes,' Arthur replied, sounding more relaxed than Victor suspected he was. 'Just running through everything.'

They settled back into silence, the uneasiness still present, Arthur still not speaking except to thank Wendy, sitting in the back with Sam, for her conviction that everything would be fine, which she offered each time

Arthur assured Sam, who kept reminding him he didn't have to do this if he didn't want to, that he did, indeed, want to.

This newfound sense of calm evaporated, however, when Victor navigated a bend and the road opened out into the wider, straighter stretch leading into the village. Cars were parked up and down the lane, pitching up on the grass verge on either side, leaving little more than a car's width through which to manoeuvre – a task made infinitely more difficult by the number of people walking along the road toward the village.

'Bloody hell,' whispered Victor when he first saw the line of people. He repeated this sentiment a number of times as he rode the brakes for the rest of the journey until the village green in front of the church unfolded in front of them and he opted instead for the much more dramatic and, given the circumstances, wholly inappropriate, 'Jesus suffering Christ!' Not even Wendy, so stunned was she by the sight which lay before them, could find it in her to rebuke him. All four stared, dumbstruck, at the huge crowd.

It didn't take long for one of the people making their way up the lane to spot Arthur. They let out an astonished cry and, immediately, the news that Arthur was arriving started to weave through the crowd much faster than the car itself was able to. An unmistakable sense of rising excitement filled the air and, as a result, Victor had to drive the rest of the way through a guard of honour made up of Arthur's followers as they cheered, applauded and waved homemade banners and placards. Eventually, they made it to the church, where a line of people wearing high-visibility vests prevented those in attendance from entering the grounds. The line parted and Victor was directed towards a muddy lane to the side of the church and into an area behind the building. Victor, Arthur, Sam and Wendy exited the car. They were met by a small party of Arthur's followers and one very grumpy looking police officer.

Arthur's followers were the first to approach. There were four of them. The one who appeared to be in charge introduced herself as Faye. She told Arthur what a pleasure it was to meet him and explained that she had been the one who sent the invitation. She was also the person who set up the crowdfunding campaign to make today possible and had taken care of the purchase of the building with the proceeds raised. She was not what Victor had expected. He was not sure what he had been expecting, exactly, but had vaguely anticipated youthful naivety and tie dyed clothes or bright pink hair or an abundance of piercings or tattoos – something designed to broadcast an identity that was, if not full-on hippie or punk, at least proudly non-mainstream. Instead, he was looking at a middle-aged woman who was... well, normal, for want of a better word. Her hair was cut the shorter side of mid-length and was well on its way to turning grey. She smiled warmly, spoke with a soft and geographically anonymous middle class accent, and dressed smartly yet unassumingly. She looked like she would be more at home walking in the countryside than at a protest or mixed up with the kind of crowds that had recently been camping on his doorstep. The rest of the group were not quite so measured in their approach. Faye introduced them but Victor didn't catch their names. He was too busy gaping as they each took it in turns to fawn over Arthur and tell him what an honour it was to meet him, much to Arthur's polite embarrassment.

'We're planning to get started in a few minutes,' said Faye, adding, 'if it's okay with you, Arthur. If you need a little time to prepare, we can probably put things off for a little longer.'

Victor watched Arthur closely for any sign he might be feeling uncomfortable or having second thoughts, but saw no real reason for concern beyond him seeming a little more reserved than usual, which was understandable in the circumstances. Arthur assured her he was ready whenever she was.

'Great,' said Faye. 'Then I suppose we should go and get ready.'

'Not just yet, thank you very much,' announced a gruff voice. It belonged to the police officer and, if possible, conveyed even more grumpiness than his expression. He had spent the duration of Arthur's conversation with Faye standing at the back of an open police van, talking animatedly to someone inside it and glancing frequently in Victor and Arthur's direction throughout the exchange. The moment he realised it was over, he had cut his conversation short and marched over to them. 'You must be Arthur,' he said.

'Correct,' said Arthur.

The police officer turned to Victor. 'And you're the scientist,' he said, looking Victor up and down.

'I'm *a* scientist,' said Victor.

'Okay,' said the policeman. 'And I'm *a* Chief Inspector. Chief Inspector Hullett, Specialist Firearms Unit. We're here because our intelligence says there is a potential threat to human life.' He turned to Arthur and said, 'Yours, in particular, sir,' in a tone which suggested he felt this was very much Arthur's fault.

'Oh,' said Arthur, and then, 'hmm.'

'What kind of threat?' asked Sam.

'I'm afraid I can't share specific details, ma'am.'

'Because you're not at liberty to, or because you don't have any?' asked Victor, who had decided on the spot he didn't like the man.

Hullett, who had made a similar, reciprocal decision, eyed him with loathing. 'I am afraid,' he said, 'I can't share specific details, sir. What I can tell you is we have excellent coverage of the crowd and have personnel deployed in and around the area, so if anything were to occur, we are as well positioned to respond to it as possible.' He turned to Arthur. 'That being said, I am duty bound to inform you, in situations like this, any number of things can happen and it's impossible to completely guarantee your safety at this time. It's your decision, sir, but I recommend you call off your plans to address this crowd and leave immediately to ensure your own and your companions' safety.'

'Er... right,' said Arthur, before falling silent and staring into the distance for a short while. He turned to his companions. 'What do you think I should do?'

Sam placed a hand on his arm. 'We can't tell you what to do here, Arthur,' she said. 'But we'll support you with whatever you choose.'

Arthur nodded, then turned to Victor. 'What would you do?'

Victor sighed, glanced at his shoes, raised his head, made to speak, sighed again. 'I don't know, Arthur. Maybe it's time to reconsider. Is it worth putting yourself in harm's way?'

Wendy rolled her eyes and tutted loudly, then stepped forward and took Arthur by the hand. 'We can't tell you what you should do Arthur. But I can tell you what I would do. I'd speak. I'm not trying to pressure you. I wouldn't judge you if you decided not to. You don't owe these people anything. But even so, I'd still do it.'

'May I ask why?' asked Arthur.

'Because, quite frankly, 'she said, 'fuck whoever wants to hurt you.'

Victor's eyes nearly bulged out of his head. He'd never heard Wendy so much as raise her voice in frustration, let alone swear.

'Threatening to harm people in an attempt to silence them,' Wendy continued, 'is repugnant. Once someone makes that kind of threat, it doesn't even matter what it is you want to say. It isn't about that anymore. It's about showing people violence will not get them what they want. He knows that only too well,' she said, jabbing a finger towards Victor.

'Now, hold on,' Victor began. It was as far as he got.

'Oh don't start, Victor,' snapped Wendy. 'You've spent half your life publically attacking people for their beliefs. How much abuse have you received? How many death threats? How often has some journalist with an axe to grind smeared you all over the papers because you've said something to offend them? And have you ever let them stop you? Have you ever relented in your criticism? Of course not. Yet here you are now, the great Victor Dennett – the man who can't say enough about the contradictions and inconsistencies and the hypocrisy in the actions and attitudes of the religious advising someone else to do what he would never dream of doing and letting an extremist alter their decisions. Shame on you.'

All eyes turned to Victor – even Victor's – though his were fixed on his shoes so as to avoid meeting anyone's gaze.

Hullett, motivated more by impatience than a desire to alleviate the tension, was the first to speak. 'So, does that mean you're staying, then?'

'Yes,' said Arthur.

'Great,' said Hullett, and he skulked back to his van.

And so, Victor Dennett, the famous and outspoken atheist, found himself standing on a stage in front of a church to offer moral support to the man who created the universe as he prepared to address a crowd of several thousand people who had chosen to follow him as their god. To say it was a surreal moment would have been a grotesque understatement. He surveyed the crowd with a mix of disbelief and... something else. He couldn't quite put his finger on it. Was it satisfaction? Maybe. His gaze kept returning to Arthur, who was watching Faye intently as she ran through an introduction about what an inspiring turnout it was, what an incredible moment, what an important day, and so on.

Then she introduced Arthur, who stepped forward and waited patiently for the noise to die down before leaning into the microphone.

'Hello,' he said. 'As you know, my name is Arthur Fowler. I have to say, today is a very strange day indeed for me. It has been difficult for me to make sense of this movement and I confess I am still unsure what to make of it all. I have done my best to try and learn as much as I can about what motivates the people on this planet. In my study of human civilisation, I have read a great deal about religion. Much of what I read left me feeling very uncomfortable with the idea of being part of one in any way whatsoever, let alone being the subject of one. Yet here we are.

'Before I begin, I would like to say thank you to the three people standing behind me. They have been incredibly supportive over the last few weeks. They have suffered a great deal of disruption to their lives to ensure I was sheltered, clothed and fed. Without them I would have certainly been cast adrift to fend for myself on this planet I have inadvertently created. I suspect I would not have thrived had that happened.

'They are very different from one another, which has been to my benefit, for it has meant each has offered a different type of support. In addition to the enormous sacrifices Victor has made in opening up his home to me, he has taught me much about your society and helped me to navigate the complex interactions and peculiarities of life on Earth, or this little corner of it, at least. He is a man of great intelligence and great warmth. He is also, and he may not thank me for saying so, a very emotionally driven man. He may consider himself to be wholly driven by reason and rationality. Indeed, he has built a public reputation on this very thing. But the fact remains I have witnessed in Victor evidence that even the brightest minds in this world can be prone to a higher degree of emotional decision making than I am used to. At first, I thought this a shortcoming in his character, in your species, even, but I understand now how wrong I was. He would be a lesser man without this side to his personality. You all would. Emotional behaviour has its benefits as well as its disadvantages. While he was, at times, frustrated, he was also sympathetic. Although he was angry, he was also kind. Perhaps a person cannot have the positives without the negatives. Like all things, it is a question of balance. Were he purely rational, he might never have taken me in – it would have made sense, logically, for him to have turned me away. Instead, he brought me into his home. Your propensity for emotional behaviour gives you the capacity to act in a way that is not merely sensible, but good and decent. Victor Dennett epitomises this.'

There was a short round of polite applause, which Victor acknowledged with a brief wave to the crowd and a nod to Arthur. Arthur let it dissipate before continuing.

'Samantha has been an unwavering voice of reason, an advocate for me from the moment I arrived, even if she was a rather reluctant one at first. She has been supportive and kind without exception and without hesitation throughout my time here. She is a remarkable person, and it is easy to see why she is such a popular documentary presenter. She can take the most complex ideas, understand them fully, and then explain them in the most straightforward terms so they may be easily understood by all. She helps you to understand your universe. She has done precisely this for me, too.'

There was another round of applause. It was clear, judging by the duration and volume, that Sam had quite a few fans of her own in attendance. Much more at ease in the limelight than Victor, she received it more comfortably, smiling at Arthur, and then stepping forward to give him a brief hug. As Sam stepped back in line with the others, Arthur turned to look at Wendy. He was smiling as he turned his attention back to the crowd.

'I believe it is through Wendy that I have learnt most of all – much of it about myself. I didn't expect to after our first few encounters. It may seem strange that a close friendship might develop between a Christian and myself, but it most certainly has. And it has done so despite my early dismissive attitude to her faith, despite my early belief I would never find common ground with someone who, to my shame, I thought completely lacking in logic and reason. How ignorant I was. I have learnt through her how vulnerable humans are rendered by their emotions. You suffer much more than I believe I am capable of suffering. When you do, you can become so overcome with pain that you abandon all reason. I didn't understand this at first, and so I thought her foolish. But she is far from it. Wendy doesn't deserve derision. She deserves respect. She deserves support and sympathy, but not pity. She has suffered as much as I think a person can and yet her positivity is still dominant. She is kind. She listens. She is compassionate. If her faith is a means of maintaining this, then I say it should be celebrated.' Arthur turned to face all three and said, 'Thank you.' A final smattering of applause rang out.

'Now, on to the business at hand. There is, I am sure, a degree of anticipation regarding what I am going to say here today. I suspect there is also a great deal of expectation, because that seems to be a hallmark of any religion. It's strange – religion masquerades as a set of expectations a deity has of its followers. Yet, in practice, it seems more accurate to call it a set of expectations that the people who subscribe to it have of others. Indeed, since my arrival, I have found everyone to be far more preoccupied with their expectations of me than whatever expectations they think I have of them. As a result, I fear I am destined to disappoint you all. I have nothing profound to offer you. I am no wiser about what you call the big questions than you are. I don't know why we are here. I don't know if there is a 'why'. I wouldn't presume to tell you what to do with your life, nor can I tell you where that life came from. I can, of course, explain how your universe was created, but I cannot do the same for my own. Perhaps it too is contained within a larger one. Perhaps there are millions of universes within universes. But what of the outermost one? The answer to the question of first cause will, I think, always evade us. And, if I am wrong, who is to say the answer would be meaningful? Perhaps everything is a giant accident. It doesn't matter. All that matters is that we are. It doesn't matter why we are, or how we are. We should stop seeking to understand these things and embrace the uncertainty of our existence. I think many of this planet's problems would be resolved, or at least reduced, if people were a little less certain about how much they think they know. That doesn't mean you need to start doubting observable facts, of course. Right and wrong are not the same as true and false. But if you live with more uncertainty, and can enjoy doing so, you may find yourselves more tolerant and more tolerable, more forgiving and more easily forgiven, kinder and more deserving of kindness.'

Another ripple of applause floated across the crowd. Victor watched on, clapping politely as Arthur paused to wait for the noise to die back down before continuing.

'I have also realised –'

He paused, frowning, as another noise began to rise. Not the polite mumbles of tacit agreement and applause. Something else – something unsettled. And unsettling. Victor noticed it too, along with movement in the crowd. He heard people gasping and chattering. The voices, though too many to hear what any one was saying clearly, carried a quizzical tone, which quickly turned to panic. Someone screamed. Then others screamed. The movement grew, swelled, spread out like a wave, leaving one man standing alone in the center, his arm raised, a gun in his hand, pointed fixedly at Arthur.

There was a seething, rushed whisper of air, followed by a dull thud. The man lowered his arm, sank to his knees, fell face forward. There were more screams. And then, from somewhere else in the crowd, further over to their left, someone shouted two words. Instinctively, Victor threw himself to the floor. He buried his head in his arms and waited for an explosion. There was an explosion.

59

Patient in Affliction

Hospital waiting rooms, contemplated Victor, are among the very worst places on Earth. It is as though their designers have made the mistake of thinking the title refers not so much to the room's function, as to the experience the room is supposed to provide, and so, rather than being a place where one must simply wait, it is a place where one gets to feel all the waiting they are doing.

Victor was feeling every agonising moment as he tried not to think about the bruised and bloodied image of Arthur he had witnessed back at the church. The walls were a bland off-white, the chairs specially designed to prevent any sense of comfort, and distraction was prevented at every turn. Signs all over the hospital politely requested that he didn't use his phone, which he had no intention of doing anyway having switched it off to escape the incessant ringing. There were magazines, but they were, as always, of a genre which appeared to have been carefully chosen to annoy anyone desperate enough to pick one up and flick through it, leaving the reader feeling somehow taunted by the fact they could have been reading something interesting, if only it were any other magazine in existence. There was even a television, but, like all hospital televisions, it was permanently set to a muted and poorly subtitled rolling news channel, and the news currently rolling was non-stop coverage of the very explosion that he and everyone else in the room was trying not to think about. Victor and Wendy had elected to sit in the row of chairs directly beneath the screen so they didn't have to look at it.

Victor shifted in his chair and leaned forward. He scanned the selection of magazines to see if the prospect of reading about crochet, celebrity gossip, cars, or horse riding was any more appealing than it was half an hour ago. It wasn't.

Wendy and Sam, both sporting minor cuts and bruises, each coped with the boredom in their own way. Wendy, true to herself, divided up her time between silently praying and sipping unpleasant tea from a cardboard cup, all the time fighting her desire to ask if anyone needed anything or to assure them, yet again, that everything would be okay.

Sam stood at the window, people-watching. She gazed down at the car park and quietly pondered how difficult it was to tell by each person's demeanour who was leaving with good news – an all clear, a newborn, a successful operation – and who was leaving with bad. They had all reached the point where a person decides the situation cannot possibly get any worse when Chief Inspector Hullett entered the room. He regarded each of them coyly, unsure how to behave in a situation where even he knew belligerence was not an appropriate approach.

'Any news?' he asked. He spoke timidly, directing the question to no-one in particular.

'He's still in surgery,' said Sam. 'No word so far.'

'Oh.' He shuffled his feet.

'What about your end?' asked Victor.

'We're starting to get an idea of the full picture,' said Hullett. The picture, as far as the police understood it, looked like this. The man with the gun had been easy to identify. He was a born-again Christian and, in Hullett's words, 'a bit of a nutjob'. The police had spoken to a few members of his church and learnt that he was regarded as a quiet oddball with some strong views, though there was a general sense of surprise that he would go and do something like this. Victor could see the headlines already – a loner with mental health issues, the standard write up for a white Christian. Hullett told them some people in the crowd must have seen the gun, hence the initial panic. This drew the attention of the firearms officers, who were able to identify him as a threat and, when the space opened up around him and a clean shot was available, he was 'dealt with', as Hullett delicately put it. Unfortunately, he was not the only person there with designs on killing Arthur. Another attacker, 'of an Islamic persuasion', to use Hullett's tragic attempt at a politically correct term, had turned up with the intention of blowing himself and Arthur up. The current working theory was that he was making his way to the front of the crowd when the first attack was foiled. All the screaming and confusion must have made him panic, or perhaps he thought he'd been rumbled. Either way, it looked like he decided to detonate the nail-bomb he had in his backpack there and then. Those closest to him never stood a chance. Although the attacker was some distance away when he detonated, the elevated position of those on the stage meant they were subjected to some of the shrapnel. Victor, having dropped to the floor, was unscathed. Wendy and Sam, standing towards the back, had received a handful of minor injuries between them. It was Arthur, standing front and centre, who was most vulnerable. The death toll so far stood at nineteen, though it was sure to rise given the number of critically injured people fighting for their lives. They wouldn't all make it. Before they could truly register everything Hullett had said, a doctor entered the waiting room and they braced themselves to discover whether or not Arthur was one of those who would pull through.

60

Resurrection

Five days passed before Arthur finally woke up. He had sustained only superficial injuries from the few pieces of shrapnel that had struck him, but the force of the blast had thrown him backwards clean off the stage and onto the gravel path in front of the church. He was found unconscious and with only the faintest of pulses, worryingly close to the concrete steps at the entrance. The enormous bruise and pool of blood left little doubt he had struck his head with some force. He had been rushed straight into surgery, where he spent a total of sixteen hours. There were very real doubts about his chances of survival, and the updates about his condition all featured that most unhelpful hospital vocabulary made up of words like "uncertainty", "critical", and "serious". There was talk of possible brain damage. In the end, Arthur had been placed in an induced coma to reduce the pressure on his brain.

Victor and Wendy were at his bedside as often as the hospital would allow and for some considerable time that they wouldn't. They left only when Arthur's nurses needed to do whatever it was they did when they drew the curtain and after it had been explained to them, painstakingly clearly, that they really ought to get a move on because visiting hours ended over an hour ago, thank you very much.

When they were at home, both of their houses were mercifully free of the crowds they had grown accustomed to avoiding, though Victor found this merely emphasised the silence and solitude he now found himself surrounded by.

The crowds, along with the news crews that had started following them around with even more zeal since the attack, had migrated to the street outside the hospital, where a permanent vigil had been set up by Arthur's more devoted followers. The cards and flowers dotted around Arthur's hospital bed were nothing compared to those that had been deposited on the pavement and tied to railings up and down the street.

As he approached the hospital on the second day of Arthur's stay, Victor was momentarily surprised by the absence of people accosting him to ask for updates about Arthur's condition. Surveying the scene, he quickly realised that every last member of the crowd had their head bowed while someone led a prayer. He crept by, shaking his head at the sheer stupidity of praying for the health of a man they believed created the universe, knowing full well he could not, by his own admission, answer or even hear their prayers. Perhaps Arthur was right – maybe there was no way of starting something new without it quickly reverting to the old thing it was meant to replace.

Three days after the coma was induced, Arthur's doctors felt confident it was safe to stop administering the sedative keeping him under. Wendy and Victor were told Arthur could wake up fairly quickly, but his age and the amount of morphine he was on would likely delay this, so they should brace themselves for a wait that could last for days.

It was a long three days, full of pacing and fretting and waiting and waiting and waiting, punctuated by moments of heightened anxiety, such as when Arthur's ventilator was removed and Wendy, Sam and Victor sat in silence because they didn't dare voice their fear Arthur may not manage to resume breathing unassisted. There was a brief moment of relief at the news he had, in fact, done so, though this was short lived and they all returned to melancholy reflection as Arthur stubbornly refused to open his eyes for another twenty hours.

And then, he did. He had been showing some positive signs for a while, offering a nurse the faintest of hand squeezes when asked to, his fingers and toes twitching ever so slightly following a request to move them, banishing some of their silent fear and replacing it with a hope that went just as unspoken until, finally, Arthur woke.

Sam noticed first, and informed the others with a gentle gasp.

'Arthur!' exclaimed Wendy.

'I'll get someone,' said Victor, running from the room.

Wendy and Sam sat down at either side of the bed and each took one of Arthur's hands in theirs.

'Arthur? Can you hear me?' asked Sam. Arthur's eyes drifted slowly to her.

'How are you feeling?' asked Wendy. Laboriously, Arthur turned his head, his eyes swimming until they eventually met hers. There was a flicker at the corners of his mouth – an attempt at a smile, perhaps.

Victor returned. 'Someone is coming,' he said. 'How's he doing?'

Wendy and Sam both turned back to Arthur. Arthur regarded each of them in turn, his gaze eventually settling on Victor. In a rasping, laboured whisper, he said, 'I'd like to go home now,' and then he fell back to sleep.

61

Salvation

Arthur had to wait another two weeks before he was finally discharged. It was far from the most interesting or enjoyable two weeks he spent on Earth, but the staff were pleasant enough and went out of their way to ensure he had everything he needed, and he was visited daily by Wendy or Victor or Sam. They brought him books and food and news about what was going on in the wider world – how the general public had warmed to him and were hoping for his recovery, how the church was growing ever larger as a result, how public figures were falling over themselves to capitalise on his popularity by wishing him well whenever a camera was pointed at them. Arthur knew much of what they told him already – Victor had provided him with a laptop and had paid through the nose for daily internet access – but Arthur let them tell him anyway. It was nice just to talk with them.

When he was alone, he continued reading and blogging, though he kept things much lighter, thanking people for their kind wishes, wishing his growing following all the best with the new church (but declining to play any further role within it), and, most of all, making the case for allowing him to use the plans he had drawn up to attempt to return to his home. He became quite excited that it might actually happen when a protest movement started to gather momentum. It was mostly an online affair – one of those causes that made people change their social media profile pictures so they felt like they were doing something, but there was a significant number of people prepared to put in real time and effort. There were even a couple of actual physical protests – one at the hospital and one outside Parliament. Victor did his best to let him down gently. If there was one thing that protests outside Westminster Palace had in common, he told him, it was that they were almost universally ignored by the people who worked inside it. It didn't matter how many people protested on his behalf, those with the power to make such an attempt happen simply would not do so.

Or so he thought.

A few days later, the very same day Arthur was told he could go home, or, at least, go back to Victor's, Victor brought some interesting news. A man called Eli Rush had been in touch. He was, in Victor's words, 'some crazy billionaire who owned a load of tech companies', and there was a very real possibility he might be able to help.

Sam was dubious. She couldn't see why he would help. Why would he risk his reputation on such a venture? What if it all went wrong? Was he really so rich he considered himself *that* untouchable? The answer to this last question was, unsurprisingly, 'yes, actually.' But there was another reason. It turned out, when he wasn't filling his head with the complete history of human civilisation, or blogging about the absurdities of it in its current guise, or responding to the riots and protests his observations provoked, or starting a new religion, Arthur had been exchanging emails with this man.

62

ArthurFowlerBlog: Entry 21

The first time I met a man from Earth, I slapped him round the face. I have since learnt that this is not the type of behaviour you might expect from the creator of your universe. But then, there are a great many things you seem to expect of your creator, and almost none of them make any sense to me. However, I do appreciate that there exist some people who might object to such a violent act, so I would like to offer something in the way of a defence; there was no malice in it whatsoever. I only hit him because I thought he was having a heart attack.

I have not been here very long, but I have learnt a great deal since those first confusing moments. In fact, I do not think it is an overstatement to say I shall never be the same again. You are a quite fascinating bunch, really, not least because you are so full of contradictions. You are equal parts fascinating and terrifying; inspiring and infuriating; intelligent, yet relentlessly simple. I have enjoyed my time here tremendously, and I am infinitely more proud of my creation to know you are here living and loving and laughing and struggling and suffering within it.

Obviously, I had no idea of any of this when I created it. How could I have? You are, after all, such a terribly small part of it. I was merely happy to have finally created a universe stable enough to not collapse in on itself. For the first time in countless attempts, I had built one that held its shape. All of my previous attempts failed within a few seconds. It was always the same – calibrate the chamber, set the dials, charge the accelerator, flick the switch, and watch in disappointment as a faint flash of light and a barely audible pop and crackle announced that I would have to start the whole process again. But not this time. This time it was magnificent. Well, I say magnificent, but that one may be an overstatement. There are people far more talented than I who have turned universe creation into a fine art. I am a mere amateur – a hobbyist. Very rarely, one of these masters may create something that truly deserves the label 'magnificent'. Perhaps a humble 'very good' would be a more fitting assessment of my own creation. Regardless, as much as I have enjoyed my time here – and I truly have – what I want, more than anything else, is to go home. And now, finally, I can. I fear I am expected to say something profound – something that will render my time here more meaningful in some way. My 'final message' has been the subject of much speculation. Words have been written regarding the importance of my legacy, as though it were possible, through some mere eloquent and erudite phrase, to secure humanity's posterity. Truth be told, I think the most important thing I can say is nothing. Indeed, I wish to make a point of doing so. I have no final words of wisdom to help guide you to a brighter future, no tenets that must be adhered to, and no lasting inalienable principals. I have said enough. I have studied your society to the best of my ability in my short time here. I have observed, analysed, commented, advised, and criticised. And, every time, I have done more harm than good. You are a deeply and dangerously divided people. This is not a problem that can be solved quickly or simply. You cannot take shortcuts. Treating my word as law would, just as it is with any religion, be an attempt at such a shortcut. I will not allow anyone to absolve themselves of the responsibility of working out the kindest, fairest, most logical course of action to take in any given circumstances by claiming it is what I want. I must not intervene – you must earn your future for yourselves. Know this. Know that I make no requests of you. Know that I have no expectations. Know that nothing done in my name is truly done in my name – it is done in your own. You must decide the kind of person, the kind of people, you think you should be. Do not try to meet the expectations of others. Take responsibility for setting your own and meet those, and never pretend they are anyone else's. You may never hide your true selves behind me the way the men who tried to end my life hid behind their own gods. This will not prevent similar acts of barbarism in the future – there will be more. But it may, in time, help to prevent others from identifying with them on the grounds of a shared god. Such attacks demonstrate the ugliest side of your nature. And, make no mistake, it is part of your nature. You can embrace it or you can overcome it, but you must do so alone.

Know also that there is nothing remarkable about my survival. Some have likened my recovery to a resurrection. I do hope they were joking, but there is little left to surprise me when it comes to what humans will believe with sincerity. My continued existence is the result of an arbitrary combination of random events falling in my favour. True, I owe my life to the medical professionals who saved me, but those fine people would no doubt have done everything they could for anyone else who happened to find themselves in their care. The fact that I ended up on their operating table is of no significance. Similarly, those who died were not destined to. It was not 'their time', as some of you like to suggest. They happened to be standing in a random place at a random time that meant they randomly fell victim to the whims of a psychopath and the laws of physics. Do not seek to diminish the tragedy of their deaths by attempting to imbue them with meaning as the desire of some supernatural agent. There is no meaning. It was a wholly senseless act. Accepting this will do much more to prevent similar attacks than thoughts and prayers.

That is it. There is nothing left to say now but goodbye, thank you, and good luck.

63

Deus in Machina

The control room was impressive, there was no denying it. For all of the PR spin about E Equals being one of the most advanced scientific facilities in the world, it was still built on a budget. Admittedly, it was a huge budget – huge enough to provoke questions about whether or not that kind of money would be better spent on education or policing or the NHS, for example – but it was still restrictive given what they were trying to achieve. As a result, while E Equals was technically advanced, all expenses were spared when it came to workspace practicality and aesthetics. Rush's lab didn't suffer from this at all. The floor was a dark, polished marble, which was covered in designer ergonomic desks and chairs. The computer stations each had two, three or sometimes four monitors. These were mirrored on a giant display on the far wall so that every single one could be observed by anyone else from their own station. It looked like a cross between a NASA mission control room and a Bond villain's headquarters. Rush could survey everything that was happening from the back of the room. With a word, he could have any one of the monitors in the room take up the vast display in its entirety, and he did so now. He claimed he wanted to check something and fired a couple of questions at the person working at the station, though it came to nothing and struck Victor as unnecessary, leading him to conclude Rush was merely showing off.

Rush turned to Victor. 'Impressive, huh?' he asked, as though he had read Victor's mind and decided to confirm the suspicion.

'Yes,' said Victor, adding, 'if a bit Big Brother.'

'Oh, it's nothing like that. They are in control,' said Rush, gesturing to his staff. 'They can set the stations to personal mode if they want to use them for their own purposes. And, even when they are set to display up there, any time they open a tab or a website or piece of software they've added to their 'personal' list, the feed to the big screen cuts out. Look,' he said, pointing to an area that had suddenly turned dark. 'There you go. Someone must be checking their emails.'

Try as he might, Victor found it hard to dislike the man. He was charismatic and intelligent and, despite the desire to impress, surprisingly humble. This was just as well, given that Victor now worked for him. This was the price of helping Arthur. This was the upside to all of the risk that Sam couldn't work out – if they wanted Rush to help Arthur, they would have to leave E Equals and come and work for him. Sam took some convincing. She had been worried about uprooting her family. As it turned out, they were more than happy. They could live comfortably on her salary alone, so it wouldn't matter if her husband couldn't find work, and her children were bouncing off the walls with excitement about moving to America. When Rush assured her she could continue her television career, there seemed no reason to refuse.

Though he had no ties keeping him in the UK, and though he found the thought of telling Kyle where to stick his job very appealing, Victor also wrestled with it at first. It still didn't add up. Were they really worth it, he and Sam? If

Rush delivered on his promise, there was a very real chance Arthur would be killed. Was he really so desperate to secure Sam and Victor's services that he considered this an acceptable risk? Did Victor really want to work for someone who did?

'Oh, I get more from this than you two,' Rush told him. 'We're doing this because this is how we make progress. And it's the right thing to do. And I think it'll work. And because I can. And maybe,' he said, leaning in and lowering his voice to a conspiratorial whisper, 'I really believe in Arthur.'

Victor cast him a doubtful look.

'Okay,' said Rush, laughing. 'Or maybe Arthur offered to share knowledge we couldn't possibly hope to obtain for ourselves in the next fifty years at our current rate of progress in exchange for helping him.' He noted Victor's expression. 'Do I detect a hint of disappointment?'

Victor sighed. 'Maybe. Maybe surprise is more accurate. He could have done that all along. He could have shared his knowledge with everyone. Wouldn't that be the decent thing to do?'

Rush laughed again and threw his arm around Victor. 'He thought you'd feel that way,' he said. 'He said everyone here on Earth had the power to help him, but they didn't – he had to rely on me. He said 'do unto others' was another one of those ideas people don't really subscribe to as much as they should. He's a smart man, Victor. A very smart man.'

There was a brief lull in the conversation before Rush spoke again with what felt to Victor like forced nonchalance. 'It's not too late to back out if you're not comfortable. I'm sure you can smooth things over with your boss back home.'

'I doubt it,' said Victor. 'The last thing I said to him was that he needed to pull his head out of his arse so he had room to shove his job up it.'

Rush laughed again – a huge, guttural belly laugh this time. A handful of staff stopped what they were doing for a moment and turned to see what was going on. Seeing nothing especially out of the ordinary, they shrugged their shoulders at each other and returned to what they were doing. 'Damn, Victor! Good for you.'

'I hope so.'

'You know it is! I meant what I said – no financial constraints. No government red tape beyond the legal issues, and I'm pretty good at finding my way around those. No applications for funding. No justifying the need for the research to people who don't understand it. If you tell me it's worth doing, it gets done. You have full autonomy.'

Not knowing what to say, Victor fell silent and watched the staff making their final preparations. After a while, Rush gestured down to Victor's side. 'Can I ask?'

Victor raised his hand. 'This?' he said. 'A gift from Arthur. He made it. Or at least, he was making it when I brought him here.' He gazed at the marionette he had been absently clasping all the while and recalled his parting with Arthur at the door to the detector that would serve as Arthur's vehicle back home.

They had exchanged few words. Victor decided not to tell him what he and Sam had agreed to do to make this happen. They thanked each other. Victor apologised for bringing Arthur to Earth and putting him through all of this. Arthur told him there was no need. As he gifted him the marionette, he said, 'I'm glad it was you, Victor. It had to be someone. This experiment would have taken place at some point. So far as anything can be, this was destined to happen. Scientists always build on the work of others. The path they follow is pre-ordained by the simple fact each step forward is made by uncovering a universal truth. There are no crossroads. There is merely a badly-lit path heading in one direction. Your species has been on it from the outset. I am fortunate that the specimen that took this step happened to be so kind. I will miss you, Victor. I wish you happiness.'

'I hope you get home safely,' said Victor.

'I will,' said Arthur. 'Goodbye, Victor.'

'Goodbye.'

He was shaken from his reverie by Rush's voice booming across the control room. 'Okay, folks, this is it. Last minute checks everyone. We're about to make history here. Do not screw it up. The last thing you want to be remembered for is being the person who killed God because you forgot to carry the one.' He laughed to himself again.

The buzz of the control room picked up again amidst a flurry of activity as the staff collectively began the routine of powering up the detector. Somewhere, someone started to count backwards from ten.

A little over a hundred metres below all of this activity, Arthur sat in the silence and darkness of the detector. He waited. And, given that there was little else to do, he thought. He thought about what it would be like to return to his attic and look at his universe and know that everyone he had met would be gone before he could blink. Centuries would have passed on Earth before he completed his first breath. But the universe would continue, for a while at least. He thought about his wife, and how he would go and wish her goodnight and how she would be none the wiser about any of this. Later, he'd come back to the attic. Maybe the universe would still be there. Maybe it wouldn't. Oh well. In an uncharacteristic moment, he spoke to his wife, even though there was no way she could hear him. 'I'm coming home,' he said. 'Don't worry. I'll be back soon. Everything will be fine.' He closed his eyes and waited a little longer.

There was a sound like a million zips all at once.

Epilogue

It is almost bedtime. A handcrafted wooden cross rests on a nightstand. A control without a marionette. A gift. Wendy sits up in bed with her hands clasped, her head bowed, her eyes closed. She talks to God. It matters not that she uses the wrong name – Arthur doesn't believe in blasphemy. She talks of her hopes and fears. Exactly what she says is not for us to know. It is between her and God. They are her hopes and her fears. We should respect that. She doesn't speculate as to what God's response may be. Instead, she waits to hear an ethereal voice that will never come. But this doesn't matter either. All that matters is it helps her to face the difficulties of her life and deal with her problems and grow ever stronger and happier.

It is way past bedtime. Victor sits on his sofa. He talks to Arthur. There is no reply – Arthur cannot hear him. But, now that he knows him, Victor can speculate about how he might respond. He does just that, and they have a lengthy discussion in Victor's head. It ends abruptly when Arthur tells him he really should go to bed. They have been having lots of these discussions lately. The things Victor imagines him saying are almost as irritating as the real thing. They help Victor to act more compassionately, show more tolerance, and get less frustrated by the little things. And the big things. He talks to Arthur almost as often as he does his wife. He likes to think that they help him. And, because he thinks it, they do.

Acknowledgements

If you made it this far, thank you. There were times when I wasn't sure I'd get here myself. Yet, here we are, in no small part thanks to the support, kindness, patience and effort of the following handful of people.

Thank you to John Lee, my friend and former Deputy Headteacher and the first person to ever read about Arthur and Victor. Not far behind were Abi Reeley, Steffan Mallard and Rebecca Hennahane, who all offered crucial opinions, feedback, advice and headaches in the form of glaring plot-holes and conflicting views about what the story needed. Thank you. Without your contributions, I never would have wrestled this thing into shape. Thanks, also, to the friends too numerous to mention individually who read bits and pieces of this novel or indulged my need to bounce ideas around with you in what must have been tedious conversation.

Kristiana Reed was the last person to read this before the final sweep of edits. Anyone who has read it owes her thanks for catching the several million unnecessary uses of the words 'just' and 'that', as well as a selection of other equally amateurish mistakes.

The earliest seed of this story is many years old. It began with a conversation with my childhood friend, Scott. The idea we bounced around bears no resemblance to this story: it was a story about God meticulously creating and attempting to maintain the universe. This task was thwarted at every turn by Stanley, God's irritating younger brother, who was always touching things he shouldn't be and making things go wrong, especially on one particular planet that was God's pride and joy. *'Stanley's Big Brother'* never saw the light of day. I didn't get close to finishing it. But, in a roundabout way, it led to me writing this story. I've since lost touch with Scott, which I must bear all the blame for. I've tried to commemorate our friendship and our original idea by naming the young man in chapter three after our early protagonist.

Of course, the biggest thanks must go to my family. To my mum, for ensuring I spent enough of my childhood in Clacton library that I had no shortage of books or passion for reading them. To my dad, for reading those first few pages of *'Stanley's Big Brother'* and telling me I had to keep writing. To my Aunty Ann, who once told me that writing was my calling (albeit as a journalist). To my incredible girls, who give me a reason to get up every morning. I've been writing this longer than you've been alive, but you're the reason I've finished it. I'll be gone one day. But you'll still have this. Maybe you'll have more... And, finally, to my wife, Izzy. You have had to put up with me talking about this damn book for years. You went to bed alone far too often because I stayed up to work on it. You woke up alone because I got up early to write. You came home to an untidy house because I'd been staring at a screen instead of pulling my weight and through it all you've been nothing but supportive. Thank you. For everything. It's finally done now. I hope you think it was worth it, especially since I've got an idea for another story...

About the Author

David Wiley is a secondary school English teacher, which is another name for a person who wishes they were an author. He spends his time tearing his hair out at his students, tearing his hair out at his children, and tearing his hair out at his own fictional characters - all because none of them ever want to do what he tells them to. To give his hair a break, he spends the rest of his time gardening, running in the countryside, and dreaming of the day when he'll have time to watch films and play video games again. The Church of Arthur Fowler is his debut novel.

Follow on Twitter: @DaveWil82
Sign up for email updates here:
https://mailchi.mp/ea303b2f5254/davewilauthor

Printed in Great Britain
by Amazon